I0713162

eve of samhain

a novel by
LISA SANCHEZ

OMNIFIC PUBLISHING
DALLAS

Copyright © 2010 by Lisa Sanchez
All Rights Reserved. Except as permitted under the U.S. Copyright Act of 1976,
no part of this publication may be reproduced, distributed, or transmitted
in any form or by any means, or stored in a database or retrieval system,
without prior written permission of the publisher.

Omnific Publishing
P.O. Box 793871, Dallas, TX 75379
www.omnificpublishing.com

First Omnific eBook edition, May 2010
First Omnific trade paperback edition, May 2010

The characters and events in this book are fictitious.
Any similarity to real persons, living or dead,
is coincidental and not intended by the author.

Library of Congress Cataloguing-in-Publication Data

Sanchez, Lisa
    Eve of Samhain / Lisa Sanchez – 1st ed.
    ISBN 978-1-936305-20-9
    1. Faerie—Fiction. 2. Curse—Fiction. 3. Gancanagh—Fiction.
    4. Love—Fiction. I. Title

10 9 8 7 6 5 4 3 2 1

Book Cover Design by Amy Brokaw
Book Interior Design by Barbara Hallworth

Printed in the United States of America

For you, Quinn.
I loved you from the start.
Thank you for gracing my life with your light.

chapter 1

All men are assholes. No, wait… let me rephrase that. The dude I'm forced to wait on, the greasy, arrogant tool sitting at table nine, is an asshole. Unfortunately for me, ninety percent of the guys who frequent the club I work in are just like him: total douchebags.

I fought back the urge to smack him with my serving tray and flashed him a set of pearly whites. "Is there anything else I can get you?" Loud bass music blared throughout the club, filling my ears and rattling my skull.

The oversexed twenty-something took a swig from the beer I'd just served him, treated me to a ridiculous smile and palmed my ass, giving it a painful squeeze. His cheap cologne permeated the air around him, burning my eyes and stinging the inside of my nose.

"Just your number, sweet thang." His pathetic attempt at seduction crashed and burned before he'd even achieved liftoff.

Who the hell does this guy think he is? Sweet thang? Please!

The fake smile I kept plastered to my face while I worked disappeared instantly, and I peeled the sweaty palm of my unwanted suitor from my behind.

Stupid, freaking booty shorts. I hate my uniform!

I took another look at the overly libidinous customer who sat in front of me and gagged. "Really? I mean… seriously? You expect me to respond to that?" I glared at him with a look that clearly conveyed my answer: *Hell no!*

Apparently my "not in this lifetime, buddy" response was not what the asshat was shooting for. He stood up, his lips pulled down into a scowl, and muttered a low "whatever, bitch." He knocked my drink tray out of my hands and stepped away from the table, bumping knuckles with a random gawker who just happened to be watching the entire scene play out.

Numbnuts and Gawker Boy totally reaffirmed my belief that all men are, indeed, worms.

"The Fates hate me," I mumbled and bent down to retrieve my drink tray off the floor. I shook my head and sighed. It was always the same. Each night the club filled to capacity with arrogant, self-indulgent frat boys who thought they were God's gift to women, and each night I brought them booze and pretzels while they pinched, prodded, groped, and propositioned me. I was a cross between a maid and a freaking pincushion. The fact I needed the job to pay for my schooling was the only thing keeping me from whacking the grabby jerks over the head and telling the Powers That Be to "take this job and shove it!"

Fire and Ice was the hottest nightclub in town. The pay was good, the tips were great, and I made enough money to pay for school with quite a bit left over. So for the time being, I'd suck it up and deal. And the ass grabbing? Yeah... the next loser who tried was losing a finger. Maybe two.

With a deep breath, I put on my game face and went back to work, checking on the rest of the tables in my section. I jotted down my last drink order: one Buttery Nipple and a Red Headed Slut for the couple at table ten, who needed a private room far more than another round of drinks. I wheeled around to head back to the bar when a warm, delicious tingling sensation danced across my skin.

I turned, my vision accosted by a Malibu Barbie wannabe, complete with over-processed hair and a man-made rack, walking toward me. Following Little Miss Plastic was, without a doubt, the most handsome man I'd ever seen. Stop. Scratch that. Handsome didn't cut it. Beautiful wouldn't be an accurate description either. Gorgeous, engaging, hunky... nope. None of those words came close to describing the divine, godlike creature stalking toward me.

My breath caught. My feet fused with the floor and I stood frozen in place, mouth open and mute. He strolled past me, taking a seat at the empty table just to my left.

Oh. My. God.

Tall and blond, with a skull-trimmed haircut and a strong jaw, his aura literally screamed sex.

Extremely fit, evidenced by the muscles in his chest and arms straining against his black t-shirt, he wore a pair of low slung jeans that hugged a primo ass and allowed just a hint of his extremely cut abs to show.

I swallowed hard, a hot flush blazing a trail across my skin. Reminded me of that old television show, *Bonanza*. You know, the one with the burning map and the lively western tune? Yeah, my skin was that map, but the song blaring in my head leaned more toward a bow-chick-a-wow-wow sound than anything else. Hormone overload!

This otherworldly creature was not only a walking advertisement for sinful behavior, but a mystical weapon of lust and desire sent to destroy me.

A Celtic tribal tattoo circled his right bicep. Did I mention earlier I had a thing for tatts? Yeah… they drive me wild. His large eyes, the deep color of blue sapphires, captivated me and drew me to him, pulling me into their depths. I was mesmerized not only by their beauty, but by something else. A hint of sadness floated just under the surface. The sorrow tugged at my soul, overpowering me with the urge to wrap my arms around him and tell him everything would be all right.

Gah…get a grip, Ryann. He's a stranger. Still…

Thank God no one needed my help. Lost to the world, I stood mesmerized by his brilliance. Truly, he was the most handsome creature I'd ever seen. A powerful Sex God sent from above to tempt my virtue and threaten my virginity. I froze, ramrod straight, unable to move while images of him ravishing my mouth with his own overpowered me. Those full, beautiful lips…

"You there, get us some booze, eh?"

My daydream burst when he opened his pie hole. Was he talking to me? "Excuse me?"

The corner of his mouth turned up and he swiped his thumb over his lower lip, I assumed to keep from laughing. "I said, get us some booze. You're a bit thick, are ye?"

His deep voice floated across my skin like warm liquid chocolate, smooth and appealing with a sexy Irish accent. His words were another story. They ruffled my feathers, making my temper flare.

Despite his blatant show of rudeness, my palms began to sweat and my heart danced a quickstep inside my chest. Apparently, my mind took offense to being insulted, but my body—yeah, it didn't seem to care.

Thank God my brain kicked into gear. He struck a nerve when he called me stupid and I bristled. "If by thick, you mean dumb, then no, I'm not. What type of *booze* can I get you? Olde English? Steel Reserve?" I narrowed my eyes and rattled off the list of cheap beer I often saw homeless men drinking just outside the club.

I mean, really… who referred to liquor as "booze" any more? Who the hell was this guy? Where the hell was he from?

"Maybe you'd like a brown bag to hide your Ripple? In case you haven't noticed, you're in a nightclub, not a liquor store. If you want, I'll happily direct you to one around here." I glared down at the handsome source of my irritation, treating him to a haughty stare and my sharpest sarcasm. I didn't care if I was being caustic. After the ass grab earlier, I'd decided enough was enough. I wasn't taking any more crap from anyone else tonight.

The handsome Sex God gave a low chuckle and sat back in his seat. He kicked his feet out in front of him, crossing his arms over his large chest. A wide, panty-dropping grin crossed his face, and it was clear to me he found my frustration with him funny.

"You can bring me a pint. Guinness. The lady will have a Coke."

I bit the inside of my cheek, stifling the urge to lift my arm, extend my middle finger and let the patron saint of pissed off servers fly. Biting back a nasty barrage of insults, I gave him a terse nod and fled the scene. I made my way over to the bar and handed my drink tickets to the bartender, Gabriel.

While I waited for the Sex God's *booze,* I stole a glance at my discourteous customer and the set of boobs he brought in with him. She'd plastered herself to him, placing tiny kisses at the base of his neck, looking as though she wanted to rip his clothes off and get down to business. He, on the other hand, wore an expression of pure boredom. This guy was a player.

Just when I thought for certain she was going to rip her top off and swing it about her head à la *Girls Gone Wild,* Boobs disentangled herself from the Sex God, stood up, and strolled off toward the bathroom.

Unable to put off the inevitable, I grabbed my tray full of drinks and walked back to my section, serving his table last.

"Thick headed or not, you're a fine piece of stuff, aren't you?" One eyebrow shot up and an appreciative smile crossed his mouth as he openly stared at my chest. Really stared.

Seriously? Was this guy for real? I didn't bother to respond to his unwanted observation, opting to scowl at him instead while I served him his drinks.

The Sex God drummed his fingers on the top of the table. "Don't go getting your panties in a bunch. I was just admiring you." He returned my scowl with one of his own. "Most women like it when I compliment them."

I stiffened. "Calling me a fine piece of stuff, while your girlfriend is in the can, is hardly what I'd call a compliment. I am *not* like other women."

"Aye, I can see that," he said, treating me to a rakish grin. His smile lit up his entire face, and for a brief moment, there was a playful air about him. Then he started speaking again. "Are you going to just keep staring at me like that? Truly, I don't mind, but I think my date might."

Jerk! I liked this guy much better when his trap was shut.

"Don't flatter yourself. I wasn't staring," I lied. He'd caught me ogling him for sure, but I wasn't about to own up to it. This guy's over inflated ego didn't need any more padding. "I'll come back in a bit to check on your drinks." I white-knuckled my tray and turned to leave.

"Nice arse you've got there."

I froze. *Oh no, he didn't.*

Someone was about to lose a finger. On fire, I whirled around to face the handsome source of my annoyance and gave him my very best death stare. If it were at all possible to shoot lasers from my eyes, the beautiful jerk would've been a pile of ash.

Amused by my frustration, he laughed openly, while staring at me with those piercing blue eyes.

I cursed my two-timing body. My knees went soft and my treasonous heart thumped like a jackhammer all over again. What was it about this guy that sent my hormones through the roof? I marched back toward him, slamming my empty tray onto the table with a loud thwack. "I don't like you," I hissed.

His eyes blazed hot and he met my angry stare head on. "Oh, but really, you do."

"No, I don't." My cheeks burned from the anger flooding my system, and my body took on similar characteristics to a volcano. I was damn sure I'd explode.

He leaned forward in his seat and curled his finger toward me like he wanted to tell me a secret. "You're fooling yourself, lass. It's no matter, though. Even if you weren't attracted to me, I could have you."

My head snapped back and my jaw dropped in disgust. I was no mere object to be had. I didn't care how good-looking he was, this guy was a total bastard. I narrowed my eyes at him in anger. "Never." My body was a different story altogether. It didn't seem to care whether or not the guy was an assface. My breathing hitched, my nipples hardened to diamonds under my tank, and my girlie bits cried out for him to touch me. My body warred with my mind. I was completely out of control.

The Sex God leaned forward over the table and grabbed hold of my wrist. I gasped. I wasn't expecting the instant reaction that came from the contact. The moment his skin touched mine, an electric shock jolted through my body, sending a slow, delicious burn racing through my veins. The pleasant sensation grew from my center, radiating outward. A warm flush danced across my skin, and I felt dizzy, desperately sucking in precious air. His touch was euphoric.

He released his hold on my wrist, and the lusty high disappeared, leaving me angry, confused, unsatisfied, and horny.

"What the hell?" I breathed, rubbing the spot on my wrist, and cursing my body, which still longed for his touch.

He flashed me a bland I-told-you-so look. "Aye, I warned you. If I want you, I'll have you. Just not tonight."

I opened my mouth to tell him what he could have and where he could stick it, when Boobs magically returned and slid into her seat beside him.

Not wanting to create a scene, I decided it was best to get the hell out of Dodge. "Enjoy your drinks," I said, sliding my tray from the table and hightailing it out of my section.

"Thank you. We will." His Irish accent wafted over me, sending butterflies fluttering throughout my stomach. Cursing my body's knee-jerk reaction to him, I looked over my shoulder. He watched me with a devilish grin sprawled across his rugged, yet beautiful, face.

Agitated and unsettled, I chucked my drink tray onto the bar with a bit more force than necessary, sending it crashing onto the floor behind the bar. I needed to get hold of myself, and quick.

Gabriel eyeballed me with a wary look and plucked it from the floor as he filled drink orders.

I snatched up a nearby rag and wiped down the bar, completely disgusted with how my body reacted to the handsome, but annoying, jerk. He was a womanizer and represented everything I loathed in a man. But his touch—it was electric, powerful, and drew me to him in a raw, animalistic way.

I chanced a look over to where the Sex God sat with Boobs. They were holding hands and leaning in close to one another. To a casual observer, they looked like a happy couple basking in the feel of new love. I made a "pssh" sound. I knew better. My eyes stayed on him, riveted when he placed a hand on each side of her face and stared deeply into her eyes. What was he doing? Putting her in a trance? The strange, uninterrupted eye contact went on for a while until, finally, he leaned forward and kissed her forehead. He tossed a wad of cash onto the table and made for the exit. What had I just witnessed?

A high-pitched gasp resonated throughout the bar area. "Get your hands off me!"

Oh great. Not again. I looked over to the bar and my stomach rolled.

A two-hundred-plus pound, steroid junkie with messy brown hair and a crap-load of attitude towered over a petite blonde, slurring drunken words at her. "C'mon, baby. Let me buy you a drink." Pissed to the gills, the drunken ass leaned forward, grabbed the tiny barfly and went in for a kiss.

"I said no!" The loud smack of her palm hitting his fleshy cheek filled the bar. My heart jumped into my throat while I watched the meathead shove her into a nearby server, sending beer bottles, glasses, and liquor flying everywhere as they crashed to the floor.

"Stupid bitch. Get up." Grabbing a fistful of her shirt, the drunken oaf yanked the blonde off the floor, rearing his arm back to hit her.

Panic surged. I opened my mouth to shout for Gabriel when the Sex God suddenly appeared out of nowhere, alongside the abusive jerk.

His jaw was clenched, his eyes on fire and full of rage. He caught the asshole's fist mid-punch and twisted his arm behind his back. Grabbing a handful of brown hair, he shoved the inebriated jerk into the bar with an obscene amount of force and growled. "Only insecure mollies beat their women." His lips curled back into a snarl and he pulled the asshole's head back by the hair, slamming his face into the hard wooden surface of the bar.

Angry Muscle Man went limp and hit the floor.

Holy… My jaw dropped, and I stared openmouthed at the unexpected scene in front of me. Mr. Sex God was a conceited ass, for sure. But he didn't put up with lowlife bastards who hurt their women, and that made him one of the good guys in my book. I suddenly didn't feel so bad about the fantasy I'd had about him just a few minutes before.

Satisfied the drunken bodybuilder was down for the count, Mr. Sex God turned and knelt down alongside the blonde who sat cowering near the shaken server. "Are ye all right, lassies?" He reached out to help the women to their feet and suddenly pulled his hand back before making contact, cursing under his breath. Lifting his arm up, he turned toward the bar. "Can we get some help over here?"

Gabriel hopped over the smooth wooden surface, and ushered both women to a nearby table.

The Sex God stood and glowered over the meathead, who whimpered like a baby while nursing a bloody nose and trying to peel himself off the floor. "Let's go, arsehole. You're done for the night." Grabbing the bodybuilder by the scruff of the neck, he hauled him off the ground and shoved him toward the bouncers who were closing in.

With morbid curiosity, I watched the Sex God search the bar, his eyebrows furrowed in concentration. The moment his eyes found mine, his expression softened. His jaw relaxed, his eyes lit up, and the corners of his mouth turned into a lust-inspiring smile. "See you around, love." With a wink and a nod, he turned toward the crowd.

I looked away momentarily, embarrassed by the blush creeping up my neck and onto my cheeks.

Stupid hormonal body. I will not react this way.

I craned my head toward the exit, desperately trying to find him, but came up short. He was nowhere to be seen. He'd vanished. Impossible! I only looked down for a second.

Without thinking, I rounded the bar and hurried to the exit, barreling out the doors and peering down the street. The sidewalk was empty in both directions. I let out a frustrated huff as I continued scanning the area. There was no one on the opposite side of the street either. Where the hell did he go? People don't just disappear. Damn. I'd freaking lost my mind.

With a sigh, I walked back inside and over to the table where Boobs still sat, staring off into the ether. "Are you okay?" I asked. She looked like a space cadet.

Boobs turned her head slightly to look at me, but remained silent.

Maybe if I tried a different tack. I got right in front of her face and spoke with slow, concise words. "Where did your boyfriend go?" Yeah, okay, my tone was a bit patronizing. I'll admit it. But what was I supposed to do? Girlfriend was out of whack and stuck in some sort of trance. I needed to help her.

A crease formed over Boob's brow.

Aha! Synapses are firing. Boobs does have a brain.

"Huh? Boyfriend? I'm not seeing anyone right now."

Okay… she's either playing games or she's high.

Now I was concerned. She was clearly confused and out of it. "Are you feeling all right?"

Boobs shifted in her seat and cast me a nervous glance. "I'm fine. Why?"

I gripped the back of the chair opposite hers and continued. "Well, you seem to have forgotten about the guy you came in here with."

She looked at me like I was crazy. "I didn't come in here with anyone. Actually, I don't really remember how I got here."

Weird. Maybe she is high. Maybe the Sex God drugged her.

"Well, you came in a bit ago with a very good-looking, albeit viper-tongued, man. You two seemed very close, and now you're telling me you don't remember any of it?"

She narrowed her eyes and made a face. "Look, I don't know what you're talking about. Leave me alone." She stood up with a huff and stormed out, grumbling the entire way.

Okay…

Too tired to give Boobs another thought, I finished out my shift. After clocking out, I changed into my pink velour tracksuit, grabbed a cup of black coffee from the break room, and put the bizarre evening behind me. I had an appointment with the Sandman, and the slight lag in my step told me I didn't want to be late.

Walking home at two in the morning probably wasn't the smartest thing to do, especially after the break-in at my apartment last week. I'd endured an hour-long diatribe from my roommate earlier in the day about the various dregs of society roaming the streets of Hanaford Park. My reasoning for walking was simple. I lived nearby, the fresh air would help clear my head after the bizarre evening I had, and dammit, I wasn't going to live my life in fear. If I wanted to walk home, I would.

Aside from the ass grab and my run in with Mr. Sex God Extraordinaire, the evening hadn't been *all* bad. My feet didn't hurt, and for once, no one spilled beer on me. I'd also made a killing in tips; one older man with a beard and potbelly left me a cool fifty. Woo-hoo! I suppose the craptastic booty shorts we were forced to wear while on duty weren't all bad, even if they barely covered my Titanic tushy. At least they spawned good tips.

One more year. The phrase played on an automatic loop in my brain, over and over again. I needed the job at the club long enough to get me through my senior year of college. After graduation, I'd move on to bigger and better things. No more slinging beer and hot wings. No more lecherous stares, crappy come-ons, and unwanted groping. Majoring in psychology, I fully planned on being a therapist one day. I couldn't wait to get the hell outta Hanaford Park.

The piercing blue eyes of Mr. Sex God kept popping in and out of my conscious thoughts while my mind replayed the events of the evening. I rolled my eyes at the nickname I'd given him. "Mr. Sex God. Humph! I wonder what your name is." I heaved a sigh. "Those eyes… behind all that arrogance, they were so sad."

A warm, yellow glow illuminated the courtyard of my apartment building and a twinge of relief washed through me. I picked up my pace, eager to get home. Precious sleep was just a few moments away, and I could almost feel the softness of my sheets against my skin.

Out of nowhere, an eerie feeling crawled up my spine, and a terrible sense of paranoia stole my breath away. Someone was watching me.

I fished my keys out of my Coach bag, gripping them in my hand to use as a weapon. "Damn." I cursed myself for forgetting to throw my pepper spray in when I'd changed bags earlier. I'd stab someone with my keys if I had to, but much preferred the idea of hosing down any attacker from several feet away. My body seized up, shook, and swayed as I turned, and scanned the area. I was completely alone.

Unable to shake the feeling there was someone spying on me, I called out. "Is anyone there?"

Nothing.

I took a deep breath and blew it out forcefully. Stupidity was not a quality I admired, especially not in myself.

Get a grip, buckshot. There's not a soul out here.

With a frustrated sigh, I turned back toward my apartment and reached for the door, all the while sensing a pair of eyes boring into my back.

chapter 2

The loud, buzzing sound of my alarm clock wrenched me from my sleep. My roommate's mother purchased the annoying but necessary contraption for me. Reaching across to my nightstand, I hit the snooze button, then rolled onto my back and stared at the ceiling. I rubbed my eyes, which were still heavy from sleep, took a deep breath and groaned.

After a measly four hours of sleep, the thought of crawling out of bed for an early morning run made me want to cry. Getting up at six a.m. on days where I hadn't worked the night before was easy. But with classes starting up again, dragging my ass out to run on a mere four hours of shut-eye was hard. Damn hard. I'd do it anyway, regardless of how groggy I felt and how cranky I knew I'd be. People have told me on more than one occasion I have masochistic tendencies.

My profuse hatred for running did nothing to sway my resolve. Sucky as it may be, I knew it was the best way to get in a great cardio workout. I may sling beer for a living, but I rarely drank the ass-expanding crap. At least, not anymore. Did I mention before I have a badonkadonk-sized kiester? No? Let's just say that if I don't run, and often, my backside will blow up to roughly the size of Texas. My roommate, Jessica? The skinny little thing's got zero in the booty department. She suffers from what I like to call FAS, or Falling Ass Syndrome. Her pants, my God, she's constantly yanking them up. Saggy jeans? Yeah … not so much of a problem for me. At five-foot-seven, most of my one hundred thirty-five pounds is spread between my ginormous boobs, which are my best feature, and a J-Lo booty that wouldn't be *so* bad if it didn't come with the accompanying cellulite. I liked my cottage cheese in a plastic tub, not on my thighs.

Thanks to a wild freshman year of scarfing down fatty commons food and guzzling Coors Lite every chance I got, I became the victim of what many refer to as the "freshman fifteen." I'd been battling excess poundage for the past four years. At a size eight, I wasn't chunky, but a bit thicker than I liked. If I went out, I always drank clear liquor, and I'd run my ass off the next morning to keep the excess pounds away. And carbs? Yeah... carbs were the devil as far as I was concerned.

The alarm clock buzzed at me again.

"All right. I'm up." I reached over and slapped my hand down on the early morning torture device a bit harder than I should have. The annoying POS crashed to the floor.

The next thing I knew, the door to my room flew open, and Jessica stood glaring at me from the doorway. Half her blond hair was plastered to the side of her head, the other half stood on end, making her look like a wild woman on the verge of a rage attack. "Do you have to blare your alarm clock so loudly? Turn that thing down! Some of us need to sleep, *thankyouverymuch!*" She stared at me with one eye closed and ran her hand through her messy hair. "What are you doing up so early anyway? You worked late, and class starts today."

I scrubbed my hand over my face. Why was I up so early? Oh yeah... "Gotta run. Sorry about the alarm clock. Try to go back to sleep." I felt like a shmuck for waking her up. No doubt I'd hear about it later.

She mumbled something incoherent, leveling a harsh stare at me, complete with pointed finger and scowl, before turning to leave. I'd have to change the volume setting on my alarm clock pronto or she was liable to bash me over the head with it. Jess was a sweetheart but needed her sleep and became downright violent when she didn't get it. Just because I got up at the ass crack of dawn didn't mean she needed to.

I forced myself from my warm cocoon and lumbered over to my closet, stubbing my toe along the way. A few choice words, most of which would cause a sailor to blush, blew past my lips as I hopped in place, clutching my injured digit. Not a great way to start the day. After pulling on two sports bras (Yes, two. Big boobs + running = black eyes), a t-shirt, sweats, and sneakers, I snatched my keys out of my bag, pulled the stretchy keychain onto my wrist, grabbed my iPod, and headed out the door.

Rays from the early morning sun bounced off the side of the apartment building and through the tall oak sitting in the middle of the courtyard. A blanket of yellow and brown leaves covered the pavement, reminding me that even though it wasn't cold yet, it wasn't summer anymore. Autumn in Hanaford Park, California, was my favorite time of year.

The crisp morning air was refreshing, and my body came alive as I filled my lungs. Placing my earbuds in my ears, I scrolled through my playlists until I found what I was looking for: Linkin Park.

Jogging across the courtyard and out onto the street, I decided to circle the outer perimeter of the campus, which conveniently sat one block away from my apartment. Yep. You read that right. School: one block away. Work: two blocks away. My entire life took place within a two-mile radius. I was a real globetrotter.

I picked up my pace. Since today was the first day of class, I wanted to make sure I'd have enough time to shower and get ready. Rank armpits and greasy hair on top of a large ass were a definite no-no. I didn't possess a magical shrink ray to reduce the size of my backside, but what I did have was a great sense of style, and I would make damn sure I looked put together.

I circled the campus quicker than I anticipated (woo-hoo!) and decided to go another round before heading home.

The unsettling sense that someone watched me struck halfway into my second lap. Pants-pissing scared, every hair on my body stood at attention and an icy shiver shot up my spine. I'd experienced a similar feeling of being watched the night before, but this... this was different. A sick feeling of dread slithered across my flesh, making me want to jump out of my skin.

Wigged, I scanned the area and stepped up my pace. There were a few other students jogging, and a deliveryman pushing crates of milk toward the campus dining hall. None of them paid any attention to me, and once again I felt like a member of the forty-watt club.

My imagination was obviously running wild, probably a result of the measly four hours of sleep. The urge to slap myself for acting like an idiot was strong, and I hauled ass across the street, through the courtyard, and into the sanctuary of my apartment.

Once inside, I tiptoed down the hallway, doing my level best to be quiet and not wake Jessica. My efforts were in vain. I tripped over a random shoe and tumbled ass-over-tea-kettle onto the floor with a loud "Oomph!"

The door to Jessica's room flew open. "Ryann?" She flipped on the hall light and rubbed her eyes furiously. "Are you all right?"

I lay sprawled out in the middle of the floor, unable to contain my laughter.

"Ryann, are you really okay?" she asked, trying to hold back her own giggling.

"I'm fine," I replied, gasping for air as I continued to snicker. "Sorry to wake you…again. I left the hall light off, hoping to go unnoticed. I was tiptoeing to my room and tripped over this," I said, holding up one of Jessica's shoes, which as usual, were strewn about the apartment willy-nilly.

She reached for the offending footwear with a sheepish look on her face. "Oh, God. I'm sorry. I thought I moved all of my shoes out of the hallway last night. I guess I missed one."

"Don't worry about it," I said, waving her off as I got to my feet. Glancing through my doorway toward my alarm clock, I saw it was a few minutes after seven. "Oh snap. I have to shower or I'm gonna be late. My first class is at eight."

After hightailing it into my room and grabbing a set of fresh chonies and my robe, I made a mad dash toward the bathroom.

Thirty minutes later, I darted across the hallway into my room with my hair dried and styled, and my makeup done to perfection. Digging through my packed (yeah, I like to shop, sue me) and extremely cramped closet, I decided on a pair of low-rise Lucky jeans that looked great as long as I didn't bend or move too much in them, and a white Hollister t-shirt. I slid my feet into my favorite gold pair of Steve Madden flip flops and frantically searched for my large gold hoops and watch to match. Slightly OCD about matching accessories, I'd switch out the tiny stud in my nose daily, just so it would match the rest of my ensemble. That particular piece of jewelry was safe today as the tiny cubic zirconia stud matched my outfit perfectly.

"Ooh, cute sandals," Jessica said, admiring my footwear from the doorway as she sipped her morning coffee. "And your hair…I absolutely love the cut. You didn't tell me you were going to take that much off. I'd be too scared to cut mine that short."

My hands automatically reached for my new shorter hair. "Thanks." I'd gone in before work the previous day and cut my longer, brunette locks into a trendier A-line style. My hair was now stacked in the back, angled down to two wicked points in the front, and sported several chunky gold highlights. My stylist, Jolene, was the bomb. Now, if I could do something about my shit brown eyes and oversized chest, I'd be in business. No luck there, though. The thought of touching my eyeballs turned my stomach, so contacts were a definite no-go. And yeah, I may know how to flaunt my girls, but given the chance, I'd gladly trade them in for a set of B cups. I wasn't looking forward to my golden years when my twins would be hanging down to my knees.

"When is your first class?" I asked.

Jess looked at me like I'd flashed in from another planet. "English Lit at ten. Duh. We both have it, dummy. We picked our classes together, remember?"

I bent down and snatched my bag from the floor, groaning, because it looked like I'd be vacuuming later in the day. "I'm functioning on four hours of sleep here, Jess. Work with me."

"Besides," she said, scrunching her nose up and grimacing. "I am *not* a morning person, so I made sure my first class didn't start until later. Honestly, I don't know how you do it. Mornings are the worst."

"Coffee helps," I said and grabbed the half full mug of java out of her hand, downing it in one large gulp. I stuck my tongue out. "Needs sugar."

Jessica let out a large gasp and yanked the empty mug out of my hands, while she glowered at me. "Ryann! That was …" She fidgeted in place, eyes darting left and right as she racked her brain for a put down. "You're a … a …"

I sighed. Watching her struggle was painful. Jess wasn't proficient like I was in the insult department, and she fought to come up with something witty. Never one to back down from an opportunity to mock others, or myself, I jumped right in. "Crappy-ass roommate? Janky ho?" I tried to keep a straight face and failed. Jess flushed scarlet. A product of her mother's good upbringing, curse words and slander didn't come easy for her. It took two years of constant teasing to get her to say the word "ass" instead of "bottom," and she still referred to her box as her "private place."

Jessica had been my best friend for as long as I could remember. We'd met in junior high at the town's local All Star cheer gym. Though she wasn't tall at five foot five, her shoulder length, blond hair and bright blue eyes gave her an open invitation into the popular crowd. Despite the opportunities afforded by her appearance, she was far from plastic. A spattering of freckles crossed her nose and her entire face lit up when she smiled. She alone knew of my all-consuming obsession with bags and shoes, and my love/hate relationship with dairy foods and carbs. I've heard it said, time and time again, how you could count your good friends on one hand. Jess was the first finger on my one hand, and I loved her dearly.

With a snicker, I grabbed the empty mug, dropping it into the kitchen sink on my way out.

I heard her holler as I reached the front door of the apartment. "I hope that coffee burned your mouth, stinker!" *Ooh… scathing comeback!*

I laughed and threw her a quick wave. "See you at ten!" With a smirk, I closed the door behind me and burned rubber to class.

Ninety minutes later, I strolled into the quad at the center of campus, taking a seat on one of the hard, metal benches. My stomach growled and I eyed the small coffee cart a few feet away, trying to decide if the mile-long line snaking its way around the quad was worth it or not. Frustrated, I craned my head to get a better look at what they were pushing and groaned. Frappucinos and… donuts. Why? Why couldn't they peddle fruit? Hell, I'd even settle for a bran muffin. Regularity is a thing of beauty. But donuts? If I so much as sniffed one, my butt would take on beach front property, and extra Zumba classes were a no-go. I was Zumba'd out. I took a deep breath and sighed. Looked like I'd be practicing restraint.

My cell phone buzzed, and I pulled it from my tote to see Jessica's face flashing across the screen. "What's up? You know, my mouth feels fine. Your coffee didn't burn it at all." I giggled silently to myself. My sarcasm had me on a fast track straight to Hades.

"Where are you?" she asked. "We need to talk. I'm not so sure about our new roomie."

Sick of tiny, cramped dorm rooms with no privacy, and completely uninterested in rushing sororities, Jessica and I had pooled our resources and opted to rent an apartment. Our place was roomy, private, and conveniently close to campus and my work, which saved on the golden fluid flowing into my tank. They should throw diamonds into that shit for what they charge!

Jessica's mom, Karen, covered all of her expenses, insisting school should be her main focus until graduation.

A product of the foster care system after losing my parents at the early age of two, I had no one to cover my expenses and had learned early on how to take care of myself. I'd worked since I was fifteen and managed to put a decent chunk of money into a savings account over the years, and even earned enough to buy a car. "I'm sitting in the quad. What's the matter?"

"I'll tell you when I get there. I'll see you in a minute or two." She hung up before I could get another word out.

I sat lost in thought for a moment, wondering what she wanted to talk about, when an icy chill shot up my spine. My lungs went on strike, struggling to pull in air, and I felt an overwhelming sense that someone or some *thing* monumentally evil lurked just out of sight, waiting to pounce. Swallowing hard, I turned, half expecting to see some crazed mental ward escapee jumping out at me, but, as before, saw nothing out of the ordinary. I let out the breath I hadn't known I was holding. What the hell was going on?

My phone buzzed again. I didn't bother to look at the screen, assuming it was Jessica. "Hey. What did you forget?" I asked as I continued to scan the area. Something wasn't right. The tiny hairs on the back of my neck stood on end, leaving me with a sick, nervous feeling in the pit of my stomach. I wasn't expecting the voice that carried over the phone.

"Hey, Ryann." It was Stan, the new manager from the club. His high-pitched, nasally voice irritated every one of my senses and threatened to make my ears bleed. Despite his horribly annoying articulation, he was a friendly, albeit somewhat geeky, guy.

My paranoia eased up a bit, and I relaxed into the bench. "Oh," I said, slightly surprised. "Hey, Stan. What's up? Do you need me to come in tonight?" I couldn't think of another reason for his call. I liked Stan. He was a decent boss who always treated me with respect. If he needed me to work more hours, I was all for it. College tuition didn't come cheap.

He shouted through the tiny speaker on my cell. "Yeah, actually I do. There's also a big shipment coming in this afternoon. Think you can come in early and help me with it?"

His request took me by surprise. Servers didn't normally help with the shipments, but hey, hours were hours. "Yeah. Sure. No problem."

There was an awkward pause. Stan's heavy breathing sounded through the line. If I hadn't known who was on the other end, I might have been creeped out. With Stan, I was more worried he'd maybe dropped his inhaler. "Stan, you okay? You sound … out of breath."

"Yeah, sorry. I'm fine. I'll see you at five." I heard the line click and go dead.

What was up with the heavy breathing? I clamped my eyes shut and shook my head. On second thought, I didn't want to know.

"Who were you talking to?"

I jumped in my seat with a loud yelp. I looked up to see a smiling Jessica staring down at me with a curious look on her face.

I clutched my chest with my hand. "Wha—Oh, for … Crap. You scared me. That was Stan, the new manager from the club. He needs me to pick up an extra shift tonight." I paused while she sat down next to me. I angled my body so I faced her. "About this morning. I'm sorry I woke you. You have my permission to kick my ass if I do it again."

She flashed me a wry smile.

I tossed my phone into my bag and got down to business. "So, what's wrong with the new girl?"

Jess and I had enough money to cover our apartment ourselves, but, being the smart, cash-conscious girls we were, opted to take on another roommate. Splitting the bills three ways instead of two was better all around.

Our new roommate, Martha, dropped off a bunch of boxes over the weekend, but had officially moved in this morning, while I was in class.

"I knew something was up with her when she told me her full name. I mean, seriously … Martha Stewart? Who names their kid after Ms. Hospital Corners?" Jessica's eyes grew wide, and her expression held a mix of annoyance and fear. I wondered why she would be afraid of our crafty new roommate.

"She's not that bad," I said, trying to talk Jessica down. Truth was, our new roommate was more than a little odd, but out of the applicants we'd interviewed, she was the least offensive. "What did she do? Bake you a quiche and tell you it was a 'good thing'?" I snickered at my own bad joke.

"No," Jessica scoffed. "You saw her. She's nothing like her television counterpart." She shook her head and raised her eyebrows. "To be honest with you, I'm not sure what we got ourselves into. She scares me. Have you seen her goth clothing? Who dresses like that nowadays, anyway? And that scary, emo haircut and black lipstick?" She made a face. "Honestly, I'm afraid to sleep with her in the apartment. She might perform some kind of weird ritual on us or something."

I choked back a laugh. "You've been watching too much TV. No more *Buffy* marathons for you. You never know, she could end up being really cool. You shouldn't judge a book by its cover."

Jessica slumped back against the bench, folding her arms across her chest. "Geez … You sound like my mother."

"Besides," I said, "she signed a contract. The room is hers for the rest of the school year."

"Humph," she grumbled and looked away for a moment. "Hey, what time is it?"

I looked down at my watch and felt my stomach lurch. "Oh crap. Class starts in five minutes. We need to book it."

My heart jumped in my chest as we approached the entrance to our English Lit class. Standing near the entrance to the lecture hall was none other than the Sex God. A leggy brunette stood plastered to his side, whispering something in his ear and giggling. Much like the night before, he looked completely uninterested in the female's attention.

His head snapped around and those gorgeous blue eyes of his burned a hole right through me. Recognition flashed across his beautiful face, and he treated me to a flirtatious smile and a slight nod of the head.

I swear it was like I blew a head gasket the moment I laid eyes on him. My breath hitched and my heart stopped. I hated my body's automatic reaction, but I couldn't see how that could be helped. Dressed casually in a pair of worn jeans and a white t-shirt that hugged his muscular physique, he was the very picture of perfection.

He called out to me from where he stood. "See something you like, love?"

"Jackass," I muttered under my breath. Turning my embarrassment at being caught ogling him into hostility, I threw him a few angry eye darts as I passed by. Just as I crossed the threshold into the classroom, he spoke again.

"Oh, and to answer your question: my name is Quinn. Quinn Donegan." He pegged me with another devilish grin.

"I never asked you what your name was." I stared at him, one eyebrow raised. I hadn't said a word to him.

"Aye, lass, you did." He raked his eyes over me from head to foot, then strode into the classroom before me, pulling Lusty Long Legs behind him.

I stood still for a moment, trying to process what happened. When, if ever, did I inquire about his name? I hadn't. Pretty boy had lost his ever loving …

I froze. Awareness crashed over me, sending a tingling shiver up my spine. I had asked his name last night, as I walked home from work. But I'd been alone, hadn't I? How could he possibly know? "Quinn," I whispered under my breath. Just the mention of his name sent blood racing through my veins.

I traipsed into the large classroom, followed by Jessica, who looked as though she might burst out of her skin with curiosity over my brief conversation with Quinn. We took our seats near the front of the class, where she bombarded me with questions.

"Who was that, Ryann?" Jessica probed. "He's hot. Spill."

"Calm down." I hushed her. "He's nobody … just some random jerk-off that came into the club last night."

"Jerk or no jerk, he's one fine specimen. Did you see the tatt on his arm? Sexy." She gave me a playful swat on the back and turned around to look for him.

I tugged at her arm. "Stop. Don't look at him." I didn't want him to know we were talking about him.

"Why not? He's staring at you, Ryann, and good Lord … he's beautiful."

I turned in my seat to see Quinn seated a few rows up and to the left. Jess was right. He was beautiful. I couldn't put my finger on what it was about him that made him different. But different he surely was. From his smooth, sun-kissed skin to the lethal gait he carried himself with, Quinn was unearthly attractive and altogether mysterious.

He stared at me with a wide grin on his face. Legs, who sat next to him, desperately tried to gain his attention and came up short. Quinn's attention was focused solely on me.

I turned back around just as the professor began the lecture.

The following ninety minutes were pure torture. Concentrating on the lesson was impossible with Quinn's eyes boring into the back of my head. I heard nothing but the pounding of my own heartbeat, and sat flushed and agitated in my seat, unable to do anything about it. I wanted to get the hell out of the building.

Despite my disgust for the garbage that came out of his mouth, I couldn't ignore the physical pull I felt toward him. It was strong, possibly the strongest attraction I'd ever experienced. I was appalled. How could I possibly lust after someone who had such little respect for women? Both times I saw him, he had a different girl draped across him and seemed indifferent to them both. What was that all about?

Lost in thought, I didn't notice class had been dismissed.

"Ryann. Hello? Earth to Ryann." Jessica waved her hands in front of my face. "Class is over. Did you hear anything the professor said?" There was a hint of worry in her voice.

"Um … No?" I felt a little loopy and searched her face with a pleading look. "A little help? Please?"

"No worries. Everything you need to know for the first assignment is right here," she explained while handing me the class syllabus.

I gave it a once-over and groaned. "We have to write a paper on a historical legend?"

"Yep, and it's due next week," Jessica added. "Want to hit the library this afternoon?"

I shook my head. "Can't. I have to work tonight, remember? I need to get a nap in or I'll never make it through my shift. I'll have to go tomorrow before work." I held up the sheet and gave her a nod of appreciation. "Thanks for filling me in. I don't know what's wrong with me. I'm not usually so out of it," I lied. I knew exactly what was wrong with me, or rather who. Quinn had my panties all tied up in knots, and I didn't like it one bit.

Jess and I parted ways. She had one more class to get to, and I seriously needed to sleep. I felt like a walking zombie and probably looked much the same. Lack of sleep made for tired, baggy eyes, and the last thing I wanted was to look like I could carry around extra luggage beneath my peepers. I made it home in record time. Man, I was thankful we lived so close to campus.

Famished from not eating anything but a banana earlier, I raided my refrigerator, throwing together a sandwich in record time. I scarfed it down in three large bites, glad no one was around to watch me make a pig of myself. After downing a glass of water, I ambled down the narrow hallway that led to my room, threw open the door, and literally fell into bed. I eyed the alarm clock on my nightstand with contempt before rolling over and succumbing to sleep.

Vaguely aware I was dreaming, I watched myself jog through the courtyard and across the busy street toward campus. My pace was impressive, and I smiled to myself as I completed the first lap in record time, continuing on for a second circuit.

Approaching the halfway marker, I noticed a dark figure lurking among the trees. Whoever it was went unnoticed by Dream-Ryann as she jogged. I swooped down from above and closed in on the ominous figure to get a closer look. Terror covered me like an icy blanket, freezing me in place.

The mysterious lurker was a man dressed in all black, complete with a trench coat that billowed in the early morning breeze. Except, there was no breeze. The air surrounding us felt unusually still. His coal black hair fell to his shoulders, and his skin was unnaturally pale, almost translucent in the early morning light. Black, spidery veins crept across his face and neck, but it was his eyes that frightened me the most. A pair of sinister black holes stared at me. Two gaping orifices ready to suck the very soul from my body.

Dread wormed its way through my gut, filling every cell, every inch of me. Looking toward my dream self, I saw the fear in my eyes as I scanned the area looking for the source of my unease. How could I have missed such a sinister, creepy-looking character? I turned to face my fugly stalker and fought to pull air into my lungs. He trailed several yards behind me as I jogged toward my apartment. With terror filled eyes, I watched as he raised a long bony finger toward me and uttered a single word. "Mine."

I screamed and thrashed awake. Panting and out of breath, I looked at my clock. It read four thirty. I still had fifteen minutes to rest.

The hell if I'm closing my eyes after that dream!

I sat up, doing my best to shake off the fear and adrenaline pumping through me. Desperate to rid my thoughts of the creepy nightmare, I changed into my shiteous, booty-flashing uniform, grabbed my purse and left for work.

❧

Still anxious from my earlier dream, I crossed through the empty club and made my way into the staff room, tossing my purse into my locker and straightening my hair in the mirror. It felt odd showing up at the club so early. It wasn't customary for servers to come in to help with the alcohol shipments. That job was primarily left for the bartenders or Stan, and I wondered briefly who I was covering for.

Thankful for the hours, regardless of the reason, I made my way out of the locker room and over toward the back entrance where the shipments were brought in. I pursed my lips as I eyed a whole lot of empty space. There were no boxes, no load of goods, and not a soul around. The place was eerily silent.

What is going on?

"Hey there, Ryann."

I let out a breathy yelp and spun around to see Gabriel, the bartender, choking back a laugh, his golden eyes bright with surprise.

People needed to stop sneaking up on me. "Crap. You scared me," I managed to say while clutching my hands over my heart.

His caramel eyes were full of suspicion. "What are you doing here so early?" His Latin accent was buttery smooth and altogether lovely. "Your shift doesn't start until ten, and, come to think of it, isn't today your day off?"

"Yeah," I said, starting to feel a bit uncomfortable. "Stan called earlier and said he needed me to cover a shift tonight. He said he needed help with a shipment this afternoon."

Gabriel narrowed his eyebrows. "Huh." He shrugged. "Well, he's in charge of the scheduling, so if he says we need an extra body tonight, then I'm sure we do. But I have no idea why he asked you to come in and help with a shipment. We're not expecting anything until tomorrow. He's new. Dumbshit must have got the days mixed up," he said with a chuckle. "You might as well stay since you're here and see if Stan will let you help us take inventory."

I nodded and made my way to the storage room where Stan was already at work, counting cases of beer and liquor.

I shuffled forward, feeling awkward and uncomfortable. "So ... there was no shipment today." I felt like an idiot for pointing out the obvious and hoped he wouldn't send me home. I needed a diversion after that creepy dream.

Stan looked up from his clipboard and pushed his glasses higher up onto the bridge of his nose. "Yeah, sorry about that." His voice cracked as he spoke. "Guess I got the days mixed up. But hey," he thrust his clipboard in my direction, "you're here. You might as well pick up some extra hours. Maybe when we finish with the inventory, I can show you how to mix some drinks?"

"I'm cool with that," I said, doing my best to make the most of the bizarre situation.

He smiled, raking his fingers through his short, spiky hair, and tucked the hem of his polo shirt back into his saggy jeans. Stan was the quintessential wannabe. Impossibly tall and thin, he wore Coke-bottle glasses and tried way too hard to fit in with the rest of the staff. Though annoying at times, Stan was harmless and one of the only men in the bar who looked me in the eye instead of straight at my chest.

With the two of us working together, we finished the inventory quickly. This allowed time for a fast meal, and gave Stan plenty of time to school me in the fine art of mixology before my shift started.

Serious about his work, almost to the point of being anal, Stan threw out names of various drinks at rapid fire pace, eyeing me with eager anticipation until I shouted their various ingredients.

"Masturbating Butterfly," he squeaked, his cheeks turning a bright pink as soon as the vulgar name escaped his mouth.

I knew this one. "Midori, Absolut Vodka, sour mix…» I paused, holding my hand up, warning him not to help me as the last two ingredients were on the tip of my tongue. "I know. Sprite and Jaeger!"

Stan looked at me like a proud father whose child just brought home a report card full of A's. "Very good, Ryann. I have a feeling you have a bright future in bartending. The club is about to open, so let's get to work."

I fought the urge to stand at attention and salute him shouting, "Aye aye, Captain!" There was no way I was going to work in a bar for the rest of my days, but I wasn't about to burst his bubble. I kept my trap shut and got busy.

An hour into my shift, I delivered a huge tray of beer and Jaeger shots to a table of sorority girls who were already several drinks in and annihilated. I'd just set down my tray when a warm, familiar tingle shot up the length of my spine. *Quinn.*

I whirled around to see him walking toward me, accompanied by the same pair of perfect, size double zero legs that sat with him during our English class that morning. My heart sank to the floor. Quinn obviously liked his women pencil thin.

"Hello there, Ryann." His thick Irish accent was music to my ears. Turning to face Legs, he pointed toward the same table he'd sat at the previous evening and said, "Sit." Legs obeyed wordlessly as if she had no will of her own.

Quinn turned to face me once again and let loose the full force of his glorious smile. "So, Ryann, how are you this evening?"

What? What the hell is he up to?

I wasn't into playing games. Especially not with a gorgeous Casanova, regardless of how blue his eyes were, or how good his ass looked in his jeans.

Gah. Be strong, Ryann. You are not attracted to this man.

I narrowed my eyes as I drank him in. "Why are you here?"

He pulled a brown bag from his back pocket and flashed me a toothy grin. "I was in the mood for some Ripple. If you've got the booze, I've got the bag." Those gorgeous baby blues of his shone bright with humor.

I choked back a laugh, not wanting to give him the satisfaction of knowing I found him funny. "Have a seat then. What can I get you and your mindless pair of legs?"

Oh my God. I can't believe I just said that. Get a grip, Ryann.

"Mindless pair of legs, eh?" He chuckled, his eyebrows raised in apparent concern for the poor customer service I provided.

Needing my job, I backpedaled. "Look, I'm sorry. That was out of line. When I'm around you, I get flustered. It's no excuse, but it's all I've got. Now, can I get you something to drink?" I hated my stammering, and flushed red, painfully embarrassed by the verbal diarrhea spewing from my mouth.

He dismissed me with a wave. "Don't go worryin' about it. We're cool. Give me the same as yesterday, please."

Did he just say please? Yesterday he comments on my butt and acts like a total pig, and today he's friendly and polite. Who the hell is this guy?

I gave him a nod, went about taking orders for the rest of my section, and headed over to the bar, where Gabriel was darting back and forth, filling orders.

Suddenly self-conscious, I craned my neck, looking into the mirror behind the bar, and straightened my hair. Both of the women Quinn had come in with had long, flowing hair and zero body fat. I glanced down at my legs. "I wonder if he likes…" I paused, inwardly cursing myself. "Oh my God. Idiot." I shook my head, disgusted with myself for worrying over whether Mr. Sex God Extraordinaire may or may not like my thunder thighs.

Grabbing my tray full of drinks, I hotfooted it over to my section, determined to concentrate on my job and nothing else. "Here you go." I reached out, placing the tall pint of Guinness atop a drink napkin on the table before him. His hand brushed mine as he went for his drink.

I gasped. The same electric shock I felt before shot up my arm, through my chest, and straight down to my overexcited hoo-hah. My breath caught in my chest as I stared at him, eyes wide.

He broke contact, pulling his arm back, and placed his hands in his lap. "Thank you, Ryann." His lips broke into a glorious smile.

I stood frozen, struck mute by the effect of his touch and the sheer beauty of his smile. My kitty? Yeah ... it was begging for release. Who was this guy? No. Scratch that. *What* was this guy? I gaped at him.

It wasn't until a customer at a nearby table hollered at me that I was able to tear myself from his mesmerizing presence. I went about my work, painfully aroused I might add, and watched from the corner of my eye as he downed his Guinness in one long gulp. He set his glass down and then once again placed both hands on either side of his nameless date's face. After staring into her eyes for what seemed like an eternity, he gave her a peck on the cheek, tossed a wad of cash onto the table and got up from his seat, strolling past me once again, heading for the exit.

"See ya later, love." He rewarded me with a toothy grin, eyes gleaming.

"What? Wait," I called out to him. "What about your friend? Are you just going to leave her there?" I glanced over to see Legs staring off into space, completely unaware of her surroundings. "Is she all right?" I didn't know why I was so concerned with Quinn and his dazed companion, but I couldn't let it go.

He waved me off with a look that clearly showed he wasn't worried in the least. "Don't worry about her, lass. She'll be just fine."

I wasn't inclined to agree with him and pressed further. "What did you do to her?"

He shrugged. "I let her off easy. Nothing more than that. Later." He pressed two fingers to his lips and made a gesture of throwing me a kiss before disappearing into the crowd once more.

Let her off easy? Putting her into a trance and leaving her alone is letting her off easy?

Suddenly, Legs stood up, looking extremely out of sorts, and made a beeline for the exit.

I couldn't help myself and hollered in her direction. "Excuse me? Where did your friend go? You know, the guy you came in with?"

Rattled by my question, Legs gave me a look that suggested I was crazy. "Um ... I don't remember how I got here. I don't remember coming here with anyone." Her high-pitched voice wavered.

Uh-huh ...

I continued grilling her despite my better judgment. "What about English Lit this morning? Do you remember the guy you were sitting with?"

"Uh … I don't remember going to class this morning. Leave me alone." She glared at me and fled the bar.

I stared after her, frustrated and bewildered by the entire situation. What the hell was going on, why did I care, and why, oh why, did I not carry a pocket rocket in my purse? My girlie bits were still on fire, screaming for release after Mr. Sex God's orgasmic touch.

Something was up with Quinn. I chewed on the inside of my lip as I tried to figure him out. The past two days he'd managed to dazzle a pair of women into forgetting his very existence, leaving them alone and confused in the process. Quinn was an enigma, beautiful, sexy, and infuriating all at the same time, and I was completely enthralled by him.

With a sigh, I went about my work. The remainder of my shift crawled by at a snail's pace. Horny and unable to focus on my job with images of Quinn shooting rapid fire through my head, I botched two orders and spilled an entire tray of drinks in front of the bar, which won me a thunderous wave of applause from everyone who saw it happen. By the time two a.m. rolled around, I had a pounding headache and was more than ready to leave. Grabbing a bag of trash in each hand, I lugged the garbage to the alley outside and tossed it into the giant Dumpster that sat behind the club. I took a deep breath of the outdoor air and closed my eyes, filling my lungs, hoping to clear my headache.

An eerie sense of foreboding hit me once again, my heart rate jumping from zero to sixty in all of two seconds. My palms felt sweaty and my knees shaky. Spooked, but not scared enough to run, I opened my eyes and peered down the dark alley to see a large black dog standing several feet away, staring at me. The ill-boding canine took a few steps closer, stepping into a small ray of light that shone into the narrow alley from a nearby streetlamp. Petrified with fear, I moved to turn and get the hell out of the alley, only to find my feet glued to the cement pavement, each extremity feeling as though it weighed a metric ton. I stood, trapped in place, paralyzed with fear as the dog's obsidian eyes bore into me.

I gasped. *Those eyes …* They were identical to those of the dark figure from my dream. Crippling fear wormed its way in, slithering around my insides, chilling me to the bone. Unable to move, I opened my mouth to scream, but all that came out was a breathy garbled noise. The dog stalked forward until it stood directly in front of me, baring its grisly teeth and uttering a lone, spine chilling word. "Mine."

Everything went black.

chapter 3

Ryann!"

I shifted in place, faintly aware someone was shouting my name. Whoever it was sounded muffled, as if a heavy door blocked their voice. My mind struggled to break through the haze holding me under, making my thoughts fuzzy and scattered. Where was I? What happened?

As I fought to recall what the hell was going on, an icy tremor wracked my body. Stone cold, through and through, I reached out with my right hand and slid my fingers against a gritty, hard surface. Was I lying on the ground?

The worried voice called my name again, and I willed my heavy eyes to open. No such luck. They stubbornly remained closed. Suddenly, my body took on a feeling of weightlessness and the chills subsided. Was I flying?

Warm breath wafted across my face, and a low, masculine voice filled my ear. "No, love, I'm carrying you."

The muscles in my body relaxed the moment I heard the reassuring tone of my chivalrous helper. That voice... it was so familiar. I rolled my head toward the source of the comforting sound, letting it rest against his shoulder.

No longer blocked by the annoying haze, my thoughts cleared, and I realized I was indoors, cradled in the arms of my personal aid. I felt a rustle of movement as whoever held me sat down. Several troubled voices spoke at once.

"Ryann, mi dulce, are you okay?" It was Gabriel. His voice sounded strained with worry.

I wanted to tell him I was all right, but I couldn't find my voice and my stubborn eyelids remained weighted down and uncooperative   "Ryann." The pleasant, familiar voice sent waves of comfort through my veins, easing me further.

"Hmmm?" I managed with a bit of effort.

"Ryann, *a ghrá*. Open your eyes."

Why is that voice so familiar? I know that voice.

The large, warm hand that cupped my cheek slammed me back into reality like a powerful wave breaking against a jagged ocean rock. *Quinn*. His touch sent swell upon swell of wanton desire throughout my body and wet heat pooling between my thighs.

My eyes flew open and I gasped, staring up into Quinn's brilliant, yet somber, blue eyes. I lay cradled in his arms, surrounded by Stan and Gabriel. Their words meshed together, garbled and unintelligible, as they both spoke over the other. Not that I was paying attention to anything they said. I couldn't tear myself away from Quinn's gaze. I could barely catch my breath.

Quinn dropped his head and, with a hiss, looked away momentarily before lifting me off his lap and placing me on the loveseat. He knelt down, taking great care to keep our bodies apart. Did he know the effect his touch had on me? Why did he look so sad? I wasn't sad. I was hot, ready, and oh-so-willing.

Struck with the powerful need to comfort him, I lifted my hand to caress his face and winced when he moved away, avoiding my touch. I raised my eyebrows in question.

He met my silent inquiry with a long sigh. "Later. I promise."

I nodded, telling myself I'd hold him to his word. I was desperate to know what magic kept throwing us together.

Stan lurched into view. "Ryann, thank goodness you're all right." His pitchy voice strained with worry. "You scared me to death. I saw you carrying the trash out and thought I would come back to see if you needed any help. When I came outside, you were laying on the ground, unconscious, with this guy," he pointed to Quinn, "hovering over you. What happened?"

I didn't know how to answer him. I wasn't exactly sure what happened myself. "Um … well, there was a dog."

Gabriel stepped forward. "A dog?" His deep Latin voice held a hint of incredulity, and he gaped at me like I was some kind of lunatic.

I stiffened, switching into defense mode. "Yes, a dog."

Stan eyeballed me like I'd lost my grip on reality. "Do you normally swoon at the sight of canines?" His tone was patronizing and I flashed him a nasty look.

"No, I do not normally faint at the sight of dogs. I love animals. This dog was creepy. There was something wrong with its eyes." I winced, remembering the soulless black orbs. I turned my attention back to Quinn, meeting his gaze head on.

He didn't appear to share my coworkers disbelieving sentiments with regard to the dog. Or if he did, he didn't let it show, and for that I was thankful. Instead, he stared right through me, his powerful jaw clenched and rigid, his brows furrowed as though he were deep in thought.

"I didn't see any dog, Ryann, just him." Stan pointed toward Quinn again. "How do we know he didn't attack you?" Behind the thick Coke-bottle glasses he wore, his eyes were full of distrust.

Quinn remained stone-faced and silent, like an impressive marble statue, flawless and still.

I pushed up onto my elbows and sat up, a wave of dizziness hitting me as I swung my legs off the small loveseat. "He didn't attack me, Stan. He wasn't even there. I told you, there was a creepy black dog and it scared me. That's all."

"Enough." Quinn stood up, his massive six foot three, two-hundred-plus pound frame towering over Stan. "I'll be taking Ryann home now."

The room fell silent, Quinn's thunderous command still echoing throughout the small space. Stan, who looked as though he might wet himself as he stared up at Quinn's hulking build, nodded in agreement and spoke with a shaky voice.

"Yes, I agree with your friend, Ryann, you should get home and rest. Are you comfortable leaving with ...?" Stan turned his head in the direction of my handsome new hero.

"Quinn. His name is Quinn, and yes, I'm comfortable leaving with him. He's a friend."

At least I think he is.

Regardless of who or what he was, I wanted some answers, and the best way to get them was to spend time with him. What had he been doing skulking around an alleyway at two in the morning?

I faltered a bit as I stood, still weak from my recent swoon, and gathered my belongings from my locker, feeling more than a little embarrassed. What the hell was going on? I never fainted. I never lost control.

"Feel better, Ryann," Stan called as I made my way to the exit, where Quinn stood waiting for me.

I threw my gangly boss and Gabriel a halfhearted wave, and mouthed a quick thanks as I left.

An uncomfortable silence grew between us as we walked up the street toward my apartment. Quinn's mood flipped a one-eighty yet again, changing from his earlier polite and courteous state of being, to silent and brooding.

And God, he did the brooding thing well. Dressed in a black leather jacket that screamed badass, a white t-shirt and a pair of worn jeans that clung to his muscular body as though they were designed specifically for him, his aura screamed "don't fuck with me." The muscles in his face were taut, etched into a mask of seriousness that looked an awful lot like agony.

The look of pain he wore tore at my heart. It didn't matter that I barely knew him; I had to ease him. Unable to bear the silence, I blurted out the first thing that came to mind. "So what were you doing in the alley? I thought you'd left the club?"

He glanced at me. "I was taking a walk when I heard you scream. I followed the sound and found you, passed out on the ground."

My eyes widened in shock and disbelief. "You were taking a walk? At two in the morning? Why? And really? You heard me scream?" How was that possible? I'd barely been able to make a sound, I was so scared.

"Aye, I've got good ears."

I frowned. "Did you see the dog?" I knew what I saw, but regardless of Stan's earlier comments, it would be nice to hear someone else confirm my recollection.

His lips drew into a thin line and the thick muscles in his neck twitched and pulsated. "Yes."

I couldn't help but think he was keeping something from me, what with the short, truncated answers. "What are you not telling me?" I stopped and crossed my arms, refusing to take another step until he opened up.

"Look," he said with a sigh. "I don't want you walking home from work at this late hour by yourself. It's not safe. I got a very bad feeling when I walked down that alley and found you." His deep voice sounded troubled, his Irish accent thick.

"Listen, I'm well aware that walking around after-hours is not ideal, but I live just a few streets away, so there's no point in driving to work. Walking makes more sense. I'm a big girl; I can take care of myself."

"Jaysus! Are you daft? Prancing about during the wee hours of the morning is just asking to get picked off! You're as dense as bottled shite!"

Asshole!

My blood boiled. "Excuse me? Bottled shite? You know, that's the second time you've referred to me as stupid and I don't appreciate it. I want to know why you're so concerned for my well-being. You don't know me from Adam. Explain please, and without insulting me." I glared at him with my hands on my hips, hoping he'd slip up and insult me again, so I could rip him a new asshole.

Still scowling, Quinn let out an aggravated huff and pierced me with a hot glare. "I sensed an evil presence in the alley. I'm concerned for your safety."

An evil presence? Who does he think he is, Nostradamus?

I eyed him warily. "Oh-kay. I'm not gonna lie to you, you're creeping me out with the evil talk."

He opened his mouth to say something, then slammed it shut. After a minute, he tried again. "Sorry, *a ghrá*, I was just trying to be honest with you."

I folded my arms across my chest and raised an eyebrow. "You know, I don't get you. When we first met, you acted like a complete tool, flirting with me and checking out my ass in front of your girlfriend. The next time we cross paths, you're a pompous jerk at first, only to do a complete one-eighty and come to my rescue later in the day. What gives? I can't keep up with this hot and cold crap."

Quinn brought out a huge mix of conflicting emotions in me. In the short time I'd known him, I'd wanted to both slap him silly and jump his bones. Our little argument did nothing to sway my feelings. Angry or not, I was fiercely attracted to him.

Stupid jerk!

He met my eyes before scanning the area as he spoke. "Look, I'm sorry, okay? I don't know what you want me to tell you."

He was holding back, refusing to meet my eyes, and it annoyed the crap out of me. "How about the truth?"

He took a deep breath and sighed, running a hand over the back of his skull-trimmed head. "I'm not a nice guy. What can I say? I am trying, though. Truly, I am." His voice was softer now, the harsh *ima-beat-you-senseless* tone gone from when he shouted just moments ago.

Searching his features, I found nothing but remorse looking out at me through his vibrant blue eyes. "I believe you. God help me. I don't know why, but I do."

The muscles in his face and neck relaxed, no longer twitching and straining with frustration. "Thank you," he breathed. "I still don't like you traipsing about all on your own." He inclined his head up the street. "Let's get you home, shall we?"

A radiant smile lit up his face, and he raised his eyebrows and shoved his hands in his pockets. The muscles in his arms flexed, corded and powerful, and I fought to keep myself from staring at them. A fleeting thought raced through my mind, of what those arms would feel like wrapped around me.

Gah. Get a grip, Ryann.

He stared at me with a smug grin on his face. "Enjoying the view, are we?"

With my arms still crossed, I leaned back on one hip and beamed him with a whole lot of *shut-your-pie-hole.* "You're doing it again."

He coughed, trying unsuccessfully to stifle a laugh. "What? Oh, come on, I'm sorry. Can I take you home now? Please?"

"Yeah, okay." I jabbed a finger in his direction. "Just try not to insult me again or I might have to shank you." I tacked on a playful grin for good measure. My apartment building was just up the street and I inwardly cursed its close proximity to my work. I wanted to spend more time with Quinn.

He flashed me a wry smile and waved his hand across his body, urging me to walk with him. "Well, well, well … I guess I'll just have to mind my p's and q's when I'm around you. You're a feisty wee thing, aren't you?"

His voice was incredibly deep, with an almost raspy tone, and incredibly sexy. I hung on his every word, wishing he would speak more, even if it were to fight with me.

I didn't respond, other than to smile, and bit the inside of my lip to stop myself from laughing. I'd turned into a giggling teenager. Butterflies raced through my stomach and my already sweaty palms felt stickier. I felt giddy, like a schoolgirl experiencing her first crush. God, I was pathetic.

"So this is my place." I motioned to the three-story apartment building behind me, secretly wishing I lived across town. If I had any brain at all, I would have feigned amnesia and wandered aimlessly around the city just so I could spend more time with him.

He looked toward the building and then back to me. "Aye, I can see that. So … when do you plan on working on your project for Lit?"

Crap. I'd totally forgotten about our assignment. Hell, I'd forgotten about everyone and every *thing* except for the divine creature standing in front of me. "I'll be hitting the campus library tomorrow afternoon, before I go in to work."

He gave me a nod, his deep, penetrating eyes boring into me, lighting my skin on fire. "I'll be on my way then. Sleep well, *a ghrá*."

I blushed pink and glanced down at my feet for a moment. Why was I so affected by him? He was a stranger, for crap's sake. The pull I felt toward him was…God, incredible. I'd never given much credence to love at first sight, but after meeting Quinn, I was a firm believer in lust at first sight. Stranger or no, I wanted him badly.

"Good night." I looked back up to find Quinn gone, having magically disappeared once again.

How the hell does he keep doing that?

Thankful sleep came easy for once, my exhausted body slept in until well past ten. I didn't have any classes, so I lazed around the apartment most of the day, cleaning, organizing (something Jessica never did), and hoping to get a glimpse of our elusive new roommate, Martha. Much to my chagrin, her door remained closed, and I never saw her.

Unable to put off the inevitable, I grabbed my purse and headed out the door for the library, deciding I'd grab something to eat after I did my research. After making sure the deadbolt was secure, I slammed into a two-hundred-plus pound wall of solid muscle head on. The wind flew out of me with a loud "Ooof!"

"Quinn?" My body came alive in his presence. My heart skipped a beat, and blood pooled to some of the more intimate areas of my anatomy. "What…what are you doing here?" I asked, shocked to see him. I unwillingly peeled myself from the steely expanse of his magnificent body, wishing to God I could somehow morph myself into a pair of low-rise jeans so I could hug his ass all day long.

He stared down at me with a wicked grin. "I'm taking you to the library."

I frowned. "Quinn, I'm a big girl. I don't need a babysitter. I can make it to the library just fine on my own." As much as I craved his presence and secretly wanted to figure out what was going on with him, I sure as hell didn't need a keeper. I'd taken care of myself for as long as I could remember, and did a damn fine job of it too.

Quinn's smile curled into an exasperated frown. "Don't get your knickers in a twist. I know you can take care of yourself just fine. I need to do some research of my own. I have a paper due as well, you know."

My knickers in a twist? Where the hell was this guy from, and what the heck were knickers? "You're not going to budge on this, are you?"

He widened his stance, crossed his arms, and shook his head.

"Fine then," I said with a sigh. "Let's go."

The walk to the university library was brief and chock-full of prolonged, painful silence. Quinn stared at me the entire way, watching me as though some crazed lunatic might jump out at any moment and steal me away. It was unnerving, albeit slightly flattering, that he cared enough to bother.

Once inside, I found a secluded table near the back of the library and set my purse down. "Crap." I'd forgotten my notebook. I let out an irritated groan, which won me a loud "shush" from a couple of nearby students who then gave me eye daggers as I passed them on my way to the stacks.

I heard a low snicker and turned to see Quinn fighting back a laugh. "Careful, lass. You've upset the nerd herd."

I stifled the urge to flip him the bird. I noticed I wasn't the only ill-prepared student out of the two of us. Unless Quinn had somehow managed to smuggle a laptop in under his leather jacket without my knowing, he was empty-handed and didn't seem to care. If the man had a photographic memory, I was going to hang him by his toenails. Some of us had to write shit down. I raised an eyebrow and scrutinized him.

"What?" He shrugged his shoulders, feigning innocence.

I bit my lip and grumbled. "Nothing." Arguing with him would do nothing but get me worked up. The stacks, a popular place for playing hide-the-pickle, was not on my list of top places to get pelvic. Not that I anticipated sex with Quinn in any way. Both women I'd seen him with previously had been paper thin waifs, and well... I was a Marilyn. My hourglass figure was the complete opposite of what he seemed to like.

Frustrated, I pulled a thick book from the shelf and made my way back to the table. I sat down, opening the timeworn volume, and flipped through the pages, looking for something that piqued my interest.

A few minutes later, he came up alongside me. "So if you're a psychology major, why are you taking a Lit class?"

"I've got English as a minor. Wait—" I looked up from my book. "How did you know I was majoring in psych? I never told you that." We'd only had a small handful of conversations, none of which had anything to do with my schooling.

He ignored my question and focused on the book in my hands. "What have you got there?" Quinn pulled out a seat next to me and made himself comfortable with a volume of his own.

I lifted the book, enabling him to read the title on the binding.

An impish smirk crossed his mouth. "Irish Mythology, eh?"

Heat scorched my cheeks. "Yeah, you could say my interest in Irish heritage has been recently piqued." *Oh, God. Lame!*

My admission was met with an audible "humph" as he went about reading his selection. I couldn't be sure, but I thought I caught him hiding a smile.

His rugged beauty swept me away once again as I sat and watched him read. Quinn was magnificently made. His closely shaven hair allowed for a generous view of his profile, keeping nothing hidden from my hungry eyes. Everything about him was perfect, from his strong jaw to his flawlessly full lips. And his physique! Adonis had nothing on Quinn. All masculine, hard-bodied, and sensual, he was a deadly weapon sent by the gods to drive women mad, and a walking billboard for all things wicked and carnal. *Orgasms! Get your orgasms here. Hot and juicy! Just how you like 'em!*

As I continued eye-fucking him, my eyes came across something I hadn't noticed before: another tattoo. Centered on the back of his neck, partially obstructed by his shirt, was an enormous tattoo of the Celtic Tree of Life. The intricate detail of the body art was wicked cool. I battled the urge to tug at the neckline of his shirt so I could see the entire thing.

He looked up from his book and smiled. "I thought you needed to do a bit of research?"

Damn. Caught with my hand in the cookie jar.

His satisfied smile made it painfully obvious he enjoyed the fact I'd been drooling over him. *Smug bastard.*

"I am researching. Look here. I'm learning about Bloody Bones." I shoved my face into my book and began reading aloud. "Oh... oh, God," I said as I read the horrible description of that particular story. "Listen to this. Also known as Rawhead, Bloody Bones is said to live near places of water and under sink pipes. Bloody Bones terrorizes naughty children by dragging them down the sink pipes and drowning them in water. He is also said to be able to turn the children into objects, such as pieces of trash, which are then mistakenly thrown out by the unwitting parents."

I looked up at Quinn, horror stricken. "That's a horrible myth, way creepy." After reading that little gem, I was sure to have nightmares.

"Yeah, he's a real pile of shite, that one." He went back to reading, but I noticed his skin had paled and a tic had formed in his jaw. If I had to venture a guess, I'd say he looked nervous, though I had no idea why.

I refocused on my book. "Hmm…this one doesn't seem quite as bloody as the last. Have you heard of the Gancanagh?"

Quinn's head shot up from his book and he stared at me wide eyed for a moment before regaining his composure. "That's not a very interesting tale. Why don't you read about banshees or the Dullahan? He's the inspiration for the Headless Horseman tale."

I shook my head. Scary didn't interest me. Especially not after the tale I'd just skimmed. "This one sounds pretty interesting, but there isn't much information about it."

Figures. I find something I'm interested in, and there's barely any info on it.

I pulled the book closer and lifted it off the table. "The Gancanagh, or Love Talker, is a male faerie in Irish mythology, known for seducing women. The Gancanagh is thought to have an addictive property to his skin, which charms the women he seduces into a deadly obsession. The affected women typically die from withdrawal, pining away for his love, or fighting each other to the death for him."

I looked up to see Quinn staring at the table. His fists were clenched alongside his book, his jaw rigid and the muscles in his neck rippling and flexing.

"How awful! A man-whoring faerie that loves 'em and leaves 'em. Well…at least it's not bloody."

Quinn slammed his book shut and shoved it across the table. "I wouldn't call him a man-whore. There's a bit more to that particular myth than what you've read." He rested an elbow on the table and placed his head in his hand. Apparently, I'd hit a nerve.

I leaned forward. "You know this story?"

He closed his eyes and breathed in a long, slow breath through his nose. "Yes, I'm quite familiar with it."

I grew more uncomfortable by the second and had the sinking feeling I'd insulted him somehow. Obviously, I needed to be careful with my words when discussing anything about Irish culture with him. "I'm sorry. I didn't mean to offend you or your heritage. I'd love to hear more about this particular myth, if you wouldn't mind telling me."

He lifted his head from his hand and turned to face me. "You aren't going to let this go, are you?" he asked, mimicking my words from our walk earlier.

I shook my head with a large grin. "No."

He drew in a deep breath, sighed, and turned in his chair so his entire body faced me. "Very well, then. Where to begin?" He drummed his fingers on the table. "How much do you know about Irish mythology? Faeries, their queen?" He pursed his lips and waited for my response.

I shook my head. "Nothing. I don't know a thing."

"I see," he said, and he sat back in his chair. "I suppose I should begin with a bit of history then. The Fae were an ancient race of beings that came from the great islands of the North. After being defeated in a series of battles with numerous otherworldly beings, as well as the ancestors of those who currently inhabit Ireland, the Fae retreated to the Isle of Apples, or Avalon, as you may have heard it referred to."

My eyes narrowed in confusion. I'd never heard jack about the Fae, which I assumed were faeries. "Avalon? Like from the Arthurian legend?"

"Yes," he said with a nod.

Huh ... you learn something new every day. "So, uh ... where's that located?"

"Avalon? In the Otherworld, of course."

I felt like smacking myself on the forehead. *Oh, of course. The Otherworld. I should have known!* I squelched my sarcasm and let him continue.

"The Fae queen, Morgana, was eternally young and beautiful, and desired by many, including one young and foolish courtier. Exceedingly handsome and gifted with the ability to charm those around him, the young libertine ravished his way through Morgana's female courtiers, wooing them into his bed one by one. Narcissistic in the extreme, the young faerie cared not for the feelings of the women he took advantage of, and he boasted openly about his conquests to all who would listen.

"He was, in fact, so sure of himself, the vainglorious idiot attempted to beguile the beautiful queen, claiming she would be his greatest conquest. Upon hearing his plan, the queen became enraged, cursing the young faerie. For five hundred years he would walk the earth, seducing women, a slave to their passion, driving them to insanity with lust and the illusion of love. His touch brought about a euphoric reaction to the women he courted, filling them with desire and longing." He stared at his hands as he spoke, as though they were the spawn of the devil, and hastily placed them in his lap, out of his line of sight.

Hot and dizzy, I inhaled sharply, unaware I'd been holding my breath. I stared at Quinn, willing him with my eyes to continue, as my breath came in shallow pants.

"Nothing he did was real; it was all an illusion. Every touch, a lie. Never would he know true love or passion, as every woman he came across fell prey to the magic of the curse." He paused for a moment and stared off into space as if he were remembering the story firsthand. Darkness flashed in his eyes. "For a time, he became angry, indifferent to the plight of the women. After ravishing them, he left, letting them pine away for his touch. There were a few women who became deadly, killing any other that dared to cross their unrequited love's path."

He stopped talking when he heard me gasp, and looked down, refusing to meet my eyes.

"What ... what happened?" I asked, my voice barely registering above a whisper. His story was riveting.

"The faerie was unable to live with the destruction that lay in his wake. He discovered he had a few other talents that enabled him to strip the memories of those he seduced, saving them from their inevitable spiral into madness."

"So he sleeps with his prey, and then erases their memories?" My hand shot up to my mouth.

"Yes," Quinn replied quietly, his voice filled with shame. His head hung low, and he refused to meet my eyes as he spoke.

I reached out to him, wondering why he was so worked up over a work of fiction. "Quinn, it's all right. It's just a myth. Th—"

"No." He shot up out of his seat, jaw clenched in anger. "It's not all right. It's torture." His voice broke. His whole body shook, throwing off waves of anger, frustration, and sorrow. "To know every moment of your existence is a lie, a farce. To live each day knowing the women you touch will either have no memory of you when it's all said and done, or suffer mindless insanity is pure, unadulterated agony!" He threw back his chair and stormed off, leaving me shocked and speechless.

My mind reeled. *No way, Ryann. Don't even go there. You like to reside in a little place called reality, where there are no such things as faeries.*

His story was so compelling, though. The tale he wove seemed to meet all my unanswered questions about him. Not to mention, he spoke with such conviction, as though he lived it himself.

Could it be?

Twice I'd seen him at the bar with some random Betty, and twice he'd left them in a whacked out, hypnotic state. Could he have swiped their memories from them? Seemed a bit farfetched to me. Well … okay, it seemed a lot farfetched. But with nothing else to go on, his description of the cursed faerie seemed pretty convincing. Not to mention that orgasmic touch of his. Just thinking about it got my juices flowing.

I had to find him. Gathering up my purse, I tucked the book under my arm and raced out of the library, searching for answers from the only person who could give them to me: Quinn.

chapter 4

"Quinn!" I ran out of the library, frantic and shouting.

I ignored the annoyed stares and disapproving looks of several strangers as I darted down the front steps and onto the grassy area in front of the building. Standing on a bench to get a better view of my surroundings, I craned my head in search of Quinn. He couldn't have gotten far. I left the library just a few moments after he did. This bizarre disappearing act was becoming somewhat of a habit where he was concerned. I thought back to the first day I met him at the bar. He'd vanished then as well.

Well… if he's a faerie, he'd be able to do things like disappear.

I shook my head to clear the crazed thoughts taking over. I needed to get a damn grip.

There's no such thing as faeries, Ryann. Pull it together, girl, or someone's going to send you to the nut house!

Disappointed with my inability to find Quinn, I stepped off the bench with a sigh and took a seat. My stomach twisted and churned, defeat quickly becoming my new best buddy. Had I offended my new friend? Friend. Is that what we were? I wasn't sure how to define our few brief interactions. We didn't have much of a relationship. We'd only been together a handful of times.

Still, despite our rocky start, there were definitely feelings between us, something I wanted to explore more than anything. I didn't normally argue so much with members of the opposite sex—ass grabbers not included. I was generally pretty agreeable. There was just something about Quinn that drove me insane, causing me to call him out whenever he acted cocky.

Was I trying to hide my attraction to him with defensive behavior, like some sort of bizarre foreplay or something?

Foreplay? Was that what our arguing and attitude was?

Whatever the case, I hoped my chances of getting to know him better weren't destroyed. I needed to work on my impulse control. I was always sticking my foot in my mouth.

I stood, gathered my purse and my accidentally pilfered library book, and decided to head home. Quinn was most likely pissed and not coming back, and I was done making a spectacle of myself. I'd trudged all of ten feet before I heard a loud "Ahem" from behind me.

When I turned, there was Quinn, shooting daggers at me with his beautiful baby blues.

"Have I not told you that it isn't safe to be walking about on your own?"

I let out a loud huff. Bad Boy sounded like Yoda. *Safe to be outdoors, it is not.* "Excuse me. You left. What was I supposed to do? Sit and wait in the library until you decided to come back? It was obvious you were angry and didn't want to talk. I mean … you did storm out of the library like a man on fire."

He gaped at me like I'd grown another head. "I didn't leave. I just needed a few moments to myself. I'm not mad at you either. It's just that damn, fucking legend … I … ugh!"

The angrier he became, the more pronounced his accent grew. When he spoke the word "not" it sounded like "no." I had a thing for Irish and Scottish accents, and his was like liquid sex cascading over every inch of my body.

I stepped forward and raised my arm, wanting desperately to comfort him with my touch.

He shrank away, leaving me with an overwhelming sense of rejection.

My arm felt like it weighed ten tons as it fell to my side. "Fine then," I said while burning him with a hot stare. "I won't touch you. I only wanted to comfort you. My mistake … *won't* happen again." I bit the inside of my cheek and turned my back to him, fighting the urge to do something stupid like slap him. It was easier to let my anger take over than to admit I was hurting because he didn't want me near him. I was done making a fool of myself. "I am *so* out of here."

"Ryann, stop!"

Curse my wretched body. My legs stopped moving, my feet frozen in place by his words. I wanted to run. I wanted to stay. I wanted to scream. Mostly I just wanted to know what the hell was going on.

Why was I so freakishly drawn to him? I hardly knew him. The mix of emotions I felt were too much, an overload. Hot traitor tears welled in my eyes, spilling down my cheeks. I didn't turn to face him, but I didn't walk away either. There was no way I'd let him see me cry. I'd never give him that satisfaction.

In an instant, he stood behind me. My body jumped as warm breath wafted across my ear and down my neck. "I want you to touch me."

His close proximity, combined with the delicious minty scent of his warm breath, sent a fevered chill over my skin. I spun on my heels to face him, once again reaching out.

"You can't!" he shouted, stepping back. His eyes went wild, the muscles in his neck straining as he cursed to himself.

I gaped at him, confused. "But you just said—"

"I said I want you to touch me," he interrupted, "but that doesn't mean you can." He shook his head and paced back and forth, scrubbing at his closely shaven head with his hands.

"I don't understand." It was the understatement of the century. "Why not?"

"Because … I have feelings for you." Quinn's voice broke, sounding as though he were crushed.

I ran my hand through my hair and took a step forward. "You're not making any sense."

Quinn held up his hands in caution. "Please, just stop and listen." He grimaced and balled his hands into fists. "Fuck! I've gone and made a right hash of it, haven't I? Goddamned, bloody idiot!"

I stood closed mouthed, not wanting to further aggravate him, and watched as he paced like a madman. I feared for the concrete if he kept up with the back and forth. He'd dig a hole to China before the night was over.

Finally, he stopped and pierced me with his eyes. "I am he."

My head snapped back. "Huh? You're who?"

"The Gancanagh. I am the Gancanagh. The legend is real."

His words hung in the air as the world had gone still. Had I heard him right? If my ears were indeed working correctly, then I'd just witnessed Quinn admit he was a mythical being. He'd confirmed my suspicions that there was something more to him than met the eye, but a faerie? I was crazy for even thinking it. He was insane for believing it about himself. Hell, we were both cuckoo. Maybe we deserved each other.

I stood gawking at him for what seemed like an eternity. Speechless for once, I didn't know what to do.

Quinn growled in frustration. "Say something!"

I hesitated for a moment before jutting out my chin and lowering my eyelids. "Prove it." If he was who he said he was, my little challenge should be small potatoes for him. "This is insane. Faeries aren't real. Mythical creatures don't exist. I mean … Seriously? You really expect me to believe you're a faerie?"

My head was screaming at me to run, to get away from the crazy man who thought he was a mythical being. My heart? Yeah, it had other ideas. An intense ache tore through my chest as I chanted over and over to myself. *Please be real. Please be real. Please, please, please be real.*

Quinn hesitated for a moment, opening his mouth to speak and then closing it again moments later. He scanned the area, shook his head, and frowned. "Too many people. Follow me."

My mouth felt dry as I trailed him to a more secluded area behind the library, free of curious onlookers and random gawkers. What the hell was he going to do? Perform parlor tricks? Uncertainty became my new best friend, and I didn't like it.

He stopped in the center of a small, bench-lined clearing and turned. I watched in awe as he broke into a glorious smile. "Now you see me." He vanished into thin air. "Now you don't."

"Holy shit!" I picked my jaw off the ground and spun around, searching for him while my mind tried to come up with some sort of rational explanation for what I just saw.

"Aye, that's 'bout right." I whirled around. He stood a mere two feet from me. With his head lowered, he looked at me through his lashes and pursed his lips. It was evident he was waiting for a response from me.

Shaking, I opened my mouth only to slam it shut moments later. What do you say when someone disappears before your very eyes?

He scrubbed at his face and groaned. "Say something. I'm shittin' bricks here!"

My voice barely registered above a whisper. "Impossible."

"Impossible? Maybe. But very true, nonetheless." He evaporated before my eyes again and reappeared seconds later, standing on a nearby bench.

My mind spun, and I felt like I was trapped in some kind of bizarre sci-fi reality show. Was I being punked? "Amazing! How are you doing that? Is it like time travel?" My mind couldn't wrap itself around what I'd witnessed.

"No, I'm not traveling through time. I wish." He let out a nervous laugh. "If I could travel through time, I'd go back and stop myself from trying to seduce the queen, and prevent this wretched curse. No … I merely have the ability to render myself invisible."

Merely? He spoke of his mind-blowing ability as if it were no big deal, like rolling your tongue or snapping your fingers.

"Is there anything else?" I asked, unsure of how much more my mind could absorb.

A priceless, shit-eating grin lit up his face, and for a split second, the sadness behind his eyes dimmed. It was like an enormous weight had been lifted from him, and his newfound ability to share with me set him free. After a quick scan to ensure we were alone, Quinn hopped off of the bench, and picked it up with his left hand, raising it high above his head as if it weighed no more than a piece of paper.

The loud clanking noise filling the air? Yeah, that was my jaw hitting the floor again. The solid steel bench had been anchored to the ground.

Quinn smiled at my reaction. "I've got a fair bit of strength." After placing the bench back where it belonged, he appeared in front of me, moving so quickly all my eyes registered was a faint blur. He stared down at me and took off again toward the center of the lawn area at light speed.

I shook my head, desperately trying to come to terms with what I knew was possible, and what I was seeing play out in front of me. Quinn had mad super powers. "Oh. My. God."

In a flash, he stood a few feet in front of me again, as if by magic. "Nope, not God. Just a horny faerie." He raised his eyebrows suggestively.

I sucked in a breath. "You heard me? I barely whispered and you were yards away."

"Aye," he said, pointing to his ears. "Told ye. I've got good hearing."

Was there no end to his abilities? I'd lost my mind. There was no other explanation. This couldn't be real. I'd had an aneurism or something. I was trapped in a dream, and I just wasn't waking up.

Did I really want to, though? Here was this incredible being, standing a scant two feet away, who admitted he harbored feelings for me. No. I'd happily reside in the Land-of-the-Loonies if it allowed me to be with Quinn.

I held up my hand while I struggled to pull my thoughts together. "Let me get this straight. You have the power of invisibility. You've got mad strength, super speed, and have crazy good hearing?"

He laughed, and the musical sound of it sent my heart flying. "Among other things, but yes, that about sums it up."

I swallowed hard. "Other…things?" What else could there be? X-ray vision? Mind reading abilities? *Only one way to find out.* With my mouth clamped shut, I focused on his godlike features and sent him a wordless proposition. *I want your body like a fat kid wants chocolate cake. Kiss me.*

Silence filled the air for a moment as I repeated my silent plea. I didn't move. I didn't breathe. Could he read my mind?

Quinn did a double take and scratched his head. "Are ye all right, lass? You look a bit…hell, I hate to even say it…constipated."

I groaned and buried my face in my hands. Okay, so he wasn't a mind reader, but now he was under the impression I suffered from irritable bowel syndrome. *Smooth move, ex-lax!*

I shook my head and waved him off. "I'm fine. Sorry. Please continue on with your laundry list of super powers."

He raised his eyebrows and grinned, but there was something else hiding behind his chipper façade: relief. He shook his head. "I cannot tell you, lass, how good it feels to finally be able to share myself with someone. Let's see…I'm pretty skilled in the art of seduction, and I'm fairly persuasive. I can also remove all traces of me from your memory if I wanted to." His voice was flat as he spoke these last words, his smile fading into a somber frown.

A shudder ran through my frame at the idea of not being able to remember him. The very thought of a world without Quinn was inconceivable to me, and I instinctively recoiled from it.

Desperate to steer the conversation on to less painful things, I reminded him of a power I'd witnessed firsthand. "There's also your love touch."

The mention of his "love touch" elicited another smile, and I was thankful I could brighten his mood so easily.

"Yes, there is that as well."

"Is it really addictive? Your touch, that is?" I thought back to the first time I'd met him at the bar and the sensation that coursed through my veins when our skin came into contact. His touch was complete, sensual bliss. My circulatory system kicked into overdrive at the memory of it, and I tried my best to calm down. Could he hear my heart racing?

My answer came with a wide, knowing grin. I couldn't keep anything hidden from him.

So not fair!

"It depends," he said.

I crossed my arms and stepped back, staring at him with my jaw tight. I expected a better answer.

He inhaled deep and stared at me with a look that clearly said he didn't want to answer my question. "Just touching you won't bring about the madness. You'd only lose your mind if I were to shag you."

"Shag me?" I said, slightly taken aback. Were we trapped in a Mike Myers film and I didn't know it?

"Sorry, *a ghrá*," he said, treating me to an eye roll. "Make love. Is that more to your liking?"

I flushed and looked down, unsure of how to answer him. Changing the subject seemed like a better idea. I shoved my thumbs into the back pockets of my jeans and bit my lip. "What is that you keep calling me? Do I even want to know? Is it Irish slang for dipshit?"

His laugh was deep and rich and rang out loud.

I gave him my best squinty-eyed glare and crossed my arms with a huff.

"Silly girl. *A ghrá* means 'my love' in Gaelic. It's a pet name often used in the old language."

"Oh." I bit my lip harder and turned away. Heat engulfed my cheeks, turning them a bright neon red. Maybe he was telling the truth when he said he had feelings for me. Why else would he refer to me as his love? Or maybe he had pet names for all of his conquests, and I was indeed being a total nub. Unsure of how to respond to his new name for me, I focused on my previous question.

"So, the women you have…" I hated to even speak the words. "… dealings with. They only lose themselves to madness if they sleep with you. Is that right?"

"Aye," he huffed.

"And those two chippies I saw you with at the bar…you slept with them and then erased their memories of it, didn't you?"

He gave a single nod. He wore a grim expression, his jaw rigid, his lips drawn into a thin line.

My stomach rolled as I conjured an image of him in the club, cradling their faces in his large hands, staring deep into their eyes. I'd witnessed him scrubbing those women's memories. I felt a little sick and a whole lot angry. But beneath all that anger, I pitied him. I felt sorry for the women, of course, but I also felt compassion for Quinn. True, his curse forced him to do deplorable things, sleep with women and then wipe away their memories or leave them to waste away, crazy. But it also left him completely and utterly alone. He'd never experienced a real relationship or felt the glory of true love. How could he? His touch brought about a false reaction, an illusion. How would he ever know if someone's feelings for him were real? I suddenly understood his earlier meltdown.

Quinn stood silent, no doubt trying to gauge my reaction. I ran the gamut of emotions from anger to pity to compassion for his horrible plight. He waited patiently while I made sense of what I was feeling, and allowed me to work through the mountain of information he'd dumped at my feet.

"Is that why you won't let me touch you?" I asked in a soft voice as tears welled in my eyes. I hated how I wore my heart on my sleeve. My body never let me hide my emotions, no matter how hard I tried.

He gave a single nod. "Aye, you're different from the others. Different from anyone I've ever come across. Women, they fall all over me, throw themselves at me without a second thought." He shook his head as he spoke. "Not you. You were so full of piss and vinegar the first time I met you. Practically radiating spunk and fire, and that was even after I touched you. I found myself wanting to talk to you, to get to know you. I can't do that if I touch you. The fucking curse won't let me. I want to keep whatever is between us real. Can you not understand that?"

It felt like all the air had been sucked from the universe. His words left me breathless and dizzy. He wanted to explore what lay between us as much as I did. I looked up at him, unable to stop smiling, and swiped at the warm tear sliding down my cheek. "Yes. Yes, I can understand that," I whispered.

Quinn closed the gap between us in a few long strides and stood dangerously close to me. So close, in fact, I felt his warm breath caressing my skin. It was intoxicating. He raised his hand so it was mere inches from my head, and slowly ran it through the air from my hairline to my cheek as he would if he were able to touch me.

His haunted, beautiful eyes bore into my own with an intensity that touched my very soul. "Don't cry, *a ghrá*."

My stomach growled a loud gurgle in response. The intensity of our little moment flew out the window as we both laughed.

"Hungry, are we?"

I thought back to the pitiful handful of grapes I'd had for lunch. Hell, yes, I was hungry. "Starving actually. I haven't eaten since noon." My tummy rumbled again in agreement.

"Aye, me as well. I could eat a baby's arse through the bars of a cot!"

Oh-kay…

I shook my head, unsure if I'd ever get used to his odd language.

"Come on, then." He strolled down the cement walkway and turned, looking back at me over his shoulder, motioning for me to follow. "Let's get some food in you."

My stomach turned somersaults, not only from hunger, but also from the realization I was going to spend more time with Quinn. I took a deep breath and followed my new friend.

chapter 5

I wasn't the least bit shocked as I trailed Quinn into The Plough and The Stars, the local Irish pub and restaurant located on the main strip. Most people flock to what's familiar, apparently even centuries old Irish faeries. I'd passed the establishment countless times, always curious about the very loud and spirited folk music blasting from the entrance, but had never entered before now.

The Plough felt homey, dark with wood paneling and a spattering of Irish political posters hanging about. A large jukebox sat toward the rear of the bar near the pool tables, pumping out a very lively song. A small stage occupied the space directly across from the bar, where both local and traveling bands could play.

A petite redheaded hostess, whose nametag read Tabitha, shamelessly drooled all over Quinn, before seating us toward the rear of the restaurant portion of the pub. Ignoring my presence, she giggled and flirted with him while rambling on about the evening's dinner specials.

I thought I might pop a vein when she leaned over and shoved her large, medically enhanced boobs in his face.

Hussy!

"Fiona will be your server this evening. Is there anything else I can do for you?" She stared at Quinn like he was a piece of meat, her overly made up eyes reminiscent of a raccoon's black mask.

I forced a fake smile. "We're just fine. Thank you so much!"

Tabitha got the hint and left reluctantly.

Unable to wipe the scowl off my face, I turned to face Quinn, who sat shaking in silent laughter.

"Jealous, are we?" The corners of his lips turned up and his eyes shone bright. His smile lit up his entire face, like an explosion of light and warmth, and I wanted nothing more than to bask in its brilliance.

"No, I'm not jealous," I said with a huff. "It's just… did you see… she…" I was impossibly tongue-tied, tripping up my words. "Boobs! She shoved them in your face. It was disgusting."

Quinn sat back against the cushy fabric of the booth as he toyed with a cardboard coaster. "Well, maybe for you. I rather enjoyed them, myself." He chuckled and ducked out of the way when I threw the rest of the coasters in his direction.

I leveled a harsh stare at him and moved to get up. "Pig!"

"C'mon now," he said, plucking one of the wayward cardboard squares off his chest. "I was only teasing you. I didn't mean it."

I glared at him with my arms crossed. He needed to put the kibosh on the crass talk.

He leaned forward with his lips pressed tight, one side pulled down into a frown. "Sit down, please. I know you're hungry, I can hear your belly rumbling."

I pegged him with a harsh glare, hoping to get my point across. "Fine, but no more ogling every pair of fake boobs that cross your path."

My response was met with a toothy grin. "I wouldn't think of it. I'd much rather ogle yours."

Truly, the man was incorrigible. I shook my head and smiled in spite of his remark. He was irresistible.

Fiona waltzed up to our table, water in hand, and placed it directly in front of Quinn. Tall, wafer-thin and blonde, she was a classy helping of filet mignon, and I was a heaping dish of down-home cooking. I shifted uncomfortably in my seat, deciding it was nothing but water and Tic Tacs for me for the month. Evidently, I was invisible as she focused all her attention on Quinn, never bothering to look in my direction.

"Hello there, handsome. My name's Fiona and I'll be your server this evening." Not only did she have her back to me, but she also sat one perfect butt cheek on the table as she spoke to Quinn, leaning toward him.

Hello! I'm right behind you.

"Good evening, Fiona." Quinn greeted her with a polite smile. "If you would be so kind as to remove your arse from the table I plan to eat off of, I'd like to see my lovely date's face."

Fiona shot off the table as if it were on fire, turning only briefly to acknowledge my presence. "I'm sorry," she said with a nervous stammer. "Can I start you off with a drink?"

"You can start by bringing us another water." Quinn pointed in my direction and winked. "I'll have a pint of Guinness. We'll order when you get back. Now off with ye." He dismissed her with a nod, and I watched as she obeyed, starry eyed and spellbound.

"Wow, you really do have the power of persuasion. She acted like a mindless robot when you told her to leave." I frowned in the direction our plastic server had gone.

Quinn shrugged off my comment like it was nothing. "Eh, it's easy to work my mojo when the person's an idiot. That one that just left, she's not the full shilling."

"Maybe not, but she's pretty." I cringed inwardly, unsure of why I'd let that little gem slip out, and regretted it instantly. The last thing I wanted him to think was that I was fishing for compliments, even if maybe I really was.

"That bird? She's a Bobfoc. Nothing for you to worry about."

"A what?" I couldn't keep up with his slang, though I loved the sound of his voice. If I had my way, I'd listen to him speak all day long, regardless of whether or not I understood anything that he said.

"A Bobfoc. Body off *Baywatch*, face off *Crimewatch*."

I drew in a loud breath in mock horror. "That's awful."

"Maybe, but it's true," he said. "Her face would drive rats from a barn!"

Fiona returned moments later with my water and Quinn's beer.

I looked down at the table and fought to contain my laughter when she asked if we were ready to order. Every time I opened my mouth, I'd start snickering and was completely unable to speak. As her attention was yet again placed solely on Quinn, it was a non-issue, except for the fact that I really needed to order. I was starving. To hell with the Tic Tacs.

Taking notice of my ridiculous fit of giggles, Quinn manned up and ordered for the both of us. "We'll have the fish and chips," he said while handing her the menus. He took a long sip from his beer and closed his eyes, oblivious to the fact that our server still gaped at him.

Spending any kind of time with Quinn was going to take some getting used to, that much was certain. He was like the Pied Piper of women. I'd have to put a bag over his head to get any alone time with him.

He opened his eyes, took one look at the server and sighed. "That'll be all, now off you go."

Fiona's overly made up face fell and she hesitated before finally turning to leave. I couldn't blame her for lingering. Quinn was like crack—thoroughly addictive.

The restaurant portion of the pub filled quickly, a loud clamor ringing out across the room that made hearing your own thoughts difficult, let alone hearing someone else speak. I leaned forward and did my best to speak just loud enough for Quinn to hear. "How is it that you are known as the Love Talker? Not to be insulting or anything, but I've got to say, pretty much everything that comes out of your mouth is far from romantic. How on earth did you get that nickname?"

In the short time I'd known him, Quinn had let loose a barrage of insults, crass humor, sexual innuendos, and curses that would put a sailor to shame. Not that he needed to speak to woo a woman. His godlike features were enough to melt any woman within a twenty-foot radius into a puddle of goo. And his voice … Lord, he had the voice of an angel. Deep and melodic, it was smooth as milk chocolate and pure music to my ears. I knew he could be sincere; he'd proven himself outside of the library earlier. But I'd yet to hear him utter anything swoonworthy and I couldn't help teasing him about it.

I wasn't prepared for what happened next. Quinn leaned forward, his smoldering blue eyes dark and serious, capturing all of my attention. I sat breathless, listening to his velvety soft words.

"How do I love thee?
I love thee to the depth and breadth and height
My soul can reach, when feeling out of sight
For the ends of Being and ideal Grace …"

He was quoting Elizabeth Barrett Browning. "How about some Shakespeare?
Shall I compare thee to a summer's day?
Thou art more lovely and more temperate."

My hand shot up. "Enough. I stand corrected." He was, without question, more than capable of reducing me to a quivering mass of flesh with his words. I suppose I should consider myself lucky he'd never unloaded his complete arsenal of talents on me, or my virginity would be no more than a fleeting thought.

Wearing a self-satisfied smile, Quinn downed the remainder of his beer, then waved to one of the servers and pointed to his empty glass.

Feeling bold, I asked another question. "So how old are you?" I'd been tossing around different possibilities since his big reveal earlier. He didn't look a day over twenty-two, but that meant absolutely nothing. Having witnessed firsthand his wondrous abilities, I knew pretty much anything was possible where Quinn was concerned. Hell, he was a faerie, for crap's sake.

"Old. Care to venture a guess?" One eyebrow rose slightly as he smiled at me.

Never one to back away from a challenge, I threw a couple of numbers at him. "How old? Two hundred years?" That was a nice large number in my book, and was a solid guess as far as I was concerned.

I watched as he spun one of the coasters between his finger and the table like a top. "Older. Try again." He grinned and started to down the new pint of Guinness one of the servers brought him.

Well, shit. Two hundred years is damn old. How old is he?

My eyes widened in shock and I sat back in my seat. "Oh-kay … um, four hundred?" That would place his birth sometime in the sixteen hundreds, Shakespeare's time. I took a sip of my water, the cool liquid sliding down my parched throat. That's when it hit me like a sledgehammer knocking me upside the head. Hello! This guy had seen an incredible amount of history. He was alive when Shakespeare wrote his famous works. He'd probably had front row seats to see Beethoven and Mozart. What the hell was he doing here, drinking beer with me?

My stomach rolled as another thought struck me, much less appealing than the first. Quinn had done more than two hundred years worth of womanizing. How had his appendage not fallen off with so much use?

I'm going to be sick!

I took a deep breath, exhaling slowly while I reminded myself he was cursed. I thought back to when he lifted the bench off of the ground as if it weighed nothing. Quinn had special abilities. My thoughts took a dirty turn. Did he have some sort of magical peen that could do tricks? Was he like the Energizer Bunny? If a mere touch from him overran my system with desire, what would happen if he kissed me? If he … Heat flooded my cheeks, and I was thankful he didn't possess the ability to read my mind.

Gah, stop it, Ryann. Get your mind out of the gutter and stop thinking about his wanker.

"You're getting warmer," he said, eyeing me with suspicion, and finished off his second pint. "I'm five hundred and twenty-one years old."

I choked on my water, half of what was in my mouth spurting out my nose. "Five hundred!" I felt bad for my outburst, but it couldn't be helped. Five hundred? For someone who'd lived over half a millennium, he looked damn sexy. The younger boys of my generation had nothing on Quinn. "Okay, Grandpa. Should I refer to you as Cro-Magnon Man? Talk about robbing the cradle." I couldn't resist, the words came out before I could stop myself.

His voice filled with sarcasm as he made a face at me. "Oh look, you made a funny. I may be as old as dirt itself, but all my parts are in fine working order."

Our conversation stopped briefly when Fiona sidled up to the table with our meal. After haphazardly chucking my plate onto the table, she turned her attention toward Quinn yet again. "Is there anything else that I can get for you?"

"That will be all, thank you." I dismissed her forcefully. I knew what she was up to, offering to get things for him. I could just imagine what her inner dialogue sounded like: coffee, tea, me? I was surprised she hadn't slipped him her phone number on one of the napkins yet.

Skank!

The delicious aroma of my piping hot dinner wafted up to my nose, and any and all sense of decorum I'd learned as a young girl flew out the window like yesterday's garbage. I inhaled my food as if it were the last meal I'd ever eat, barely bothering to chew. I wasn't a huge fan of seafood, but it didn't matter in the least. The dinner could have consisted of cardboard and rocks and I would have told you it was the best meal I'd ever had.

After gorging on three quarters of my plate, I looked up to see Quinn gaping at me with a look of surprise. "What?" I asked, feigning ignorance. I knew damn well what he was staring at: my abhorrent manners. "I'm sorry. I know I'm being a total pig, but I was absolutely starving. I hope I didn't offend you." I set my fork down and wiped my mouth with my napkin, hoping to God I didn't have food smeared across my face.

He lifted a hand, waving me off. "Stop worrying, Ryann."

Heat pooled between my thighs. I loved hearing my name roll off his tongue.

"I'll admit I was a bit shocked to see you go at your food like that, but I was happily surprised. Most women just order leafy crap when I take them out, and then move it about their plate, insisting they're not hungry, while I can plainly hear their bellies rumbling. Food is meant to be eaten and enjoyed. I'm pleased to see you taking pleasure in our meal."

I don't know how he did it, but I was actually blushing after having just made a pig of myself. Quinn wasn't lying when he said he had skills with women. After five hundred years of practice, the man was a pro.

Wait… Five hundred years?

I thought back to our conversation in the library when he told me about the myth of the Gancanagh. I remembered him saying the curse lasted five hundred years. If he was five hundred and twenty-one, and had been twenty-two when the curse was placed upon him, his torture was almost at an end.

"Oh my God, Quinn!"

He held up his hands and glared. "Easy there, lass," he said, pointing to his ears. "Super sensitive hearing, remember?"

"Sorry." I couldn't contain my excitement. "Your curse is almost over. You couldn't have been more than twenty-two when you were damned, and you've lived for five hundred years. You're almost free." I watched as he eyed the couple seated at the table next to us grimly.

"Ryann, I'd rather not have to scrub the memories of each of the patrons here. Could you maybe keep your voice down?" He shook his head at me, but I saw the corners of his mouth turn up into a smile.

"Sorry, but I'm right, aren't I?"

Tight-lipped, he averted his gaze for a moment, then met my eyes. "Not exactly."

"What do you mean 'not exactly'?" The tone of his voice made me uncomfortable.

"Look, Ryann." He sighed. "Can we just enjoy the rest of our meal, and not talk about the damn fucking curse? I'd really just like to keep it light for the rest of the evening. Would that be okay with you?" Mentally worn, his shoulders slumped and he closed his eyes while taking a deep breath. I dropped my insistent attitude. I refused to be the cause of any more pain for him.

"Okay, I'll drop it. For now anyway."

He seemed to relax at that point, easing back into his seat. I watched as he savored his food as well as the new beer one of the wait staff placed before him. He'd had several pints and looked completely normal. Were faeries not affected by alcohol?

We spent the remainder of our meal playing twenty questions. Quinn, no doubt excited at the opportunity to connect with someone on an emotional level rather than just a physical one, inundated me with a barrage of questions ranging from things as trivial as what I liked to eat, to what my goals in life were.

"And your family? Where are they?" he asked, plopping the last bite of fish into his mouth.

I looked down at my plate and pushed it aside, no longer hungry. "My parents died when I was two. I've been on my own for as long as I can remember." The carefree tone of our conversation took a turn, and the air filled with an uncomfortable tension.

The weight of his stare prompted me to look up, and my eyes were met with a soft expression. "I'm so sorry, Ryann. Losing your parents at any age is rough, but losing them as a child is doubly hard. It's made you the woman you are today, though. Strong, determined."

I nodded quietly and fiddled with my napkin.

We sat in silence for a moment, both of us avoiding the heavy issues of our pasts. At that moment, I understood his desire to keep things light for the evening. With the enormous revelations he made earlier, a little bit of levity was definitely on the menu.

I yawned unexpectedly, not realizing how tired I was. Though it wasn't late evening yet, the busyness of the past few days zapped away most of my energy.

He wiped his face with his napkin and tossed it onto his plate. "You're tired. Let's get you home."

I wasn't ready to say goodnight to him yet, but the sensible part of me knew I should get back to my apartment and at least attempt to get some sleep. I wasn't sure if that was a possibility. Being around Quinn amped me up and left me giddy and excited. I nodded in agreement. "Yeah, okay."

Quinn slapped several large bills onto the wooden table and stood. He looked down at me as I struggled to scoot toward the edge of the booth. Out of habit I'm sure, Quinn held his hand out toward me as I stood, offering his help.

I reached for him without thinking and felt crushed when he realized his mistake and yanked his hand away before we made contact.

"I'm, uh … I'm sorry about that." He rubbed the back of his neck and drew in a quick breath. "Fuck. I'm sorry, *a ghrá*. I'll try to be more careful."

The urge to scream was overwhelming. How could I spend any kind of time with him and not touch him? With the simplest of things like helping someone out of a booth being off limits, the craptastic rules forced on me were more than I could take. Especially when every fiber of my being wanted to jump him.

"It's okay," I said and forced a smile as we strolled toward the exit.

Autumn in Hanaford Park was pleasant, the evening air unseasonably warm. The streets were filled with a mix of college kids and locals alike, enjoying the last bit of nice California weather before Mother Nature got snippy and caused a dip in temperature. The short walk to my home was again quiet, yet somehow comfortable. There were still a million things I wanted to ask him. As old as he was, he possessed a wealth of knowledge, and I couldn't wait to pick his brain. He seemed so happy to finally be able to have a conversation with someone that wasn't enhanced or manipulated by his curse, so I left my questions for another time.

As we approached the entrance to my apartment, I reached into my bag, pulling out my keys to unlock the heavy door. "Well, this is goodnight, then." I looked up at him through my eyelashes and chewed on my lower lip. I wanted so badly for him to lean down and kiss me, to confirm his feelings for me in the physical sense. I knew that wasn't a possibility and fought with myself to not appear disappointed when the kiss never came.

"Sweet dreams, *a ghrá*. I'll see you tomorrow." He smiled down at me and once again held his hands inches from my face, ghosting the air just above my flesh, as he could not touch me.

I was breathless, drunk from his close proximity, but somehow managed to make it inside my apartment, hyperaware of Quinn's gaze wafting across my flesh as I slowly closed the door. Tired as I was, I didn't want to go to sleep. I was too afraid I'd wake up and realize the events of the evening had all been a dream. I opened the door to my room with a sappy smile drawn across my face and plopped down onto my bed with an excited squeal.

chapter 6

The annoying buzz of my alarm clock wrenched me from my sleep, and I rolled over quickly to silence the annoying piece of crap. I'd tossed and turned all night, replaying the events of the previous day over and over again, and felt exhausted. How I would keep Quinn's true identity a mystery was beyond me. There were no secrets between Jessica and me. I literally told her everything, and lying to her was not something I particularly wanted to do. She'd spot my deceit in a heartbeat. I was a terrible liar, and anyone who knew me well always saw through my sad attempts. But what choice did I have? None. I had to keep his secret to myself, not only to protect him, but also to keep people from thinking I was an absolute nut job.

Truth be told, the idea that I'd lost my mind still weighed heavily on me. I was either insane, or someone had slipped me a mickey while I worked, and I was lying in a drug-induced coma somewhere while my mind enacted out vivid fantasies. Whatever the case, I was screwed.

I cracked one eye open, noticing the clock read six a.m. Begrudgingly, I crawled from the warmth of my bed and stumbled to my closet. My workout clothes and sneakers were scattered on the floor, so I picked them up and headed for the bathroom. After dressing and pulling the sides of my hair back and out of my face, I grabbed my iPod and tiptoed out of the apartment. No sense waking Jessica or Martha. I wasn't ready to face them yet.

Eager to get moving, I set off at a leisurely pace toward the university, thinking if I had time after my run, I'd hit the campus gym for some weight training and ab work. I may be top-heavy and sport a meatier butt and thighs than most, but my tummy was flat, and of that, I was proud.

I picked up my pace, hyperaware of my surroundings. Still a little spooked, I grimaced, remembering the sense of unease I felt yesterday on my run, along with the creepy experience with the dog at work.

The chimes on the university clock rang. Class didn't start for an hour and a half. That left just enough time for weight training before I needed to book it back to my apartment for a shower. Placing my iPod ear buds in my ears, I scrolled down to my favorite work out playlist, letting the sounds of Britney Spears' "Womanizer" blast through the tiny speakers. I found the song oddly appropriate, given my new friendship with Quinn, and laughed quietly to myself as I grabbed a pair of free weights.

A tugging sensation pulled at my gut while I worked through my reps. Someone was watching me, and the feeling nearly bowled me over with its intensity. My already flushed skin tingled and burned, and my heartbeat kicked up a notch. The corners of my mouth automatically lifted and I sucked in an excited breath. I set the weights down and turned to scan the room. Only one person brought about that type of reaction in me: Quinn.

Only one way to find out.

"Quinn," I called out, trying my best to not look like a complete idiot. "Quinn. Are you in here?"

Silence rang through the air. I did receive a few odd looks from various meatheads and diehards who were also working out, no doubt wondering who the hell I was talking to.

Good job, Ryann. Way to look like a complete freak, talking to yourself.

Blaring the volume on my iPod, I finished up with the free weights, mentally cursing myself for forgetting to bring a towel. I was a sweaty mess and resorted to wiping myself off with my sweatshirt. Gross.

"Have a nice workout?"

I whirled around to see Quinn, leaning against the wall of the corridor I'd just entered.

He looked like he belonged in an Abercrombie ad, dressed in distressed jeans with a tight-fitting, white t-shirt clinging to his impressively sculpted chest in all the right places. The clothes accentuated his muscular body well, but it was his gaze I couldn't tear my eyes from. Quinn truly possessed the face of an angel. His sapphire eyes pierced my soul.

He smiled widely at me, flashing his pearly whites, but the intent didn't reach his eyes. Those beautiful baby blues still held an underlying hint of sadness. Something haunted him, and I needed to know what it was.

"Yeah, actually, I had a great workout." A blush crept onto my already flushed face. "Hey…were you watching me the entire time?"

Quinn didn't answer me, opting to flash me a flirtatious grin instead.

I raised an eyebrow. "And before, during my jog?"

He shrugged and continued beaming, while I stood open-mouthed and aghast.

A group of diehards exited the workout room, and I bit my lip to keep my trap shut until they were out of earshot. "Why didn't you answer me when I called out to you? I looked like a psycho calling your name and talking to myself."

He straight out laughed at that point, and I had no clue why.

My temper flared. "What is so damn funny?"

"You," he said, choking with laughter. "When you're angry, you talk with your hands and your arms flail about, this way and that. It's quite funny."

"Well. So happy to be your source of amusement." My voice filled with sarcasm, and my cheeks burned. I purposely threw my arms about for his benefit.

Damn annoying faerie.

Yeah, I was annoyed. But as pissy as I felt over his hidden voyeuristic escapade, I was equally as happy to see him smile. Those lips…that mouth…his whole Goddamn face—it lit up like the sun.

His happiness was infectious and it drew me in with its warmth and comfort.

"All right, all right," he said, holding his hands out in front of him in surrender. "Sorry, love. Where are you off to next?"

"I'm actually heading back to my place to shower before I go to class." I swiped a nervous hand over my sweaty hair and cringed. While Quinn appeared ungodly handsome and good enough to eat, I looked a rank, nasty mess.

"Let's go then. I'll walk you." He moved from the wall and took off in the direction I'd been heading earlier. His divine, powerful scent permeated the air, and I practically drooled all over myself. The man smelled delish—masculine and sexy all rolled up into one intoxicating scent. I stifled the urge to sniff him repeatedly.

"Should you maybe put your sweatshirt on?" He pointed to me with a brow raised, his oh-so-kissable lips turned down into a frown.

My stomach seized up like I'd been kicked. He thought I looked fat. On fire from my workout, I hadn't bothered to cover up and was now regretting that decision. Frankly, I was a bit shocked by his words. Size eight was on the larger end of medium, but I was certainly no contender for *The Biggest Loser*.

He opened his mouth to say something only to slam it closed seconds later. His scowl grew exponentially as he eagle-eyed my clothes and scrubbed at his head in frustration. "You're seriously not thinking of walking about outside like that, are ye?" He paced back and forth, one hand on his hip, the other rubbing the back of his nearly bald head.

I looked away, hot tears forming in my eyes. Why was he being so cruel? Most guys liked ample T and A. I glanced down at myself. Nope. No muffin top, and the cellulite was covered. I wore a pair of shorts, a full Lycra tank and a sweatshirt wrapped around my waist.

I crinkled my nose and shook my head. "Seriously? You think I look that bad?" I peered down the hallway, waiting for someone to harpoon me.

He stopped pacing the narrow hallway and stood inches from me, feet wide and arms crossed. "What? Bad? No." His eyes zeroed in on my cleavage. "Do you really think you ought to be showing off that much skin for every Tom, Dick, and Harry to see?"

Ah … now we were getting to the heart of his question. Quinn didn't want anyone looking at me dressed in skimpy workout clothes, not because he thought I looked fat, but because he thought I looked good. A rush of warmth traveled throughout my body. Quinn was jealous. My flushed skin was the only thing keeping me from exploding everywhere all at once.

I bit down on the inside of my cheek, the sharp pain squashing the urge to squeal like a kid in a candy-store. Take that, skinny bitches of the world! The hot love faerie thought I looked good. "Here. Hold this." I held out my iPod, which he took from me, taking care to not touch my hand with his own. I untied the sweatshirt from my waist and pulled it over my head. "There. Happy?"

He dropped my iPod into my outstretched hand, his face wearing a whole lot of smug satisfaction. "Quite."

"Just so you know, I work out all the time, and this," I said, sweeping my arm out in front of me, "is what I usually wear. And don't forget, my work uniform isn't much better."

Quinn shook his head and scowled. "Aye. Don't remind me. Those tiny, little…"

"Booty shorts?" I said, finishing his sentence for him. "Yeah, I have to wear those and the matching tank every time I work. Better get used to seeing a little skin." We lived in the twentieth century, and Quinn needed to get with the times. I didn't mind appeasing him here and there, but I wasn't about to revert back to the Stone Ages and cover my ankles before going outside.

He answered me with a grumble as we made our way outdoors.

"So why are you in college?" I asked as we strolled along the green lawns that led toward the quad. "I mean, you have five hundred years' worth of knowledge. What more can you learn?"

"Boredom," he said easily. "You can't imagine how absolutely monotonous life can be when you've lived as long as I have. Not to mention, there is that constant desire to connect with people. The curse…it prevents me from…really connecting to anyone. But just being around people…helps. It gets lonely sometimes," he said, trailing off.

My chest ached as I listened to him admit he felt lonely. To live as long as he had, having no one to confide in, no one to share with had to be maddening. Acting on instinct, I reached for him, wanting to offer up comfort.

Quinn shot me a warning look.

I dropped my hand to my side, my fingers flexing, crying out in agony for just one touch. "Oh, God. I forgot, sorry."

We walked for a bit in comfortable silence until we reached my apartment, stopping just in front of the door. I looked up at Quinn unsure of what to do. I took a step forward with my hand raised, then realized my mistake and let my arm fall awkwardly. Normally when parting ways with a friend, I'd treat them to a hug or kiss. With Quinn, this was impossible. Neither of us knew quite what to say or do and an uncomfortable silence filled the air.

Quinn let out a deep, aggravated sigh. "Oh, for the love of fuck! I can't take this. I'll be back later to take you to class." He motioned toward the door, wanting me to go inside before he left.

I bit down on my lower lip, nodding, as I unlocked the door and walked in. I looked over my shoulder to see him watching me, his hand held up as if to say goodbye. He was gone in an instant, vanishing into thin air. I jumped from the suddenness of it.

Damn. I don't think I'll ever get used to that.

After locking the front door, I hauled ass to the bathroom, thanking the Good Lord above it was unoccupied. I needed to hit the water locker in a bad way. The piping hot shower not only washed away the sweaty remnants of my workout, but helped ease the residual tension pent-up within me after parting ways with Quinn. As the scalding hot water rained down onto my skin, I closed my eyes, letting my subconscious mind take over my thoughts.

The sweet citrus smell of my shampoo permeated the air as I massaged the foamy suds into my scalp and down the length of my hair.

"Let me help you with that, a ghrá," Quinn's voice whispered suggestively. A pair of strong hands stroked my sudsy locks, drawing the shampoo through them in a leisurely fashion. Every inch of my body felt awake, alive, and on fire. The soft pads of his fingertips caressing my skin brought my body to life with a tingling sensation that covered me from head to toe.

"Mmmm…" I moaned in sheer delight, closing my eyes and reveling in the feel of his magical hands as they washed my hair.

My heart jumped the moment one of his hands slid down to my waist, the other moving to gently wash the skin just above my collarbone.

The air in the shower felt heavy and thick with a mixture of hot steam and growing desire.

"Lean back, Ryann. Let me wash you."

With heavy lidded eyes, I leaned into the wide expanse of Quinn's chest, the deep contours of his muscular pecs pressing against my back like a large, stone wall, solid and strong. Despite his massive size and considerable strength, he bathed me with extreme tenderness, whispering soft words from his ancient language which I couldn't understand.

A small moan escaped my lips as his fingers grazed the side of my breast, and my back arched ever so slightly, pressing my naked bottom against his large—

"Hey! You about done in there?" The sound of my very annoyed roommate wrenched me from my fantasy.

Holy crap!

"I'm almost done," I shouted, completely mortified.

Shit. What the hell was that?

"All I know is there better be some hot water left or I'm going to be seriously pissed." A loud pounding shook the bathroom door and the chafed voice continued to yammer.

I rinsed myself off at a breakneck pace, wrapping myself in a towel and exiting the shower, avoiding the annoyed stare of my somewhat phantom roommate, Martha, as I flew out the door. Visibly pissed, I was afraid she'd incinerate me with her scary, kohl-lined eyes and freaky mojo.

I darted back to my room, quickly throwing on some clothes, all the while trying to make sense of what just happened.

I just had a sex fantasy about Quinn. I'm in so much trouble.

Having only known Quinn for a couple of days, our relationship, if that's what you could call it, was in its infancy. If I was already having steamy sex fantasies about him when I barely knew him, I could only imagine the level of sexual frustration I was in for in the weeks to come, given my inability to touch him.

I sat on the edge of my bed, running a comb through my hair, when my cell phone went off. I jumped, dropping the comb onto the floor. Bending down with a groan, I plucked it from the carpet before reaching for my phone, which sat on my nightstand. Jessica's smiling face shone on the small screen.

I flipped the phone open and placed it against my ear. "What are you doing calling me? Where are you?" I asked, surprised she'd be up and out of the apartment so early. With all that had happened in the past twenty-four hours, I had a lot to tell her and was a bit disappointed she wasn't home for me to talk to.

"Hey. I'm up the street at the coffee shop. Steering clear of Martha," she said with a jittery sigh. "Do you want anything?"

I finished combing out my hair as I talked. "Thanks, but no. No time. Class starts soon and I'm running late. I need to talk to you, though. You gonna be home this afternoon?"

"Yeah. We need to talk about Martha as well. Do you know she actually told me if I touched any of her stuff, she'd put a hex on me? She's crazy!"

I snorted and placed a hand over my mouth to stifle my laughter. I felt horrible for losing it, as our roommate dilemma was really no laughing matter. "I'm sorry," I said and giggled, no longer able to contain myself. "When is it that she's giving you crap? Seriously, I *never* see her around. Ever." Martha's irritated pounding on the bathroom door a bit ago was the first real interaction I'd had with her.

"Go ahead. Laugh all you want. I caught a peek of her room, and I'm telling you, Voodoo Martha has some seriously creepy stuff floating around. She's gonna put the whammy on either one or the both of us." Jessica snickered as she spoke, and I knew that although our creepy roommate irritated the crap out of her, she was comfortable enough to make light of the situation. I knew she inevitably would be okay.

"Okay, got some reading to do. Talk to you later!" she said, and hung up.

I set my cell down, still smiling, and sat down near the outlet closest to my bed with hair dryer in hand. I wasn't about to go back into the bathroom and face Pissy Girl again, opting to dry my hair in the sanctuary of my own room.

A short while later, after deeming myself fit for human eyes (faerie eyes as well), I grabbed my book bag off the floor and headed out to class.

Ambling across the lawns toward the center of campus, my stomach cried out, demanding to be fed. The damn thing needed to shut it. Didn't it know I was watching my calorie intake?

"Jaysus, woman! Does your belly always make so much noise?"

I let out a loud squeak and jumped, dropping my book bag onto the ground in the process. I whirled around to see Quinn chuckling at my reaction.

"Ack! You scared me." I bent down to retrieve my wayward bag. "And to answer your question, yes. My stomach talks back when I'm hungry."

"Well, come on then, *mo chrói*. Let's get some food in you before you start chewing on your shoes."

chapter 7

I made it to my Human Sexuality class with five minutes to spare, fully expecting yet another awkward goodbye with Quinn at the door. Much to my surprise, he waltzed past me into the large classroom, finding two seats near the back. He raised his arm and motioned for me to sit with him.

"What are you doing?" I asked, eyeballing him skeptically. "You have this class as well?"

"I do now," Quinn said with a playful smirk. "While you were showering earlier, I persuaded the old bird working in the registrar's office to let me add this class. A few sappy words and a cheeky smile was all it took."

"Why?" I wanted to know his reasoning, though I was more than happy to have him seated next to me. Even if the subject matter of the class was embarrassing as hell.

"Well . . . for one . . . I'd like to spend more time with you."

His admission sent my heart flying. If I had my way, I'd spend every waking moment with him.

"I also couldn't pass up the opportunity to take a Human Sexuality class." He wore an impish grin as he pointed toward the front of the auditorium.

Anxiety swelled and I swallowed hard. I didn't want to turn my head, but knew I had no choice.

Raising my eyebrow in question, I glanced over my shoulder toward the front of the room to see two giant posters occupying the space on the wall behind the instructor's desk. One was a picture of an enormous flaccid penis. The other:

a large depiction of the vagina. The two were no doubt learning tools for the class, a fact that didn't help to alleviate my embarrassment.

My sharp intake of breath evidently amused Quinn, who then did his level best to muffle the snickers coming out of his mouth, while trying not to draw attention to us.

With cheeks ablaze, I turned to face Quinn. "What, may I ask, is so damn funny?"

"Sorry, *a ghrá*. It was just the look on your face when you saw the oversized genitalia. You looked as though you'd never seen a man's flute before."

Flustered beyond measure, I sat silent for a moment before speaking. I looked down at my feet, avoiding his penetrating gaze. "Um…well, that's because I haven't…you know…seen a…penis before." I felt his eyes burning a hole into my cheek, and stupid me, I raised my head to meet his eyes. The auditorium felt tiny and lacking in important things, like air.

How am I going to get through this?

Quinn wore a look of surprise on his handsome face, though he sat quietly while I continued my admission, refraining from teasing me, thank God.

Ugh! He thinks I'm a repressed freak. Better backtrack. Can someone just kill me now, please?

"That's not exactly true…uh…I've seen flashes of…um…" Crap. Why couldn't I say the word penis in front of him? I felt like a preteen learning about sex for the first time. I let out a deep sigh. "I've seen a few penises in movies, but…uh…never one so big as that, and never a real one up close."

Oh, God! Did I just look at his crotch when I said that?

"And well…I have a vagina, so I know what that looks like. Um…yeah…" Word vomit took over and I blabbered away nervously, talking in circles. My palms were sweaty and my cheeks a flaming shade of crimson. Why was there never a spare shovel around when you needed one? I briefly considered using my pencil as a makeshift spade with which to dig a hole and bury my head in.

"So you're a virgin, then?" he inquired softly.

"Yes. I, uh…I just never…" I couldn't bear to look him in the eye. Acutely embarrassed, I did my best to avoid his piercing stare. There I was, at the ripe old age of twenty-one, an inexperienced virgin, sitting next to someone who was quite possibly the most virile, sexually experienced man on the planet. What was I supposed to do with that?

It was practically unheard of for someone my age to still have their virginity intact, and it was a source of both pride and frustration for me. I had no desire to give it up to some oversexed frat boy who wouldn't remember to call me the next day. I also wasn't fond of the idea of parading around my excess flesh. I was holding out for Mr. Right, and was proud I'd never engaged in meaningless sex. On the other hand, I took a serious amount of shit from just about everyone I knew, sans Jessica, for having a cherry that was still intact.

He looked at me through tender eyes. "Shhh, *mo chrói*. No need to be embarrassed. It's refreshing to know you respect yourself enough to wait for the right person. You've just given me another example of why you are so different than most women."

I scrunched my mouth up and made a face. "Yeah, I'm different, all right." I glanced over to him with narrowed eyes. To be honest, his reaction to my abstinence was not what I'd expected. For a sexed-up love faerie who couldn't keep his sword in its sheath for five hundred years, he seemed awfully supportive of my choice to abstain. I was good and confused.

He shook his head and leveled a reassuring smile in my direction. "Different is a good thing, *mo chrói*. Trust me."

I fidgeted in my seat wanting desperately to change the subject. "What does *mo chrói* mean? I swear, I'm going to have to carry around a pocket translator just to understand you."

Quinn laughed quietly and sat back into his chair, nodding toward the front of the auditorium. As I turned my attention to the front of the classroom, I saw the instructor hastily scrawling the name Professor White, in large block lettering across the dry erase board.

I heard Quinn whisper softly under his breath. "My heart. It means my heart."

My body thrilled at his confession, a warm tingling sensation blossoming over my entire being. Unfortunately, I wasn't able to revel in the newfound knowledge of his pet name for me as the professor began speaking to the class.

"Sex!" His voice boomed so loudly I jumped in my seat. "Sex is on the forefront of society's every waking thought. A hot commodity in today's market, sex sells." He paced back and forth in front of the class as he spoke. "In this class, we will explore the different aspects of sex and sexuality as it pertains to not only society, but ourselves as individuals."

The professor passed out the class syllabus as he spoke, discussing the course outline and his expectations. My attention strayed from his speech as I read through the course summary. We'd be studying the multicultural history of sex, the male and female anatomy and physiology, as well as the various stages of arousal and response. My mouth felt unusually dry all of a sudden. I'd avoided this class for the past three years. There was no getting out of it now.

I chanced a look over at Quinn, who sat listening intently to the professor speak, acutely interested in what we'd be learning.

"Hey," I said, trying to keep my voice down. "I thought you already knew all about this stuff." Older than dirt and chock-full of life experience, Quinn probably could have taught most of the classes at the university as opposed to taking them. This class in particular.

He frowned and shook his head. "I've always focused my studies on history and literature. I've never given much thought to what makes my Johnny stand up, just feeling happy as a pig in shit that it does. This class should be bloody interesting."

I snorted. "Your Johnny?"

"The Big Bopper. Ankle Spanker. Heat Seeking Missile." He leaned back in his seat, crossed his legs at the ankles and snickered, pleased with himself.

I crossed my arms and pursed my lips. "What? Are we in high school here? Really, Quinn?"

He swiped a finger across his mouth to keep from laughing. "Well, what can I say? When you're hung like a Clydesdale, you find yourself naming your appendage." He shifted in his seat and glanced down at his crotch with a smile. "Captain Leviathan here is legendary."

I laughed before I could stop myself. My hand shot up to my mouth and I flashed Quinn a look of death while swiping my other finger across my neck, signaling him to cut it out.

"What?" He tried to feign innocence.

I dropped my hand from my mouth. "Aren't you a little old for the penis nicknames?"

He answered my question with a "humph" sound. "I don't care how old a bloke is, he'll always be happy to talk about dicks and diddies."

"Diddies?"

"Breasts. Boobies. Knockers." The corners of his mouth turned up and he flashed a perfect set of teeth.

"Ahem. We'll be discussing the female anatomy in the weeks to come. Let's try and stay focused on today's lesson, shall we?" Professor White stood a few feet from Quinn and me, arms crossed and irritated at being interrupted.

Flushed and embarrassed beyond belief, I nodded morosely and buried my nose once again into the class syllabus, hyperaware of Quinn's silent laughter next to me.

Men!

Quinn and I managed to make it through the rest of the lecture without another public reprimand, a fact I was extremely grateful for. We sauntered out of the auditorium in a leisurely fashion, paying no heed to the disapproving glare from Professor White.

Feeling guilty for making a poor first impression with one of my instructors, I resolved to be especially attentive in class from that point on.

We strolled casually to our Lit class where I found Jessica waiting for me, a look of apprehension swathed across her face. She cast me a cautious smile as I moved to sit with her. Quinn situated himself a few rows behind me, effectively giving me my space.

Class carried on, and I'd be damned if I could tell you what the lecture was about. Every bit of brainpower I possessed zeroed in on one thing or should I say one person: Quinn.

Motioning to me as we filed out of class, I walked over to where Quinn stood after telling Jess I'd meet her back at our place.

"So, where are you off to now?" he asked as we strolled through the grass toward the crowded quad. Dozens of students milled back and forth, hustling to and from their classes. A football whizzed past my head, landing a few feet from Quinn.

He picked up the wayward pigskin and launched it back at the large group of rowdy jocks who were tossing it around not far from where we stopped. The poor schlep that caught the ball flew backward and got the wind knocked out of him good.

My eyebrows shot up as I answered his question. "I'm headed home. Jess and I have some things we need to talk about. I can call you later if you'd like?" It was more of a question than a statement. I didn't have Quinn's number, and if I was being honest, I didn't even know if the man owned a phone. Quinn had a knack for showing up out of nowhere, right when I needed him.

Quinn stood in silence for a moment, obviously mulling things over in his mind, but about what I hadn't a clue.

Finally, he heaved a sigh and held out his hand. "Give me your phone, *a ghrá*. I'll plug in my number for you." He frowned when I handed him my old Nokia cell phone. "What the hell is this?" He held my phone between his thumb and finger gingerly, like it was roadkill.

"Uh, it's my phone. What's wrong with it?" I knew it was old, but the service was good and the plan was cheap.

"This is a piece of shite," he said, holding up my ancient Nokia. "This … this is a phone," he said with a smile, and pulled a sleek new iPhone from his pocket, admiring it with a shocking amount of reverence.

I rolled my eyes. "I see it makes no difference whether the male is human or a faerie, you're all still infatuated with gadgetry."

"Aye, my sweet. We're six o' one, half a dozen o' the other. We're all just the same." He met my reproving frown with a wide, toothy grin, and despite my best efforts, I found myself smiling along with him.

With a sigh, Quinn handed me back my dinosaur of a cell phone, having entered all his pertinent contact information. "Mind yourself, and keep this in your hand when you're walking about. If you sense any kind of trouble, call me." He wore a staid expression on his handsome face, and I knew he expected me to do what he said.

I scowled and shot him an annoyed glare. "I'm a big girl, Quinn. I can take care of myself. Remember?"

Quinn treated me to an impressive display of posturing and a low, dismissive growl. He stood towering over me, with arms crossed, jaw clenched, and a harsh glare. Clearly, he intended for me to follow his instructions.

"All right, all right, fine," I said, making a face. "I'll call you if anything happens. Satisfied?"

More growling followed, along with what I assumed was a string of profanity in his old language. The only thing I recognized were the words "stubborn" and "git." Scanning the area to ensure no one was looking, Quinn muttered a quick "later then" and disappeared before my eyes.

"You need to stop that," I shouted into the empty space where he previously stood.

A faint chuckle floated through the air, and I shook my head with a smile.

The hustle and bustle of the street filled my ears as I hoofed it back to my apartment. The delicious smell of coffee wafting out onto the sidewalk as I passed by the local coffee house was too tempting to resist. I found myself walking the rest of the way home with a decaf soy mocha, my drink of choice when I felt particularly indulgent.

I took a sip from my hot treat, savoring the smooth, delicious liquid as I unlocked the door to my apartment and went in. All was quiet on the western front, which meant Jess hadn't made it home yet, and I really didn't have a damn clue where Martha was. Honestly, I didn't know what Jessica's beef with her was. She was silent as the grave and never home, which, as far as roommates go, was pure gold.

Enjoying another sip of coffee, I ambled down the hallway to my room, flipped on the light switch and dropped my bag at the foot of my bed. I turned around, fully intending to head back to the kitchen to grab a snack when I froze. My coffee slipped from my hand and crashed to the floor in a sticky mess, as paralyzing fear choked the air from my lungs, rendering me immobile.

Scrawled across the mirror that hung above my dresser in ominous, blood red lettering was a single, terrifying sentence that chilled me to the bone. *I've been watching you.*

My heart pounded so forcefully in my chest it rang in my ears like a surround sound stereo blaring at full volume. The room took on a violent spin, and it was then that I realized I'd been holding my breath. With a loud gasp, I took several shallow breaths, tears flooding my eyes as I stumbled backward, falling onto my bed.

Someone had been in my room. Panic spiked and I shot off my bed. Whoever left the message on my mirror could still be in the apartment!

Near hysterical, I scanned my room in search of something—anything— that might serve as a makeshift weapon, coming up empty handed. I suddenly remembered the large Maglite I kept in the top drawer of my dresser for emergencies. Crossing the room in three large strides, I yanked open the drawer, rifling through its contents until my hands found what they were looking for.

The sick feeling that took up residence in my stomach grew as I turned my head, looking over my shoulder toward my closet. A shudder ran through me, and I white-knuckled the flashlight. Whoever had broken in could be hiding in my closet. I swallowed hard and turned, trembling and shaking, tears falling rapid pace down my cheeks as I slowly approached my storage space. Realizing it was now or never, I raised the Maglite high, ready to strike, and yanked open the door with a scream.

The closet was empty. Relief, though fleeting, washed through me at the sight of my empty storage space, and I dropped my arm, the heavy weight of the flashlight tugging on my shoulder.

"Oh my God, Ryann. What happened?"

I whirled around with a scream, swinging the large flashlight back, ready to maim the sick freak who'd broken in.

"Whoa," Jessica shouted, holding her arms up in front of her to ward me off. "Geez, Ryann. Careful with that thing."

The floodgates opened the moment I recognized it was Jessica standing in my room and not some crazed lunatic, and I dropped my makeshift weapon as a steady stream of hot tears ran down my cheeks. Unable to look at the threatening message scrawled across my mirror, I lifted my arm and pointed to the source of my panic and unease.

There was a loud gasp and the next thing I knew Jessica's arms were wrapped around me.

"Oh my God, Ryann. No wonder you're so freaked out. It'll be okay." She rubbed my back, trying to soothe me. "I'm calling the cops. Two break-ins in two weeks is ridiculous. The police need to get off their heinies and do something. "

I managed a slight nod as I stepped back, wiping away the tears from my puffy and swollen face. There would be no argument from me. I was beyond freaked out at the thought of someone watching me, of someone invading my personal space and using my home, my place of sanctuary, as a means to frighten me with.

What I wanted to do was call Quinn. He'd specifically told me to call him if anything hinky went down. Ominous lettering scrawled across my mirror certainly qualified. Still…how would I explain my relationship with him to Jessica? I heaved a deep sigh. Calling Quinn was definitely out for the time being. But bringing in the cops? Yeah, that was a damn good idea in my book.

❧

"And you say nothing's missing? What about last week?" The portly officer scanned the living room before scribbling away at his clipboard.

"No. Nothing was taken. Not this time. Not the last. Things were just—" I paused, grimacing at the memory of my ransacked room.

"Her room was torn apart," Jess said, answering for me. "Her drawers were emptied, her room pretty much turned inside out. Mine as well. There was an officer here last week. He took notes, pictures. Don't you guys have a record of it?"

The officer chewed on the inside of his lip and wheezed. "Things have been pretty busy down at the station. Whoever took the report last week most likely hasn't gotten around to finishing it up." He stared down the hallway toward Martha's room. "And what about your roommate's room?"

"Her room was empty last week. She just moved in a few days ago," Jessica said, casting a sideways glance toward Martha's door, a look of concern etched across her face. "Look. Nothing was taken or moved this time. Whoever broke in didn't touch anything but Ryann's mirror."

The officer scribbled some more at his notebook and ignored Jessica completely. "And where is your new roommate? Do you know?"

"Haven't got a clue," Jessica said while I just shrugged. I never knew where Martha was or how she spent her time. She was somewhat of a mystery.

"I was at the library," a soft voice replied smoothly.

I turned to see Martha closing the front door behind her as she stepped into view. She might be a phantom roommate, but her timing was impeccable.

Her voice, though soft, carried across the room. "What happened here?"

"Break-in," Jessica said coolly, leveling a harsh glare at our macabre roommate. Girlfriend's dander was up for sure. "But don't worry. None of your," she busted out the finger quotes, "shit was touched. You won't have to hex anyone today."

My eyes widened in surprise. Jess had actually used the "s" word.

Martha glared at Jessica, chin held high, a look of pure hatred swathed across her pale face. Though partially obstructed by a long sweep of mahogany bangs, her hazel eyes held a staggering amount of contempt.

Thank God the officer decided to pipe in. I really didn't want to find out what Martha did to people she was angry with.

"Did anyone see you at the library, Ms…?" The officer stared at Martha expectantly, waiting for her answer.

"Stewart. Martha Stewart." She looked completely un-phased by the break-in. Either nothing scared her, or she didn't care. "Yes. Plenty of people saw me. I'm not exactly hard to miss," she said, sweeping her arm out in front of her, drawing attention to her somewhat unorthodox wardrobe choice.

She'd hit the nail on the head for sure. No one would forget the sight of her dressed in a black corset top, plaid skirt and knee high Doc Martens.

"Here," she said, pulling a small stack of books from her bag. "I checked these out this afternoon. I'm sure if you speak with the librarian, she can verify my presence in the campus library."

The overweight officer scratched his head before scribbling a few more notes onto his clipboard. "I'll do just that, Ms. Stewart. Thank you for your cooperation. Now if you'd all excuse me, I need to have a few words with Ms. Pierce."

Jessica nodded and gave me a hug before heading off toward her bedroom. The icy look she sent toward Martha did not go unnoticed, and my stomach tightened. The last thing I needed to deal with was warring roommates.

Martha stood for a moment, staring at me with her brows knit together and her jaw clenched. With a scowl, she shoved her books back into her bag, spun on her heels, and walked out the front door.

I swallowed hard and stared at the portly officer. Why me? What had I done to deserve the boatload of crap currently being dealt to me? And why, oh why, did I get stuck with Elmer Fudd for an officer?

He scratched at the side of his nose for a minute and cast me a contemplative look. "Do you have any idea who might have done this?"

"No," I said, shaking my head, somewhat surprised by his question. If I had any idea who the douchebag was, I would have said something. This guy had eaten one too many donuts and had gone soft in the head.

"I'm not going to mince words, Ms. Pierce. I believe you've got yourself a stalker. Nothing was taken from the home during either break-in, and your room seems to be the main focus of the intruder's attention. Is there someone at school or your workplace that's been giving you trouble?"

I racked my brain, trying to remember if I'd dealt with any disgruntled patrons from the bar recently. Aside from the asshat who'd grabbed my butt the other night, there was no one.

About two seconds later, I had a lightbulb moment. You know what I'm talking about, right? Your mind is blank one moment and the next—BINGO!

Realization hits you like a Mack truck square between the eyes. Quinn. His friendship was the only recent change in my life. But he couldn't possibly be the intruder, could he? No. I'd only just met him a few days ago, and the first break-in occurred well over a week ago. I'd have sensed his presence if he'd been in my room, or anywhere in the apartment, for that matter. I had some sort of sixth sense where Quinn was concerned, a built-in radar of sorts. My body tingled and my kitty flamed up anytime he was near. My nether regions were stone cold right now. Quinn hadn't been here.

Besides, Quinn himself said he sensed an evil presence near the bar, and had been watching over me like a hawk the past few days. He had ample opportunity to hurt me if he wanted to, but had never been anything but protective toward me. Not to mention annoying, crass, and full of himself at times, but fiercely protective and hot as hell.

No. I was certain Quinn wasn't responsible for the ominous message left on my mirror. "No. There's no one," I replied quietly and shook my head.

Officer Ate-One-Too-Many-Donuts appeared stymied. "What about an ex-boyfriend? A new admirer?"

I shook my head. Somehow I figured telling him about the five-hundred-year-old faerie I'd recently befriended and secretly had a crush on was liable to get me thrown into a padded cell. I decided to keep that little gem to myself for the time being.

The officer gave a small grunt and shoved his pen into his pocket. "Well, then, I suggest you change your locks, make sure they are secure each and every time you leave your home, and seriously consider getting yourself some type of surveillance system."

Yeah, okay. I could have come to that conclusion on my own. Frustrated, I took a deep breath, blowing it out forcefully, and took the business card the officer handed me.

"Make sure you give me a call if anything else happens. Watch yourself, Ryann," he said as he strolled to the front door and let himself out.

I wasn't worried about watching myself. I was worried about the creep watching me. I dropped the officer's card onto the nearby coffee table and slumped down into the large brown chair that sat next to the sofa in our front room. Resting my elbows on my knees, I dropped my head into my hands and rubbed slow circles at my temples, trying to rid myself of a pounding headache brought on from my recent bout of tears.

"I cleaned the writing off your mirror for you." Jessica's worried voice startled me as she entered the room.

"Thanks," I said weakly. I felt like I'd run a marathon and came in dead last, spent, on my knees and bleeding. In other words, I felt like absolute crap.

I heard her shuffle into the kitchen as I sat, lost in thought, trying to figure out why I was the focus of some nut job's unwanted attention. It had to be someone from the club. There was no other explanation. Working in a bar put me in close contact with all types of unsavory people, one of which no doubt spawned some sort of sick attachment to me and thought it funny to scare the living piss out of me. I groaned.

Sick bastard. Get a life!

"Here." Jessica thrust a plate under my nose, complete with sandwich and cut fruit. "You need to eat something. I called the club and told them what happened. You don't have to go in to work tonight."

Crap. I'd completely forgotten about work. "Thanks," I said, grabbing the plate from her hands, not hungry in the least but taking a bite anyway to show gratitude for her nice gesture.

Jessica sat on the couch opposite me and watched quietly while I ate, taking the plate from me when I'd finished and disposing of it in the kitchen.

I grabbed a nearby throw pillow and fiddled with one of the frayed edges as Jessica walked back into the room. "So … you wanted to talk about Martha?"

She shook her head. "It can wait. Trust me. After the day you've had, you don't need anything else to worry about."

"Worry?" I clutched the pillow to my chest and hung on for dear life. God, what else could there be? Famine? Pestilence? A horde of ravenous vampires lying in wait to bleed me dry? "Just tell me, Jess. What exactly is it about Martha that I should be worried about?"

She raised her eyebrows and sighed deeply. "Don't say I didn't warn you. C'mon," she said, motioning for me to follow her.

I chucked the pillow aside, stood up from the chair, and walked down the hallway, stopping in front of Martha's closed door. We were about to invade her space. Disrespect her privacy. I didn't care.

Grasping the brass handle, Jessica opened the door, placed one hand on her hip, and pointed into the dark room. "That. That is what we need to be worried about."

"Holy … crap," I said as I stepped foot into the *Twilight Zone*.

chapter 8

Where our rooms were light and airy, Martha's was stygian, dank and devoid of any color. Scary looking posters and drawings of pentagrams adorned the walls surrounding her bed, which was also bathed in black. Stacks of archaic books, both large and small, riddled the floor around her living space, and there was a considerably large trunk situated at the foot of her bed, with a substantial looking lock keeping it safely closed.

I stood for a moment, my mouth slightly agape, taking in my bizarre surroundings.

"See what I mean?" Jessica said, wearing an I-told-you-so look. "I told you she was a weirdo freak."

I looked back at her over my shoulder, mouthing a giant "wow" before walking over and gingerly swiping a book off of one of the many stacks that lay before me. Turning the small leather bound book so the binding was visible, I read the title out loud. *"Le Grimoire."*

I turned to face Jessica, eyes wide as I spoke. "Shit. You weren't kidding. I think our girl practices witchcraft." I returned the aging book to its stack posthaste, rubbing my hands on my pants as if to remove any traces of evil, and secretly hoping Voodoo Martha never found out I had my curious hands on it.

A wave of dizziness washed over me as I absorbed the reality of our roommate situation. "You're right. I don't think I'm up for dealing with this right now." Weak and jittery, I flashed Jessica a look of apology and hurried out of the creepy room and into my own, avoiding eye contact with the mirror over my dresser. I knew the words were no longer there, but just the same, I was still spooked.

Jess followed me into my room, taking a seat at the foot of my bed.

I desperately needed to talk about something to get my mind off the break-in and Martha's nightmare room. "So … you up for some interesting gossip?" I was dying to tell her what little I could about Quinn. He was just too damn yummy to keep completely to myself. Besides, if you couldn't share deets about a hot guy with your best friend, then who could you share with?

Jessica perked up, her eyes bright with excitement. "Does it involve you and a certain muscular, sexy, tatted up Casanova?"

"Possibly." I kept my answer evasive, trying to make her crazy with curiosity.

"Spill," she squealed, and chucked one of my throw pillows at me.

"All right, all right," I said, trying to dodge the flying pillow. "So … Quinn might not be as big of a jerk as I originally thought." I sat quietly for a moment, letting her mind chew on my statement for a bit before continuing.

"Really?" Jessica narrowed her brows at me dubiously. "Wasn't it just the other day you referred to him as a … a …"

Oh, Good Lord. "Pompous ass-munch? Yes." I chucked a pillow at her face. "I meant it when I called him those names. When I first met him, he totally came off as a womanizing jerk. Then I ran into him yesterday at work, and well … I saw a different side of him."

I spent the next few minutes filling her in on my embarrassing collapse, Quinn's timely rescue, and his stubborn insistence on walking me to both school and work. Of course, I left out the part about the ominous black dog and the fact that Quinn was indeed a centuries old faerie who couldn't touch me, though I desperately wanted him to. Basically, I left out all the good stuff. I didn't know what else I could do, though. If I told her everything that actually happened, she'd probably act reassuring and supportive while secretly calling the men in white to come and carry me away in their paddy wagon. Not wanting to spend the rest of my life in a round room, I edited my story a little.

Jess didn't look convinced. "So he went from a complete …"

"Fastard," I interrupted.

She frowned. "What I was going to say was that I find it hard to believe he'd change from a jerk to a good guy in one day. And fastard? What is that?"

I looked at her with a smirk. Jessica knew I lived for slang, adopting new words weekly into my large vocabulary. I shrugged. "Fucking and bastard all rolled into one. I'm lazy, what can I say? I need my profanity to be quick and easy."

We both broke out into a fit of laughter.

Our amusement was short-lived as Voodoo Martha sidled into the room, an air of gloom traveling in her wake.

She eyeballed me sharply, with her lips pressed tightly together and her arms crossed over her chest. "Someone touched my shit." She glared at Jessica for a moment before turning her attention to me. "I'm new here so I'll let it slide this one time. Nobody touches my shit without my permission, which is something neither of you will ever have. Do it again and you'll be sorry, got it?"

I sat quiet, silently aghast at how deadly serious she appeared to be. Now I understood Jess's earlier reference to people "touching her stuff." Hell, I'd only looked at one book. Jessica had told the truth before. This girl was a certifiable freak. What the hell had we gotten ourselves into with her?

"Sorry," I said, feeling more than a little afraid. "Won't happen again."

She continued glaring at me with her face scrunched up like she was concentrating particularly hard, or trying to figure something out. If she was trying to psych me out, she was doing a great job.

"What?" I asked, completely rattled by her unyielding gaze.

"Your aura is shrouded in darkness."

My aura? Okay, sister thinks she's Sylvia Browne, I guess.

"My aura is dark? What exactly does that mean?" Why I was continuing to converse with her was beyond me, but given everything that took place in the last couple of days, I was strangely curious. The weird stuff was becoming alarmingly less shocking, much to my dismay.

Martha gave an aggravated sigh, letting me know in no uncertain terms she really didn't want to be talking to me but would answer my question anyway. "It means you're evil, or you've recently been near an evil presence."

I stared at her like a mute idiot.

Well, hell…

Jessica stood up from the bed and cast Martha a look of pure hatred. "She's not evil. You, on the other hand, I'm not so sure about."

Martha ignored Jess altogether and shrugged. "Well, then she's been around an evil presence recently."

Jessica turned to face me. "Ignore her, Ryann. She's just trying to scare you. I don't believe in that aura garbage anyways. It's just a bunch of bunk."

I only half heard Jessica as she tried to dissuade me from listening to Martha's disturbing observation. Her voice sounded muffled and distant, like she was talking to me through a thick door. Her words barely registered. My mind was focused on one thing, or should I say, one person. Someone I'd been spending the bulk of my time with the past forty-eight hours: Quinn.

He couldn't be evil, could he? I felt so safe when I was with him. Not only that, but he was so overly concerned with my safety, confessing that he himself felt a dark presence near me in the alley behind the coffee shop. No, Quinn was not the evil presence Voodoo Martha referred to. He just couldn't be. Who, or what, was it then that was stalking me?

"Ryann? Ryann? Did you hear me?" Jessica waved her hands in front of my face. "She's just trying to scare you. Ignore her. I plan to."

Martha delivered a particularly menacing scowl in Jessica's direction before heading for the door. She looked over her shoulder once more at me, uttering a quick warning. "I don't care whether you believe me or not. Something dark is seeking you out. What you do with that knowledge is your business." And with that, she was gone.

Jessica let out a loud sigh. "Oh … my God. She is such a freak. Contract or no contract, we need to find a way to make her move out."

Nodding, I stood up from the edge of the bed. The staggering urge to flee, run, get the hell away from everyone and everything was more than I could handle. Anxiety reared its ugly head and I knew if I didn't get out of the apartment I'd lose my shit altogether, go postal. "I need to get out of here." My head spun from the crapload of garbage I'd been dealt over the past few days. Escape was all I could think about.

"Yeah, okay. Where do you want to go?"

I shrugged. "Doesn't matter. Just out." Anywhere but there was all that mattered to me at the moment.

"Okay. Let me just freshen up." Jessica strode out of the room toward her own.

On edge and full of anxiety, I dug through my closet with shaky hands, changing into a pair of low-rise jeans and a grey, sleeveless top. My rationale was that if I looked good on the outside, maybe, just maybe I'd feel better on the inside. I know. My reasoning sounded stupid. Probably was too, considering my inability to breathe in the tight pants. Still, I was willing to do just about anything to make myself feel better at that point. I slipped on a pair of silver flip-flops and pulled out my cell phone, throwing my bag over my shoulder.

My skull pounded and felt like it might splinter from all the overtime my brain took on trying to figure out what Martha meant when she said something dark was after me. Nervous, despite the fact I wasn't alone, I gripped my cell phone, turning it over in my hands anxiously. I let out a loud sigh of relief as Jess entered my room, fresh and ready to go.

She pressed her lips together tightly and frowned. "Sheesh … Martha really did a number on you. Relax, Ryann. She's crazy. Don't let her get to you."

I knew Jessica was right. I may have a creepy stalker, but there was no ominous evil presence lurking around the corner ready to jump out at me. Simply put, Martha was off her rocker.

I chewed away at the inside of my lip and shook my head. What the hell happened to me? Ridiculous had somehow become my new middle name. Hi there. Name's Ryann Ridiculous Pierce. I talk to faeries and have an ominous, evil stalker tailing me. Nice to meet ya! I needed to have my head checked and possibly a bit of shock therapy on the side.

With keys in hand, we exited the apartment. "Remind me to call a locksmith," I said as I bolted the front door closed. Come this time tomorrow, there'd be an extra deadbolt, slide latch, and security screen on the door, keeping unwanted visitors out of my home. Unless the asshole who broke in had the ability to both control and manipulate matter, as well as poof himself in and out of places, my apartment would be safe.

"Oh, hey." Surprise coated Jessica's voice as she bent down to pick something up off the ground. She handed me a small brown box. "You got a package."

I felt my brows knit together. "Huh. I wonder what it is." I jiggled my keys in my palm and flipped the box over. There was no return address marked, which I found a little odd. I used my keys to score through the packing tape and open the box, all the while hoping the nut job who broke in hadn't planted a bomb in front of my apartment. Hell, with my bad luck, anything was possible.

I looked up at Jess with a wry smile. "I bet whatever it is, it's from your mother." Her mom, Karen, was addicted to shopping online, and packages were always coming to her house for someone.

Whoever sent the package had a love affair with packing tape. I wrangled with the damn box for several minutes and actually managed to work up a sweat trying to open the thing. Finally, the tape gave way and the cardboard sprang open. Inside, a rectangular shaped gift box lay wrapped to perfection in shiny red paper, and was finished off with a pretty white organza bow. A small note was attached.

Time to toss that banjaxed ball of shite you call a phone, and move into the twentieth century. Q

"No way," I shrieked. My hands shook with excited anticipation as I ripped the shiny paper to shreds and tore open the lid of the box, revealing a sleek, new iPhone and all of the accompanying accessories.

Jessica's eyes reminded me of a cartoon character as they all but shot out of her head. I half expected to hear sirens and an obnoxious "Ow-ooga" sound. "Holy…wow, girl. If my mother sent you that, she'd better be getting me one. Pronto."

I shook my head, handing her the note, which she eagerly read while I played with my shiny new toy. After playing with the expensive gadget for just two minutes, I completely understood Quinn's unholy appreciation for the contraption. The iPhone did everything but wipe your ass for you, and I bet if I looked I could find an app for that as well. The phone was wicked cool.

Jessica's loud gasp filled the air as she discovered who sent me the phone. "O.M.G.! Somebody's smitten with our Ryann."

I rolled my eyes at her while inwardly hoping she was right. "Smitten? Really? Are we in the middle of a *Leave It To Beaver* episode? Nice word, Beave."

She stuck her tongue out at me and grinned. "Whatever, potty mouth. It's better than anything you might have come up with."

"Potty mouth?" Yeah, I couldn't argue. She had me with that one. I shook my head and went back to my new phone as we shuffled out of the courtyard.

So taken with my shiny new toy, I stubbed my toe on the edge of a brick planter, tumbled into the foliage, lost a shoe, and smashed a defenseless daisy plant in the process. Apparently I was a hazard to everything around me as well as myself. Grumbling, I hopped on one foot while slipping on my wayward shoe, and stepped out of the planter, thankful I hadn't dropped my new phone.

"Walk much?" Jessica teased.

I lifted my arm, extended my third digit, and flipped her the bird, never once looking up from my new phone.

Jessica's lighthearted laughter rang through the courtyard. "Nice, Ryann. Very ladylike. Hey, let's take the Mint Mobile," she suggested. "If there's a stalker tailing you, we shouldn't be walking around."

I nodded in agreement and walked around to the side of the apartment building where my mint green convertible VW Bug was parked. My baby. The culmination of several years of hard work wrapped up in one adorable, mint green package. "Let's hit it," I said as we piled into the car.

If it was a short walk to Main Street from our apartment, it was an even shorter drive. The small time in the car was spent "oohing and ahing" over my new iPhone, which Quinn had loaded with what seemed like every song ever written.

Jess scrolled through the massive list of artists and shook her head in appreciation. "Good Lord, Ryann. Your boy has great taste in music. He could be a keeper, this one."

I focused on the road ahead of me, wearing a fat grin and the first sense of ease I'd felt since we'd left the apartment. Quinn was definitely a keeper.

As luck would have it, I found a parking space directly in front of The Plough and The Stars, quite happy I wouldn't have to trek half a mile from the parking garage located further up the street.

I grabbed my purse and climbed out of the car, but not before I heard Jess snort, "The Plough? Someone's got an Irishman on their mind." It was obvious she was trying to push my buttons.

I did my best to feign irritation as I spat out a quick "Shut up!"

The pub was hopping, full of college students and locals alike. Tabitha, the coquettish hostess who'd seated Quinn and me before, greeted us near the entrance. "Restaurant's full. You can take a seat in the bar if you'd like." She shoved two menus at me and motioned for us to seat ourselves.

I made a beeline for one of two empty tables opposite the bar. The Pogues' "Fairytale Of New York" blared throughout the packed room and I giggled to myself. I'd liked the song ever since I'd seen the movie *P.S. I Love You*. Gerard Butler is hot!

Jess followed close behind, taking in the scenery. "Wow. This place is busy."

My butt had just hit my chair when a plastic looking waitress sidled up to our table. "Can I get you ladies started with a drink? A pitcher of beer? Some wings?"

Jess gave our plastic server the once-over and rolled her eyes. "God, no, beer goes straight to the gut. I'll have an Appletini, please. Oh, and a vegetable platter." She turned to face me. "Is that cool? Will you share it with me?"

Jess and I were of like minds. We both sang about the perils of fanny-inflating foods and avoided beer at all costs. "Yeah, that's fine." I looked over my shoulder toward the server. "I'll have a Lemon Drop and an extra plate, I guess."

With a nod and a smile, the server left to fill our order.

Halfway through our shared veggie platter, the bar was just as full as the restaurant portion of the pub. The cacophony of voices and laughter made thinking difficult, let alone hearing one another over the loud din.

Thank God for Lemon Drops. After my second, the tension that had me wound up taut as a bowstring finally eased and I found myself laughing at Jessica, who I'd taken to calling "Chug-a-lug." Jess didn't let loose often, but when she did, she was a happy drunk, giggly and flirtatious. She threw several come hither looks toward a handsome college boy sitting at the bar.

Upon seeing Jessica and me, the slick-looking twenty-something signaled his two friends with a slight nod before making a beeline straight for our table.

Oh great.

"So…would you ladies care for some company?" Rico Suave was a player. I could tell not only by his voice, but by the way he waltzed over to us like he owned the place. Pimp Daddy thought he was fly. I wasn't fooled by him or by his friends. Jess? Well, she was another story.

Completely annihilated, Jessica was thoroughly incapable of forming a rational thought, let alone recognizing the player for what he was. Pissed to the gills, she sat in her seat and giggled as they approached. "Definitely!" she shouted happily, feigning a fake Australian accent. Jessica wasn't just tipsy; she was toast.

Rico and his merry band of idiots swarmed down on us like a plague of locusts, stealing unoccupied chairs from other tables.

Señor Suave spun his chair around and straddled it as he sat next to Jessica. "Cool accent." He eyeballed Jess like she was a juicy piece of steak. "Are you from Down Under?"

"Yep," Jess lied, lifting her glass toward Rico as if to say "cheers," and downed the rest of its contents.

Girlfriend was off the hook tonight. I really needed to cut her off.

Rico leered at Jess like a dog with three dicks. "Well, how about I give you an Aussie kiss?"

Oh no, he didn't!

"Excuse me?" Jessica shouted. She reached for her glass only to find it empty, then grabbed mine, dumping the remainder of its contents onto Rico's lap. "You don't get to talk to me like that, now rack off!"

All hell broke loose.

"Bitch!" Rico jumped up from his seat with a growl and towered over Jessica. "You're gonna pay for that." He clenched his hands into fists and I feared he'd lose it altogether and hit her.

Tired of asshats who had no respect for women, I grabbed a handful of vegetables and tossed them at Rico's face. "The hell she is. Get lost!" I tried to stand, but was yanked back into my seat by one of Rico's nameless companions.

"Keep your trap shut or I'll shut it for you," Nameless Guy said, doing his best to intimidate me. It worked. Adrenaline spiked and I trembled from head to toe.

"Touch her again, and I'll rip your fucking arm off and shove it down your bloody fucking throat!"

The effect of *his* voice on my body was instantaneous. My limbs stopped shaking and the fear that had placed me in a chokehold vanished. Only one person had that effect on me. *Quinn.*

I turned my head and got an eyeful of two-hundred-plus pounds of pissed off faerie. Quinn towered in front of our table with his arms crossed, jaw clenched, and a murderous look in his eyes. Beyond sexy, dressed in a skintight black t-shirt that displayed his oversized chest and biceps quite nicely, ass hugging jeans, and Doc's, he wore a deadly look upon his beautiful face. If looks could kill, Rico and his band of idiots would be dead, ten times over.

"Fuck off, Irishman!" Rico stepped forward, full of attitude and raised his arm as if to shove Quinn away. Lightening fast, Quinn took hold of Rico's hand, crushing it in his own. The sound of bones cracking sailed over the noisy crowd, and Rico hit the deck, writhing in agony.

Tweedledee and Tweedledum hopped up from beside Jessica and me, wasting no time in getting the hell away from us, leaving their fearless leader whimpering and alone.

Shocked, my eyes darted from Jess to Quinn to the crying lump of flesh moaning on the floor. I didn't quite know what to say, so I kept my trap shut.

"If you'll excuse me, ladies?" Quinn excused himself politely and hefted the now sniveling Rico off of the floor, dragging him to the nearby exit at the rear of the bar.

"Ho … ly … Wow." Jessica's eyes widened in shock. "Did you see what he did to that guy's hand?"

I fought to regain composure and stared in the direction Quinn had disappeared, completely stunned into silence.

A loud burp and the sickening sound of gagging tore my attention from the back exit. I looked over to Jess, who'd turned a brilliant shade of green.

"Oh … oh, God. I'm going to be sick." With her hand over her mouth, she shot out of her seat, sprinting for the bathroom.

I moved to follow her when Quinn suddenly appeared again.

"I leave you alone for one evening and look what happens. Jaysus!" Quinn let out a frustrated groan and sat down in Jessica's empty seat. "Fucking mollycoddles." He sat back in the chair, flashed me a toothy grin, and snatched up a celery stick, popping it into his mouth.

chapter 9

I sat openmouthed, staring at Quinn as he ravaged the last of the veggie platter, shocked at what I'd just seen. It wasn't often I witnessed the crushing of a human hand. In fact, I'd never seen anything remotely close to the type of damage Quinn inflicted on Jessica's unwanted suitor. I found it sexy as hell, which was odd since I rarely condoned violence. The more I thought about it, the more I realized I saw Quinn as my champion. Commanding and strong, he safeguarded not only me, but also my friends, from harm, and that was one powerful turn on for me.

Jess returned from the bathroom, her pale skin a violent shade of green, and took a seat opposite Quinn and me. Obviously still somewhat skeptical of my new friend, she slowly reached her hand out to greet Quinn, but changed her mind, hastily shoving it into her lap. I couldn't blame her. If I'd just witnessed a stranger crush someone's hand, I wouldn't be too keen on giving him a handshake either, even if he had saved me from a rank asshole. In truth, I was a bit relieved. Knowing what came along with Quinn's grip, I was fairly certain he'd refuse to comply, leaving Jessica hanging and confused. It was better all around if we kept strictly to conversation.

"Jess, I'd like you to meet Quinn. Quinn, this is my best friend, Jessica." I smiled, nervous, praying the two of them would get along. Knowing how skeptical Jessica was in regard to Quinn, I wasn't sure what she'd say.

"It's very nice to meet you, Quinn," Jessica said weakly, looking as though she might toss her cookies right at the table.

Thank you, God.

He gave her a nod. "Aye. You as well. Are you all right, lass? You're looking pretty … ripe."

Jessica sat quietly for a moment before her hand flew up to her mouth. She bolted once more from the table, in the direction of the bathroom.

"Well, I guess that answers my question," Quinn said with a chuckle. He turned to face me, staring intently into my eyes, and I flushed. The power those baby blues had over me was almost too much. "So, did you like your present?"

"About that." I leaned forward in my seat. "Thank you so much for the new phone. I absolutely love it. I just don't think I'll be able to afford the service for it." I hated to put a damper on his wonderful gesture, but it was the plain truth. I made good money at the club, but an expensive phone plan was just not in my budget.

"Keep your knickers on, lass. It's all taken care of." A smug smile crept across his face and he turned toward the table to our left, which was occupied by a bunch of pencil-pushing geeks. He grabbed hold of their pitcher of beer, ignoring their protests and turned to face me once again, brazenly downing half its contents.

I shook my head. The man was shameless. "Dip into your pot of gold to pay for it?" I said with a snort, laughing at my own joke. From the look on Quinn's face, I was clearly the only one who thought it was funny.

"Leprechauns!" Quinn grumbled. "Miserly ol' gimps. I'm fair sorry to call them cousins."

I gaped at him like he'd grown another head. "There are actually leprechauns?"

I'd been joking when I made the comment about the pot of gold, never thinking they might actually exist. Why it was such a stretch for me, I wasn't sure. If I could believe in the reality of a five-hundred-year-old faerie, then why were leprechauns such an impossibility? Denial seemed the safest road to travel down as far as the existence of mythical creatures. If I remained in denial, I wouldn't have to entertain the possibility there were sinister creatures lurking about, along with more charming beings such as Quinn.

"Aye, love. I'm not the only otherworldly creature roaming about. And not all of them are as handsome and charming as yours truly." He smiled broadly for a moment, then leaned forward in his seat with a grim sigh. "So quickly you seem to have forgotten about the nasty creatures you read about just the other night. There are a fair number of dark beings more than willing to bleed you dry and leave you for dead."

A chill shot up my spine and large goosebumps broke out all over my flesh as I trembled. I hadn't forgotten. Hell, it wasn't only mythical creatures that had me spooked. There were plenty of human assholes roaming around that scared the bejeesus out of me.

"Aye, that's a more appropriate reaction. You should be afraid. Especially after the evil presence I sensed near you in that alley. I was deadly serious when I told you I don't want you roaming about on your own."

My stomach lurched, nausea rolling around my belly like a pinball in an arcade machine as the memory of the ominous message scrawled on my bedroom mirror flashed through my mind. Afraid and unwilling to consider the possibility my stalker might be a supernatural creature of some sort, I sat quietly, unsure of what to say.

I was about to tell Quinn about the break-in when Jessica dragged her way to the table, slow, unsteady, and still an unsavory shade of green. A thin sheen of sweat covered her forehead from emptying her stomach. She leaned heavily on the table, looking a little bit worse with each moment that passed. She exhaled heavily. "I need to get back to the apartment. I feel like death."

"Oh God, Jess. Of course." I reached into my bag for my wallet as I stood up from my seat. "Let me just take care of the check and I'll drive us back."

Quinn stood up, pulling a thick roll of cash from his pocket and tossed a few large bills onto the table before I could retrieve my own money from my wallet. I let my frustration with him be known and scowled at him with a huff.

"No arguments." His tone was curt and authoritative, as was his expression. "Let's get your friend home, shall we?"

I wanted to get Jessica back to the apartment more than I wanted to argue with him, so I let it go. I pulled her arm over my shoulder and let her lean on me as we navigated our way through the pub toward the exit. "I'm sorry, Jess. I shouldn't have let you drink so much. I was so caught up in my own crap, I wasn't paying attention."

"Ugh," she said with a groan. "It doesn't take much to get me drunk. Plus, those jerks from the bar scared me a bit. Pigs!"

I looked up toward the heavens as we stepped outside. The sun was low on the horizon, streaks of pink and orange painting the autumn sky a wondrous color. Still pleasantly warm with just a hint of a breeze, it was a perfect California evening. Except for the fact that my car was no longer where I left it.

"Wait! Wha…what? No!" I screamed, my voice filled with anguish as I ran to the empty space where my beloved Mint Mobile was no longer parked.

"Ugh." Jessica wavered a bit, doing her best to balance herself after I'd left her on her own. She ended up sinking down onto the sidewalk in a heap.

"This…" I turned to face Quinn and Jess and held my hands out, motioning to the empty spot in which I stood. "This is not happening!" I paced back and forth maniacally.

I clamped my eyes shut nice and tight and held my breath, willing my car to magically reappear. If faeries and boogeymen existed in this world, why the hell couldn't my car materialize back to where it belonged? I cracked one eye open and faced my grim reality with a heavy heart. My car was gone and I was devastated.

Astonished by the fact that my car was stolen in broad daylight in front of the very establishment we patronized, I ran past Jessica, who sat hunched on the curb, and Quinn, who looked incensed as he paced back and forth scanning the area. Someone had to have seen something with as crowded as the pub was.

I scurried past Tabitha, ignoring her protests that I couldn't just barge into the place and interrupt people while they enjoyed their meals. I didn't care what she had to say. I needed to know if anyone saw anything. I weaved my way through the crowded dining area until I stood in front of the two tables situated in front of the window, directly across from where my car had been parked.

"Excuse me," I said, out of breath and panting. "I apologize for interrupting your meal, but my car was stolen. It was parked just outside…there." I pointed to where Jessica sat on the curb, partially blocking the now empty space. My poor, drunk friend; she heaved once again into the street, and I grimaced at having treated the poor strangers to such a sight during their meal.

A warm, tingling sensation trickled up my spine and I turned to see Quinn standing behind me, a fierce look in his eyes as he stood with his hands shoved into his pockets.

I stared at the patrons in front of the window. "Did you by chance see anything?"

The guests at the table farthest from where I stood merely shook their heads and continued shoveling food into their mouths. The older couple sitting at the table closest to me, however, stared at me like I was a certifiable nut.

Frowning at me, the old man spoke. "Yeah, I saw something. I saw you get into your car and drive away."

Me? What?

"Uh, no, I didn't move my car. I was in the bar until just a few minutes ago." The tone of my voice rose higher and higher, along with my agitation.

He pointed a bony finger at me and glowered. "Look here, little missy, I'm telling you what I saw. About twenty minutes ago, I watched you get into your car and drive off." He shook his head at me in disgust and grumbled, "That's the problem with your generation. You don't take responsibility for yourselves. Maybe you should lay off the sauce and focus more on your studies. When I was your age …"

Grandpa Kettle's words floated off into the ether as I stood amidst the crowded tables, shaking with anger.

"Ryann, come with me now," Quinn said forcefully.

I whirled around to face him. "But—"

My protest was met with a stern glare. Mr. Serious Face was not messing around.

Not wanting to argue with Quinn on top of everything else, I made my apologies to Ol' Man River and his wife, and followed Quinn outside. "What the hell?" I said once we were outside the Plough. "I'm just trying to find out what happened to my car. Apparently, I stole it myself and drove away!" I reached into my bag, pulling out my new phone, and dug around for Officer What's-His-Name's card. Dammit! I'd left it on the coffee table back at the apartment. I frantically clawed at the touch screen, trying to figure out how to make a call. "Damn thing! How the hell do you make a call on this contraption?"

Quinn stalked over to me. "Who are you trying to call?"

I blew up. "The cops! I need to report my car being stolen."

Quinn scanned the street in both directions with a deadly look on his face. "Put your phone away, *a ghrá*. The police won't be able to help you find your car."

"Why not?" I stared at him in disbelief.

"Because I think it was taken by some kind of demon. I sensed the presence of evil when we first came out here. It lingers still." Quinn took on a protective stance, positioning himself closer to me, while staring down each passerby with a shit-load of *ima-beat-you-if-you-come-any-closer* as he spoke. In fact, as he stood on the curb with a cold, lethal stare and a pair of large, sinewy arms that looked more like weapons of mass destruction crossed over his chest, Quinn was no longer the cheeky, charismatic ladies' man I'd grown to know, but a fierce warrior ready to wipe the floor with anyone or anything that came near me.

"What the hell does a demon want with my car?" Mythical creatures popped in and out of places by magic and traveled at the speed of light. Last time I checked, the boogeyman didn't drive a Prius. Hell, maybe I was the crazy one, and the past few days had been some kind of whacked out fantasy being played out in my mind.

"I've no idea. It seems the only explanation, though, what with the dark aura that's lingering about, and with the patron's account of what he saw."

"What do you mean?"

"The man in the restaurant claimed he saw you get into your car and drive away. I know you didn't as I was with you, so someone, or something, that looked like you took your car."

"Something that looks like me?"

"Aye, *mo chrói*. A shapeshifter," he said, his voice filled with disgust.

I blanched and my eyes felt like they might pop out of their sockets.

Shapeshifter?

The boundaries of what my brain could accept were being stretched way past what was acceptable to me.

I hit the wall and lost control of myself, unleashing an emotional tirade straight out of Jerry Springer. "This is insane. No, I'm insane, that's it. I've lost my freaking mind. My car, you, all of this is a manifestation of my subconscious mind. Holy Mother of God! I've cracked!" I was past upset and had ventured into the wonderful realm of hysteria. My eyes darted back and forth scanning the street, my paranoia-filled mind certain I'd be shot any moment with a tranquilizer gun and dragged away for shock treatment.

Quinn stood in front of me and glared. "Calm down, *a ghrá*. You're not crazy and—if you wouldn't mind keeping your voice down? It's really not very fun having to go around scrubbing people's memories."

"Uh…hello? Ryann?" I snapped my head around to see Jessica still sitting on the curb looking pale and sweaty. "Can we go home or should I just lay down here in the gutter?" It was plain as day Jessica felt awful, and a terrible pang of remorse stabbed me in the chest. I was a horrible friend for leaving her to sit on the curb for so long while I had a mental breakdown.

"Oh, God. I'm so sorry. Here…" I walked over and crouched down, grabbing hold of her by the arms and hauled her up to her feet. "Let's go. We'll have to walk."

"Stay where you are," Quinn said with a commanding tone while glaring at me. "That means no flitting about interrogating hapless strangers about your wayward vehicle." He stood in front of me, his body mere centimeters from mine, and got right in my face. "Sit yourself down and stay put."

"Excuse me?" I crossed my arms in front of me. I didn't particularly care for his bossy tone and I loathed being treated like a child, though I knew he meant well. I donned my best diva attitude, placing my hands on my hips, and stood still, chin up, glowering at him.

"You heard me." He pointed toward the curb, glaring at me with one eyebrow raised, all but daring me to cross him. "Stubborn as a mule you are," he grumbled and shook his head while walking away, I assumed to retrieve his car.

I looked over my shoulder toward the Plough, inwardly cursing myself for leaving the apartment, and took a seat next to Jessica on the curb. If I'd just stayed home, we wouldn't have had the run in with Rico and his band of idiots and I'd still have my car.

"I like him for you." I heard Jessica over my shoulder, trying to stifle a yawn. Alcohol even in small amounts always put her to sleep, so the fact she could speak at all, as knackered as she was, was incredible.

My jaw nearly hit the floor when I registered her drunken admission.

"Wait, did I hear you correctly? Did you just say you approve of Quinn?"

A small moan escaped her lips and she eyed me with contempt, no doubt for making her elaborate when she felt like shit. "He's feisty, and he seems to be every bit as pigheaded and commanding as you are. He's a good match for you. Plus, the way he took down that creep in the bar was beyond amazing. I know you'll be safe with him looking after you."

"Pigheaded?"

How am I pigheaded and commanding? I don't think so.

Jessica let out a gnarly sounding burp before giving me an aggravated sigh. "Yes, pigheaded. When you set your mind to something, that's it, there's no changing it. You are incredibly strong-willed and focused about everything from your schoolwork, your job, and your life goals," she raised an eyebrow, "your running."

"Humph." I didn't necessarily agree with her. I wouldn't refer to myself as pigheaded as much as I would panicked. True, I was serious about my schooling and life goals, because they were all I had. With no family to lean on, I only had myself, and I was determined to be the very best I could be. If that meant staying focused twenty-four-seven, then so be it. I didn't plan on living in Hanaford Park the rest of my life. I was meant for bigger and better things.

As I sat lost in my thoughts, I heard Jessica gasp. "Holy Moses," she muttered under her breath as a jet-black Mercedes S65 AMG pulled to a stop in front of where we sat. Sleek and shiny, the car was sex on wheels and the epitome of class and style.

I looked over to Jess, eyes wide, mouthing the word "wow."

What happened next was something straight out of the movies. The passenger side window rolled down nice and slow, treating us to a delicious view of Quinn sitting in the driver's seat, wearing a flirtatious, albeit somewhat pretentious, smile.

Damn, conceited faerie!

He knew his car was hot. He knew he was hot, and he was being smug about it.

Men!

"Get in." His deep voice carried over the loud music blaring from his, no doubt very expensive, stereo system with ease.

I stood up, brushed myself off, and helped load a very pale-looking Jessica into the back seat, before sliding into the front passenger seat alongside Quinn.

He looked over his shoulder at Jess before hitting the gas. "If you need to be sick, give a holler so I can pull over."

Jess merely groaned and slumped over, resting her head against the window and lifted her hand, motioning for us to go.

The drive back to our apartment was brief. Not only because it wasn't a great distance away, but because Quinn drove at maniacal speeds, causing me to air break every two seconds and grip the handle on the door so tightly I temporarily lost feeling in my hand.

"You know, there's a speed limit posted you're supposed to follow." My heart took up residence in my throat, and I wondered how Jessica was faring in the back seat with the quick turns and sudden starts and stops. I was too afraid to look, though, fearing she may have hurled again, this time on Quinn's perfectly upholstered seats.

Quinn dismissed my declaration with a grumble. "This car is German engineering at its finest. It's meant to be driven fast. I like fast." He flashed me a devilish grin, sending butterflies fluttering about my stomach and blood pooling to the more intimate areas of my anatomy. I returned his smile, as it was impossible not to. I was quite thoroughly mesmerized by him, and it felt wonderful.

My stomach lurched as we pulled into the parking lot of my building. The thought of sleeping in my room, knowing some strange lunatic had been in it, sickened me. I chewed on the inside of my lip, trying to decide if I should fess up, tell Quinn what happened. Would he be mad I'd kept it from him? Probably. I chickened out and didn't say a word.

We eased into a parking spot just as Jessica moaned and lurched for the door. She heaved herself from the vehicle and tossed her cookies once more alongside a yellow Cutlass Supreme.

I glanced back at Quinn, who laughed silently in his seat. "Good luck getting sleep tonight," he said in a mocking tone.

With my eyes narrowed, I stuck my tongue out at him in defiance. "Very funny." I slid out of the comfortable leather seat and closed the door behind me.

I heard him calling after me as I walked toward the dorm. "Be mindful of yourself, *mo chrói*. Don't be going off on your own."

Overcome with attitude, I stood upright and stiff, saluting him with a shout. "Sir, yes sir!"

"Stubborn, pigheaded, obstinate little girl. You'll be the death of me. I swear it!" He gripped the steering wheel tightly and took off, tires screeching as he exited the parking lot.

chapter 10

I didn't sleep well that night. In fact, I was up till the wee hours of the morning with Jessica. On top of being drunk, she was sick with the flu, having spiked a fever later in the evening. After helping her fall asleep and thoroughly sanitizing everything within reach, I lay awake in my own bed, tossing and turning, replaying the events of the day over in my mind.

The idea my stalker might be some dark creature or demon unnerved me. Whoever or whatever it was, what did it want with me? How had I become immersed in a world full of magical creatures, which, prior to meeting Quinn, I was blissfully unaware of? Did he bring this shit storm of unworldly crap on me, or was I being stalked before he came into my life, unbeknownst to me? I didn't have any answers, and that frustrated me more than anything.

I rolled over with a huff, glaring at the clock with contempt. Four forty-five a.m. I sat up, my body shaking and full of anxiety. What I needed was to go for a run. Exercise was great for getting rid of stress, and I knew there was no chance in hell I was getting more sleep.

I hesitated for a moment, knowing Quinn would no doubt disapprove of me jogging alone at this early hour. But I was desperate for some relief from the restlessness that ate away at my insides, and like an idiot, I assured myself that if I took my phone with me, I'd be fine. Stalkers had to sleep too. Right? Whoever was following me couldn't possibly tail me twenty-four-seven. Could they? I'd just call Quinn if anything out of the ordinary happened. I refused to live in constant fear. Plenty of other people went for morning jogs without centuries old faeries looking after them and they fared just fine. I was certain I could as well.

I changed into sweats and running shoes as quietly as I could, not wanting to wake poor Jessica from her much needed slumber, and clueless as to whether or not my early morning noise had any effect on Martha. Grabbing my ear buds and my fancy new phone, I quietly exited the apartment and made my way out onto the street, filling my lungs with the brisk morning air.

Jess hadn't lied when she said Quinn loaded the iPhone with a ton of music. I took a moment while stretching to scroll through the massive list of artists, impressed with his well-rounded taste in music. He'd uploaded a little bit of everything from classical to indie, to a little bit of rap and a large heaping of alternative, which was currently my favorite genre.

Choosing a fairly new alternative band, I hit the play button, slid the phone into the kangaroo pocket of my sweatshirt and took off into a slow jog.

It was still dark out, given the early hour, the only light coming from the scattered streetlamps. As per usual, I opted to jog around the perimeter of the campus, not wanting to stray too far from home.

Nervous and on edge, I scanned the area repeatedly while I ran, scoping out the perimeter, but for who or what, I wasn't sure. If evil were to approach me, would I know it? How can you tell if someone is a shapeshifter? I stifled a laugh, appalled at how ludicrous my thoughts sounded to me.

The faint echoes of my laughter rang through the air when a dark blur whooshed past me from behind and came to a halt about twenty feet away.

My heart jumped into my throat and I choked on the air I desperately tried to breathe in.

Cloaked in black, the creature's obsidian eyes seared my flesh as it stalked forward slowly. The same horrific demon from my nightmare just days before, the evil monstrosity raised its long bony arm, gesturing for me to come forward with its gaunt fingers.

"Ryann." Its spine-chilling voice had every cell in my body terrified and ready to flee.

How silly of me to think I wouldn't recognize evil when I saw it. It stood right in front of me and I was certain I was going to die.

It opened its mouth, a putrid, baleful sound ripping through my flesh. "So beautiful. So innocent. Unblemished. Untainted by today's society. Mine."

"No!" I tried to scream, but all that crossed my lips was a high-pitched squeak. "Leave me alone," I pleaded breathlessly while backing away. Reaching into my pocket, I grabbed hold of my phone, fumbling with it as my hands shook terribly, trying to make a call.

The creature let out a ghastly chuckle and moved forward again as though it were floating through the air. "Put your silly gadget away, my sweet. There is none that can help you." Just an arm's length away from me, the demon reached out, running its ice-cold finger down my cheek. Its mouth opened revealing a jagged set of teeth no human could possibly possess with its sinister smile. The smell of eternal suffering and death clouded the air, choking me.

So terrified I was sure I'd lost control of all bodily functions, I stood frozen in place, tears streaming down my face. I closed my eyes, not wanting the face of evil to be the last thing I'd ever see. Conjuring up a mental picture of Quinn, I breathed out what I believed would be my last words—an apology. I'd been so wrong to dismiss his warnings, a damn fool. So stupid to venture out on my own when I knew someone was after me. Stubborn and deluded, I'd ignored his cautioning and now suffered the horrific consequence. "Quinn," I sobbed. "Forgive me."

A thunderous roar filled the crisp morning air, and suddenly, I no longer sensed the demon standing in front of me. A familiar tingle ghosted across my skin and up the length of my spine. *Quinn.* My eyes shot open to see him standing inches from me, crouched and defensive, staring at the demon he'd thrown some fifty feet away.

"Faerie!" It hissed with a malevolent tone. "This is no concern of yours. Leave!"

Quinn didn't flinch. He stood his ground, unyielding, fierce and ready to do battle. "You made it my concern when you attacked the girl."

Like a serpentine abomination, the ominous creature slithered forward, its soulless eyes fixed on Quinn, trying to gauge his next move. "What is she to you? I know who you are, Gancanagh. You can have any woman you want. Leave this one to me."

Quinn's beautiful voice took on a harsh, menacing tone, his Irish accent thick with rage. "She is mine." Gone was the man I knew. This new Quinn was deadly, lethal and more than capable of tearing my stalker apart, piece by bloody piece.

Overcome with a mix of fear and shock, I backed away from the ensuing fight, taking shelter behind a nearby tree. With horror-filled eyes, I watched

Quinn and the demon stalk back and forth in a deadly, macabre dance, each one crouched, spine coiled, ready to pounce like the deadly predators they were.

In a movement so quick I almost didn't catch it, the demon flew at Quinn with a blood-curdling scream. The force of the demon's blow sent both sailing into the back of a nearby utility building with a deafening crash.

One second Quinn was on the ground, the next he vanished into thin air. My eyes darted back and forth in search of him, and I jumped when he reappeared again, lifting the hideous creature high above his head and then slamming him onto the ground.

A high-pitched keening filled the air along with the unearthly sound of bones crunching, snapping, and shifting. The demon shook violently on the darkened pavement before exploding into a brilliant flash of light, rendering me momentarily sightless. My hands shot up to cover my eyes, shielding myself from the blinding light.

The keening broke off, replaced by a vicious snarling. Hugging the trunk of the massive oak as if it were some sort of lifeline, I peered from behind the tree once more, my eyes still singed from the flash, to see what looked like a giant black dog baring its razor sharp teeth. It was the same fiendish canine that came at me in the alleyway just the other night.

The savage cur moved in a wide arc around Quinn, snapping and growling. My heart nearly stopped when it bent low to the ground, readying itself to spring forward and attack. Every inch of me wanted to scream, to cry out for Quinn to run, to get the hell out of there. But I dared not make a sound. A distraction from me could prove deadly, and I'd never be able to live with myself if I caused Quinn harm. So I stood in silent fear, my lips pressed together tightly, my fingernails digging into the scratchy bark of the large oak, praying to God the fight would end soon and Quinn would come out unscathed.

Quinn popped in and out of the mêlée at light speed, cloaking himself with invisibility one minute, showing himself the next.

The demon, unable to keep up with Quinn's dizzying speed, spun in a wild circle, baring its razor-sharp fangs as it growled and snapped.

With a blur of movement, Quinn magically appeared alongside the menacing beast, and with a look of single-minded ferocity, he kicked the creature as hard as his powerful leg would allow, sending it flying toward the utility building once again with a loud yelp.

"Hey! You there!" An irate voice shouted from the distance.

Warning bells rang loud and clear the moment I heard the stranger's voice. Whoever it was needed to turn around and run in the opposite direction. Didn't they know there was a supernatural smackdown taking place?

Shaken and visibly injured, the beast took advantage of the momentary distraction. It let out a low, depraved chuckle, peeled itself off the ground, and retreated into the darkness just moments before the hapless newcomer stepped into view.

The owner of the strange voice, a round, balding man in his late forties, stepped into a patch of light cast by a nearby lamp, visibly upset with Quinn. He threw up his hand and barked, "Hey, buddy. We don't take kindly to the beating of animals around here. I've a mind to call the authorities."

Unable to control his rage, Quinn blew up. "Stupid, fucking arsehole! 'Twas not a dog at all, but a devil in disguise! He's escaped and it's your doing. Leave now before I mop the floor with your fat, balding arse!" I watched his anger float off him in waves, still on a high from the throw down with my attacker.

The offended stranger yanked out his cell phone, clearly unhappy about being referred to as a "fat, balding arsehole" and began punching numbers into its keypad.

If I didn't do something, things would go from bad to worse. "Wait!" I stepped out from behind the tree, my voice breathy and feeble. "Please … don't call the police. This man …" I pointed toward Quinn with teary eyes and walked forward. "This man saved me from that … that … dog." It most certainly was not a dog. Demon, devil, underworld freak, yes; it was all those things rolled into one, an unearthly monstrosity bound and determined to claim me for its own. Quinn had saved me from the devil himself and words could not begin to express the gratitude I felt for him.

The pear-shaped stranger eyed Quinn and I dubiously, lips pursed as he wrestled with his decision to call the cops or not. Evidently satisfied I'd spoken the truth, the man grumbled a quick "fine" before walking away, shaking his head and mumbling something I couldn't make out.

Once the stranger was out of sight, I completely fell apart. Having witnessed a mythological shakedown, I was surprised I'd remained standing as long as I did. I fell to a heap on the pavement, silent tears trickling down my cheeks. Curled into a ball, I rested my head on my knees, my hands fisting huge chunks of hair as I repeated, "I'm sorry. I'm so sorry," over and over again. Mental breakdowns were becoming a regular occurrence for me.

I sensed Quinn move so that he stood over me, but I didn't look up. I couldn't face him. Not after what just took place. Before I knew what was happening, he lifted me off the ground, cradling me in his muscular arms, and whisked me away from the scene of the attack. My eyes shot open and I stared at him in shock. He was touching me, though taking care to hold me only where there was clothing in between his skin and mine. I opened my mouth to speak, but stopped short as he spoke.

"Shh, *mo chrói*. You don't ever have to be sorry with me. Hush now and close your eyes."

I gazed at him in wonder, not knowing what to say. Why would I need to keep my eyes closed?

"Trust me, lass. Keep them closed."

I did trust him—completely. As soon as I shut my peepers, the most exhilarating sensation whirled over me. Wind whipped across my face, sending my short hair flying every which way. It felt as though we were flying, though I knew that was not the case.

Doing his best to shield me from the coldness of the early morning air without coming into contact with any exposed skin, Quinn ran and ran, and when I thought he might come to a stop, he ran some more. The rapid pounding of his feet against the pavement was like a steady drumbeat, and my heart kept time right along with them. He didn't sound winded, and his pace never slowed. Quinn was a freaking machine.

Just when I was sure he planned on footing it all the way to China, we came to a stop.

I felt the delicious weight of Quinn's stare on my face as his warm breath wafted across my skin. "Open your eyes, *a ghrá*," he said as he set my feet onto the ground. His voice was gentle and surprisingly steady for having run as far and as fast as he had.

He's Superman!

When I opened my eyes, I found myself standing in front of what was possibly the largest house I'd ever seen. Tucked into the base of a large hill, surrounded by several massive oak trees and a boatload of greenery, the house was easily the most beautiful I'd ever had the chance to behold. Taking in my surroundings, I quickly deduced we were about fifteen to twenty minutes from the university, in the less populated, more rural area of town. The fact that he ran us to this location so quickly blew my mind, and I stood motionless for a moment in complete awe of him.

"Is this your house?" I pointed toward the enormous structure awkwardly as I glanced over to look at Quinn.

He gave a single nod. "Aye."

I swallowed hard. "And you ran the entire way here, holding me?"

"Aye." He frowned, annoyed with my incessant questioning.

"How did you do it without people seeing?" I knew he could render himself invisible. But me as well? Visions of me floating through the air at breakneck speeds came running through my mind and I let out a small giggle. How I was able to laugh after what just happened was beyond me. It must have been some sort of survival instinct kicking in. Whatever the case, the laughter felt good.

"I cloaked the both of us. Now, can we go inside, or would you like to continue standing out here playing twenty questions?" A wry smile adorned his handsome face, and I returned it while sweeping my arm out in front of me, motioning for him to lead the way.

As I stepped through the entryway into Quinn's home, one word came barreling into the forefront of my mind: posh. Extravagantly decorated, the house looked like it belonged on the cover of a magazine. Leather couches filled the rooms and giant flat screen TVs covered the walls as I was lead through the enormous house.

We ended up in an oversized kitchen, complete with a stainless steel Wolf range oven and an enormous refrigerator built into the wall.

"Wow," I said, taking it all in. "This," I circled my arm mid-air, "is impressive."

"Thank you." Quinn glided toward the far counter and fiddled with the buttons on a high tech machine that looked somewhat like a coffee pot.

"How did you come about acquiring a place like this? I mean, it's not like you're pulling a day job." I'd been wondering about this for quite some time, how he paid for things. If there was no pot of gold waiting for him at the end of a rainbow, where did all of his money come from?

"Ah, I wondered when this conversation would take place. Have a seat, *a ghrá*, and I'll answer some questions for you."

I pulled out an expensive looking barstool and sat down, letting my arms rest on the cool marble countertop of the massive island that sat stationed in the center of the impressive room. Seriously, his kitchen was bank and would have Martha frigging Stewart's tongue lolling out of her mouth with its high tech gadgetry and spotless décor. I felt a twinge of insecurity, sitting in his posh home in a pair of ratty sweats, but forgot my worries the moment he opened his mouth.

"So you want to know how I pay for things if I've no job, eh?"

I nodded silently, trying to keep my cool though I was bursting with curiosity.

Quinn flitted around the room, pulling out various cooking utensils. "You could say I'm a good investor. I own property all over the globe, several companies, restaurants…"

"Okay, I get it. You're smart. You've diversified your money. Where did it come from?" Deep down I knew what his answer would be, but I needed to hear him say it.

Quinn let out a sigh, no doubt resigning himself to the fact I was not going to let it go. He placed both hands on the countertop, leaned forward and spoke.

"I wasn't always the charming, good-natured bloke you see before you. There was a time, many, many years ago when I was angry, filled with bitterness and hate for what had been done to me. Before leaving the women I'd seduce, I'd persuade them to give me all of their money. Of course, I'd make sure to charm only the wealthiest—noblewomen and the like."

"Enough!" I put my hand up to stop him. It was just as I'd suspected. I couldn't let myself get angry with any of the appalling things he'd done centuries before. Well, I could, but it wouldn't do me a damn bit of good. Besides, I couldn't say I'd have behaved any better if I'd been cursed, and I felt a momentary pang of pity for his unhappy plight.

He treated me to a look that plainly said, *I told you so.* "We need to talk about what happened this morning, Ryann." His voice took on a serious tone. He bent down and rifled through his oversized refrigerator as he spoke, pulling out the makings for what looked like some sort of egg breakfast.

My eyebrows shot up. *He cooks?*

The look of astonishment on my face must have been plain as day because Quinn rolled his eyes at me before reaching up for a copper pan that hung above the stainless steel range. "Yes, I cook. I've got to eat, haven't I?" He shook his head and scrunched up his mouth and nose. "Quit trying to change the subject. Is there a reason you didn't heed my warning about going off on your own?" He slammed the pan down onto the counter and leaned forward, his expression a mask of controlled frustration. "And tell me, lass. Just what were you thinking when you decided to go for a run during the wee hours of the morning? That's just asking for someone to attack you!"

His words came out with the force of a storm, his face grim, serious, and marked with worry. This was why I'd been trying to avoid this conversation. I knew I'd disappointed him. I'd placed myself in danger, and I felt, well, I felt plain stupid. I hated being wrong, and having to admit it was even worse.

Tears of anger and frustration welled in my eyes and I blinked, desperately trying to keep them from falling. My words came out in a garbled mess. "I know... I'm sorry, okay? I was stupid... you don't have to rub it in. I just felt so awful and I didn't sleep, and well... after the break-in yesterday, and my car being stolen, I needed to do something to get rid of my anxiety." I dropped my head, lifted my shoulders, and looked up at him through my lashes like a little kid trying to talk their way out of a punishment. "I took my phone with me." And it hadn't done me a damn bit of good.

A tic formed in his jaw. "Break-in? What break-in?" His powerful voice filled the room, bouncing off the walls as he eyed me fiercely. "Start talking."

Unwilling to keep things from him any longer, I quickly filled him in on the details of both break-ins. "I should have listened to you and Voodoo Martha," I trailed off, feeling like an utter moron.

He looked at me with his brows knit together. "Voodoo Martha? Who the hell is that?"

"My new roommate. She told me I was surrounded by a dark aura and that something evil was following me."

Quinn stopped what he was doing for a moment and stared fixedly at me as I spoke. "Did she now? And how would this Voodoo lady know about such things?" He looked a bit shocked that someone else knew of my dark stalker.

I shrugged. "I think she's a witch, or she's into the dark arts. I don't know," I said, dismissing the whole Martha issue with my hand. "She doesn't matter. What does matter is that I know better now. I won't be running by myself again. I just need to figure out a safe way to get rid of my anxiety."

"I'll run with you," he offered, placing a plate with a rather large omelet on it before me. "Eat." It was more of a command than a suggestion, and I watched as he pushed a glass of orange juice next to my steaming plate.

My stomach reacted to the delicious aroma wafting from my breakfast plate and growled in excitement. I didn't need to be told twice to eat and dove into my food greedily. "You don't have to run with me. You aren't my keeper," I said with a mouth full of food. I was too hungry to be embarrassed.

He filled the large sink on the opposite side of the island with hot, soapy water and began scrubbing away at the copper pan. "No, I'm not your keeper. But I do care about you. Friends look out for one another, don't they?"

Friends: the most God-awful word in the English language. The last thing I wanted to be with Quinn was a friend. I wanted so much more from him. I thought he wanted more than friendship from me as well, but maybe I was wrong. At that point, it didn't matter to me. If friendship was all he wanted to give, I'd gladly take it.

As he dried the large copper pan with a nearby towel and hung it back on the rack overhead, I was a bit stunned that faeries did the Suzy Homemaker thing like the rest of us. "So is that what you were doing for me this morning then, looking out for me?" I couldn't imagine what else he would be doing traipsing around my apartment building that early in the morning.

How long had he been waiting around outside?

Quinn tossed the towel over his shoulder and eyed me with a panty-dropping grin. "I had a feeling your stubborn nature would win out over common sense, so I came back later in the evening to keep an eye on you."

If it were possible for my insides to actually melt, I'd have been nothing more than a spineless bag of flesh at that point. Gulping down half of my juice, I set the glass down and stared at him. I had another topic I wanted to discuss. "So you touched me this morning." I knew if I didn't mention it, the subject would never be broached. He'd held me in his arms, taking care not to touch my skin with his, and I'd felt no reaction whatsoever. Hope burst forth like water escaping from a dam.

"Aye, that I did." He stiffened a bit as he answered me, obviously not wanting to proceed down this particular path of conversation.

Hopping down off the stool, I slowly walked around the large island, one hand tracing along the edge of the marble countertop to steady me, as my knees were weak and my body shaky. In fact, my heart threw flip-flops because it knew what I intended to do. I was going to lay my hands on Quinn.

"Easy there, lass." He held his hands up in front of him as if to ward me off. "What was I supposed to do? Leave you to cry on the cold pavement? I had no choice but to touch you."

"So touch me again." I continued to stalk forward, my breaths coming in shallow pants. The mere thought of our skin making contact had me breathless.

"No."

I stopped moving. He'd shot me down. "Why not?"

"Because I have a choice now, and I choose not to." He looked pained as he spoke, torn almost.

"Why don't you want to touch me?" The sour pangs of rejection flooded my system, and doubt took over. Who was I trying to fool? Quinn was the very image of perfection, beautiful, charming, mythical, and deadly. I, on the other hand, was a very sweaty, very mortal, Big Booty Judy. I remained where I was, a mere two feet away from him, gawking at him like a complete dolt.

His expression softened. "It's not that, love. If you only knew how badly I want you, you'd never ask that question again. I choose not to touch you, because I don't trust myself. I don't know if I have the willpower to keep my hands where they should be." His sapphire eyes met mine head on and I knew he told the truth.

The butterflies returned full force and a big goofy smile made its way across my face. He wanted me as badly as I did him. That fact sent my heart soaring.

My earlier determination returned with gusto. I crossed the small gap that lay between us, standing as close as I could, without actually touching him.

Lifting my hand up toward his chest, I looked him in the eye, willing him with my heart and mind to let me try. "Please? I want so badly to touch you, to connect with you."

"Aye, I feel the same way." He spoke softly, staring at me intently.

The magnetic pull between us intensified with each passing second.

I licked my lips in anticipation, every inch of my skin screaming out for his caress. "You can touch me through my clothes. That much we found out when you carried me here. I know we can do this. I trust you. You just need to trust yourself."

He frowned for a moment as he took in my words, and then nodded quietly. "Very well, we can try."

My heart leapt the moment he gave in, and I was sure I would burst from the excitement.

Quinn seemed to enjoy my glowing mood and let out a low chuckle.

Unable to wait a second longer, I slowly raised my hand toward his muscular chest. He wore his standard black t-shirt under a black leather jacket, and my heart quickened, knowing only a thin piece of fabric lay between my fingertips and the warm flesh of his chest.

As I made contact with the cotton fabric of his shirt, a powerful surge of joy nearly swept me off my feet. His rock hard pecs, the deep ridges of his abdominals, felt amazing against my hand as I let my fingers trail down his shirt. What I didn't feel was euphoria. There were no aftereffects from his wretched curse.

"Oh…oh, God…I can touch you." I was breathless with anticipation and sure I'd burst if he didn't reciprocate soon. "Your turn. Try."

Wearing a pained look on his face, Quinn raised his hand, holding it mere inches away from my chest. My heart beat wildly as I watched him hesitate, warring with himself internally about his decision.

It felt as though time stood still. There was only the two of us in existence. I heard nothing else, saw nothing else, and smelled nothing else. Quinn enveloped each of my senses completely.

And then he touched me.

My breath caught the moment his warm hand gently came to rest over my heart. Electricity sparked, and a gentle surge of energy flowed between us, but there was no over-the-top, near orgasmic reaction from the contact. What I experienced was the normal electric attraction that came when two young people were in…love? No. It was too early to be in love. I'd only just met Quinn. Any talk of love was just crazy. Yet, as I looked at him, my heart filled, bursting with an emotion so strong, I didn't know what else to call it. It had to be love.

I gasped, awareness knocking me off my feet like a wrecking ball. I was in love with Quinn. And it wasn't some piddly, preteen crush either. I was thoroughly captivated, completely enamored, one hundred percent in love with him. I didn't care that he didn't share my feelings. The fact he was a mythical being didn't matter. The legendary creature standing before me was all I'd ever want, and I knew deep down he was essential to my survival. He was the very air I breathed.

He stared down at his hand still pasted to my chest, his eyes full of surprise, shock, and joy. His lips parted slightly and I could swear I heard his breath catch.

He felt it too.

I raised my hand, placing it gently back onto his chest. We stood a hair's breadth from each other, touching, feeling, wanting. His ancient heart thumped rapidly in his chest and, God ... I *loved* the fact I had such an effect on him. My own heart worked overtime anytime he was near. The moment was intimate, very intense, and not nearly long enough.

Quinn dropped his hand, stepped back from me, and cleared his throat.

I mirrored his action. "Um ... yeah. Wow." Words couldn't describe how I felt at that moment. Enraptured. On fire. Complete.

"We should get you home," he said with a stutter, and took another step back, scrubbing nervously at his closely shaven head. A hint of a smile peeked out of the corner of his mouth.

Having made great strides in such a short time frame, I didn't push him any further. I followed him down a long hallway and out into his large garage, where several different cars sat, all sleek, shiny, and expensive. I looked at Quinn, then back at the cars and shook my head in astonishment. The faerie was loaded.

Walking over to a particularly shiny black Porsche, he opened the door, gesturing for me to get in. "Let's get you home, little girl."

chapter 11

The ride back to my apartment was interesting, to say the least. Several major events, both incredible and shitty, took place at the start of my day and my poor body didn't know how to react. Fear, remorse, elation and hope were all interwoven and coursing through me simultaneously. I struggled to hold myself together, but images of my demon stalker burst through my conscious thoughts, shredding my psyche and wreaking havoc on my stomach.

Just when I thought the fear would chew me up and spit me out, another image, one of Quinn with his hand over my heart, would make its way to the forefront of my mind. A warm, comforting sensation would spread like wildfire over me, followed by a ditzy smile and uncontrollable giggling. The roller coaster of emotions continued until Quinn finally broke the silence.

The heat of his gaze burned like fire against my cheek. "I can sense your fear, *mo chrói*, but we really need to talk about what happened this morning." His face was serious, his jaw clenched, a hint of worry peeking out from behind his sapphire eyes.

I nodded in agreement. "I know," I said with a sigh. "What was that thing that attacked me?" Part of me didn't want to know. I kept telling myself ignorance was bliss. *Protect yourself, girl. Throw a blanket over your head and hide!* My more practical side disagreed. If I knew more about the underworld creep tailing me, I could arm myself with knowledge and be prepared if it should come after me again, which my gut told me it would.

Quinn gripped the steering wheel so tightly I feared he might rip it off its column. His eyes went wild. "I've a few ideas on what it was that came after you. Nasty fuckers, the lot o' them."

I cringed at his words. I'd grown used to hearing Quinn curse, but this was different. Warning bells rang loud and long in my ears. I looked over, questioning him with my eyes as we pulled into the parking lot just outside my building.

Quinn parked the car, kept his hands on the steering wheel and let out a long sigh, before turning to face me. His expression was one of determination and sorrow.

I knew he meant to fill me in on the finer details of what he knew, to prepare me for what was to come, but the look of sadness etched across his face tore at my heart. It was evident he knew the truth would frighten me, and was fired up by it.

Determination won out, his gaze unwavering as he readied himself to speak. "I would assume by now you would have come to accept the existence of mythical creatures in your world?"

I let out a loud sarcastic snort. I believed all right. The question was: would anyone ever believe me? Probably not.

He threw me a disapproving glare. "You're not crazy. Stay focused."

Freaking mind reader.

He went on. "Along with the more loveable creatures, such as me," he held his hand to his chest, "there are, in fact, legions of creatures walking the earth that are fiercely evil."

Legions?

Not really what I wanted to hear. "Okay," I answered, my voice shaky. I took a deep breath, never taking my eyes from his, willing him to go on.

"At first, I thought it might be some type of ghoul that came after you, since they can change their shape. Foul, mindless creatures they are. They're usually controlled by another to do their dirty work. Your demon seems to have a mind of its own, so I'm fairly certain we can rule out ghouls."

"All right," I breathed. "So ghouls are out, then." I tried my best to act nonchalant about the whole thing in an effort to keep myself from completely freaking out. But in reality my heart pounded so hard I thought it might jump out of my chest and perform show tunes.

I glanced down at my lap where my hands lay sweaty and restless. I swiped them across my sweatpants before looking up. "Are there any other types of shapeshifters?"

"Aye, there are plenty of shifty buggers prowling about, but it's identifying which one that's the trouble. Most of your basic shapeshifting demons transform from human form into birds or creatures that live in the water. Your demon chose to morph into a giant black dog. He's got power, and a lot of it."

I swallowed hard, a lump the size of Texas lodged in my throat at the mention of the shiteous creature from earlier that morning. The sound of its feral snarling still rang in my ears. "So…if my attacker wasn't your garden variety shifter, then what was it?"

"I'm fairly certain we are dealing with one of two demons: either the Ordog or the Zmeu."

Possessing the mental capacity of a box of rocks, I'd been clinging to the notion that knowledge was key. Knowing exactly what type of demon was after me would surely make me feel better. There had to be some truth to all that "know your enemy" bullshit people liked to push. Yeah, I didn't feel any better after listening to Quinn's suspicions. I was still scared shitless. "Ordog, huh? That sounds about right. I mean, it did turn into a dog."

A low chuckle escaped Quinn's lips and I scowled at him. I didn't particularly care for being laughed at, especially when it was regarding something so serious.

He took notice of my pissed off demeanor and plastered a mask of controlled seriousness across his masculine features. "Well, I suppose it could change into a dog, though I've never seen him do so. Actually, I've only encountered the shite once, a few centuries ago. It took the form of a shepherd and attempted to abduct a young farm girl."

Still cheesed over his earlier bout of laughter at my expense, I crossed my arms over my chest with a huff. "I see. And would this farm girl be someone you were trying to diddle?" I was being ridiculous. I knew it, but continued on with my mini tantrum anyway, glowering at Quinn.

"Are ye jealous?" His face scrunched up in disbelief as he scrutinized me.

"No!" I said, my face barreling past red into a deep shade of purple. I broke his gaze, embarrassed by my irrational and, might I add, stupid behavior. I had no right to be upset with him for things he did hundreds of years before we met. The past was the past, and I needed to let go.

Quinn sat back in his seat and ran his hand over his face before unleashing the full force of his charm on me. "Relax, my love. In all my five hundred years, I've never once come across anyone near the likes of you."

I turned to face him again with angry eyes and a loud "humph!" I felt like a shrew, but couldn't seem to stop my idiotic behavior.

"Let's try and get back to the issue at hand, shall we?" Quinn delivered a pleading look, successfully breaking my jealous tirade. "Personally, I'd put my money on the Zmeu being your demon."

"What do you know about it?" I asked, unsure if I really wanted an answer or not. I was fairly certain I wouldn't like what I'd hear and debated for a moment about whether or not to tell him to just forget the whole thing. Realizing I needed as much information about my attacker as possible, I put on my big girl panties, manned up and listened.

"Not much. I've never actually crossed its path. I do know its origins are in Romania, and it's known for coveting beautiful young women, who it spirits away to its underworld lair. Not only can this monster change its appearance, but it can also fly and packs one hell of a punch."

Nausea rolled around my stomach upon hearing Quinn's description of the ancient demon. I agreed with his assessment. All the characteristics seemed to fit. The demon had swooped past me while I ran as though it were flying. Much like Quinn, it had an unnatural amount of strength, which I'd witnessed firsthand during their smackdown.

"Okay, then. What does all this mean for me? I … ugh … I have to go on living. I can't run away and hide. I have school and work." Frustration took over and my voice grew louder and higher-pitched with each word I spoke. I wanted to hit something. "I refuse to let an underworld dickhead bring me down!" I'd had enough struggle and angst to last me a lifetime. I was ready for the good times to start rolling and I wanted to roll along with them. Demons, be damned!

Quinn leaned toward me and met my eyes head on. "It means I'm not letting you out of my sight. That's what it means." There was a sense of finality in his voice, one that provoked my stubborn nature, making me want to dig my heels in and protest, no matter how absurd.

"You can't possibly be with me every waking moment of the day. I refuse to be babysat. I'm not a child!"

"Then don't act like one," he shouted, slamming his hands against the wheel. At the rate our conversation was going, German engineering didn't stand a chance. He'd rip apart his precious Porsche one piece at a time. "You're bloody gone in the head if you think I'll be letting you traipse about on your own after this morning. Damn stubborn woman!" He stared at me with his lips smashed together, his nostrils flaring with each frustrated breath.

I was tempted to laugh, because for a moment, he reminded me of an angry bull ready to charge. Deciding I didn't want to know what he'd look like popping a vein, I kept my amusement hidden. "Look," I said, trying to calm my voice. "I'm not trying to piss you off. I'm just trying to maintain some level of normalcy in my life. This whole thing with the demon…you…none of it is normal."

After a few deep breaths and some more irritated swipes across his face Quinn spoke. "Let me ask you this, Ryann. If your friend Jessica was being tormented by someone, something, would you leave her to her own devices or would you do everything you could to ensure her safety?"

Damn smart faerie. He pulled the friend card.

I had no snappy comeback. He had me. If the tables were turned and my best friend was under attack, I'd move heaven and earth to help her, no matter how much she protested.

Though I'd only known him for a short period of time, I felt fiercely protective of Quinn. I knew I'd go to any length to protect him as well. He was the center of my universe.

"Point taken," I said, feeling ridiculous. What the hell was I thinking anyway, arguing with him about wanting to spend time with me? Quinn was the living, breathing embodiment of the perfect male, and everything I could ever want in a man. I needed to get my head checked.

"This isn't about me trying to control you, *mo chrói*. Friends help each other out in times of need. You need my help right now."

"Friends?" I turned my head and stared out the window, focusing on a small patch of fallen leaves that blew across the pavement. I didn't want to look at him. I thought we'd moved past the whole "friends" issue that morning when we'd finally laid hands on one another. As far as I was concerned, "friend" was the vilest word in the English language, and I considered writing a strongly worded letter to the Powers That Be about having it removed from the dictionary.

Quinn gave me an eye roll and a snort. "We're a bit more than that."

My heart sank.

He wasn't giving me what I wanted. I was starving for a declaration, an admission of his feelings for me. I was hungry for the main course, and Quinn tossed me nothing but breadcrumbs. Goddammit. *Give me the meat and potatoes, not the frigging appetizer.*

"A bit? All you feel for me is a bit more than friendship?" I knew he had feelings for me, he'd already admitted as much. It shamed me to act so needy and I vowed to shut my yap before I embarrassed myself any further.

"Look at me, Ryann."

My head turned before my mind knew what I was doing. Damn my stupid body. I had zero control over myself when I was near him.

All traces of anger and frustration were gone as Quinn captured my attention with a pair of tender eyes. "*Tá mo chrói istigh iónat.*" His voice was low and gentle, full of emotion. I didn't understand a single word of what he said, but was mesmerized all the same by its rich timbre.

Along with his expression, Quinn's mood softened exponentially, his posture easing up from the stiff pose he'd held while arguing about my demon attacker. Leaning over the center console, so his face was mere centimeters away from my own, his deep, blue eyes ensnared mine, making it impossible to look away. It was also impossible to do things like breathe, and I felt lightheaded from holding my breath.

With my heart thundering away in my chest as though it were about to break free, I spoke. "What did you just say?"

A sly smile crept across Quinn's beautifully full lips, and I wanted nothing more than to close the small distance between our faces so I could attack his mouth with my own.

"It's time for you to get inside, *mo chrói.*"

You've got to be kidding me.

All the air in my lungs rushed out in one loud whoosh. Breadcrumbs. He was still tossing me breadcrumbs.

"Good things come to those who wait, *a ghrá.* I won't let you down. You have my word." With a smirk, he exited the vehicle, rounding the sports car inhumanly fast, and opened my door for me.

Though I lacked patience, I trusted Quinn implicitly. If he promised to reveal his feelings for me, I knew he'd make good on his word.

I also knew myself well enough to know I'd be bringing the issue up again, sooner rather than later. I hadn't forgotten about our conversation during dinner at the Plough. Something was up with regard to the completion of his curse. For someone who was about to be freed from five hundred years of affliction, Quinn was way too apathetic.

After exiting the car, Quinn escorted me all the way to my front door, insisting on seeing me safely into the sanctuary of my front room.

"I'd love to hang out and chat with you," I said coyly, "but I don't want to wake Jess or Martha, and I'm in desperate need of a shower." I cringed, hoping to God I didn't stink.

With a sweeping hand motion, Quinn happily replied. "Lead the way, my love. I'd be more than happy to watch over you while you cleanse yourself."

"Yeah, I bet you would!" Images of my shower fantasy rushed through my mind, and I felt extremely relieved Quinn didn't possess the ability to read minds. He didn't need to know how hot I was for him. It wouldn't do either of us a damn bit of good. "All right, then, out." I pointed toward the door. "I can't get ready if you don't leave."

Quinn's face fell, reminding me of a little boy who didn't get the toy he begged his mother for at the store. It was heartbreaking and funny at the same time. "Very well, then. Try not to get into too much trouble while I'm away," he said playfully and made a move for the door. Hesitating for a moment, Quinn turned on his heels, taking two large steps and bridging the small gap between us. Looking down at me through his fierce, blue eyes, Quinn raised his hand above my head just as he had done a few times before, tracing the contour of my face, mere centimeters from my flesh. This time, however, instead of stopping there and backing away, he let his large hand come to rest gently against the center of my chest, just over my heart.

The moment was so poignant it stole my breath away. I mirrored his actions, and we stood for what seemed like an immeasurable amount of time, wonderful electricity flowing between us.

A small groan escaped his lips. "It would be so easy for me to lose myself in those big brown eyes of yours."

Yes! Lose yourself in me, my mind cried out. *Hold me, love me, and never let me go.*

He pulled away abruptly. "I hear your roommate tossing about in bed. She's about to get up." Walking back over to the door, Quinn looked over his shoulder, treating me to a flirtatious smile, before vanishing into thin air.

I jumped, having yet to get used to the whole disappearing act. I heard a faint chuckling.

"I'll see you later, *mo chrói.*"

chapter 12

The following month was nothing short of spectacular, and altogether the most incomparable four weeks of my life. Entirely bewitched by Quinn, I passed through my days floating on the blissful high of first love. Love (insert deep sigh). I was, without a doubt, thoroughly and completely in love with Quinn. As frustrated as I was that Quinn had yet to fully admit his feelings, I knew in my heart he felt the same way. Why else would someone go to such lengths to keep a person safe? Why else would he spend every waking moment with me, laughing, teasing, learning everything there was to know about me? It wasn't for the sex, that was for sure. Ha! We were barely able to touch one another. I knew Quinn held deep feelings for me, and I was determined to bring them out into the open one way or another.

Keeping to his word, Quinn remained by my side literally everywhere I went, from my morning jog, to my classes and work. Though it peeved me to know I was, in fact, being babysat, I shuddered to think of the alternative and gladly accepted the extra attention. Honestly, I wasn't about to complain about having the hottest man on the planet acting as my own personal champion. Truth be told, I felt downright smug about it. Not many could claim a five-hundred-year-old, muscled-up faerie with the face of an angel and exceptional sexual prowess as their own. Not that I was getting any action, but hey, one could fantasize, right?

As it was October, the mild California weather had finally taken a turn, the air cool and crisp. Large yellow and orange leaves fell from the abundant trees that lined the streets of Hanaford Park and filled the university campus. Aside from walking to and from classes, I was driven anywhere I needed to go by Quinn, who was all too happy to oblige. He had a weakness for fast cars, and he took great joy in scaring me with his maniacal driving.

Pleased with the drop in temperature, because it allowed for a wider variety of fashion, I let out a small squeal as I pulled out my favorite pair of Ugg boots to wear with my skinny jeans and sweater.

"Ooh, I love those." Jessica admired my footwear from atop my bed where she'd been lounging for the past half hour.

I glanced lovingly at my boots. "Thanks. I've been dying to wear them for a while now." I dug through the bottom of my closet in search of a bag that would match. "Ah ha! There you are." I smiled triumphantly as I yanked my dark brown Coach lunch tote from the large bin of purses at the base of my closet.

"Think you have enough bags in there, Ryann?" She laughed quietly as she questioned me, but I sensed a hint of incredulity in her voice. My purse collection was rivaled by few, and I'm sure quite a shock to anyone who didn't know me well. They were an indulgence, I know. But hey, everyone's got a vice, right? Besides, I bought all my bags and shoes at outlet stores and on eBay. I never paid full price.

I donned my best diva attitude. "Darling. One can *never* have too many bags."

I slung my tote over my shoulder and shook what the good Lord gave me while Jess shouted in the background, "Work it! Own it!"

The blaring sound of The Pogues' "Love You 'Till The End" blasted from the tiny speaker on my iPhone, interrupting my impromptu fashion show. Quinn had programmed the ringtone himself, a fact that further cemented my belief he held the same feelings for me as I did for him.

"Hey," I sang into the phone. "I'm almost done accessorizing. I'll be out in a minute."

His Irish accent carried through the cell, making me weak in the knees. "Jaysus, woman! How long can this accessorizing possibly take? Get your arse out here or you'll be late to class." I heard him chuckle over the phone before he hung up.

With an eye roll, I tossed the phone into my purse. Good fashion sense simply could not be rushed.

Jessica moved so that she sat cross-legged on my bed, with a pillow in her lap. "So how come Quinn always waits outside for you? Why doesn't he come in?"

I knew why he didn't come in, but I couldn't exactly tell her. Afraid of any accidental contact, Quinn opted to wait for me outside simply to avoid drama. Not wanting to deal with the awkwardness that would follow should one of my roommates casually touch his hand or arm, keeping a safe distance between him and my female friends seemed to be the best solution all around.

True, they might think him an antisocial bastard, but the alternative was not a scenario I ever wanted to deal with. The idea of Jessica or even Martha lusting madly after Quinn sent my stomach churning and brought my claws out. Mr. Sex God was mine.

"I don't know," I said, desperately trying to come up with an acceptable answer. "I think he's just trying to give me my space. You know, letting me have friend time with you." I didn't know what else to say. Hopefully, she'd buy my excuse.

Jess pondered my answer for a moment. "Hmm…I guess that makes sense. Well, tell him I said hi."

Halleluiah. She bought it. "Okay, I will." I waved at her as I headed for the door.

My stomach rumbled as I walked outside into the crisp autumn air. An icy chill jarred my body, and I mentally cursed myself for believing I'd be warm enough in just a sweater. The things I did in the name of fashion. Ugh!

Quinn, looking sexy as hell in dark glasses, a black leather jacket, his typical t-shirt, jeans and Docs, stood leaning against the side of the building. How I'd ever mistaken him for a mere man was beyond me. Transcendently beautiful, he was most definitely not of this world. He held a small Starbucks bag and coffee. The corners of his lips lifted as he saw me, and he pushed away from the wall, gliding over to where I stood.

"You're cold," he said, setting the bag and coffee down on a nearby bench and removed his jacket, draping it around my shoulders. It smelled like him, a deep, rich, masculine scent that had me sniffing the fabric as I shoved my arms into the sleeves.

"You're hungry, too. I heard your belly rumbling from inside your apartment. Here," he said and handed me the bag and coffee.

The warm inviting aroma of my favorite drink had me drooling as I took the cup from his hand. "God, you shouldn't have, but thanks," I said, holding up the cup before taking a sip. The sugary drink and pastry would go straight to my rump and I'd be running like a crazed Forrest Gump wannabe for the following week. I broke off a piece of muffin and groaned. "What passes the lips goes straight to the hips."

"And what lovely hips they are," he said, eying me appreciatively. "Let's get going." He motioned with a nod and we began walking.

I inhaled the contents of the bag, a cranberry orange muffin, in just a few large bites, no longer caring what Quinn thought of my abominable eating habits. The look on his face as he laughed at me affirmed my suspicions. He didn't care, and I went on stuffing my face.

"So," I said with my mouth full, trying to swallow the last remnants of my snack. "Your curse is almost over." There would be no beating around the bush this morning. He needed to be out with it, needed to open up. I had no idea when his curse would actually end, only that it was soon. "Pretty soon we'll be able to touch each other for real … you know, act like real friends."

I loathed using the friend word, but it was what he was most comfortable with at that point, and it really did the best job of describing our unconventional relationship. You couldn't classify us as lovers, since we'd never made love. I hadn't even had so much as a first kiss from him. The term "boyfriend" seemed ridiculous, given Quinn's age. Honestly, I had no clue how to describe our relationship.

"Mmph," he grumbled. Not the response I was looking for.

I craned my neck forward as we walked, trying to see his face. "Quinn?"

"We're running late to class, *a ghrá*. Let's talk about this later."

"To hell with that. I want to talk about it now." We'd sat on this particular topic long enough and for reasons that were unknown to me. I was damn tired of waiting. He should be as ecstatic as I was about being able to spend time together in a normal fashion. The mere thought of being able to cup his cheek with my hand, to kiss his impossibly full lips made me want to bust out into song and dance. I was dying for a little skin-to-skin contact.

"No." He spoke through clenched teeth and balled his hands into fists. The air surrounding us became thick with tension as we squared off, playing who's got the meaner mug.

"Why?" I needed an explanation. I was tired of Quinn keeping things from me. He held back with regard to our relationship and his true feelings for me. And now, he was hiding something else, something major about his curse. Frustration surged and I bit the inside of my cheek to keep from screaming. If he was hiding the truth from me, it had to be something bad, but what?

We'd reached the auditorium where our Human Sexuality class was held, and stood just outside the entryway.

"Now is not the time, *a ghrá*. Let it go." He stood stone-faced, unwilling to give me the answers I so desperately needed to hear.

"Fine," I snapped. I speared the air with my pointed finger. "This conversation is not over." I stormed into the building, taking a seat in the back of the room, Quinn following just a few steps behind me.

I sat down with a huff, and threw a few angry darts at Quinn, who sat motionless in his seat like a statue of Adonis. As angry as I was, I couldn't help but notice how his shirt clung to his broad shoulders, the thickness of his biceps clearly visible through the fabric. His Tree-of- Life tattoo peeked out from just beneath the collar. A pair of vibrant blue eyes cut through the wall of anger I tried desperately to maintain, and I had to look away. I wanted to smack him and lick his tattoo all at the same time.

Stupid faerie.

"There are four phases to the female sexual response!"

I jumped in my seat, startled by the professor's shouting. So wrapped up in my frustration with Quinn, I hadn't noticed Professor White begin the lecture.

"Phase one is excitement. Miss Pierce…"

Oh shit.

"I expect you did the assigned reading for this lecture. Please describe some of the physiological changes that occur during the excitement phase."

The entire classroom turned to face me along with Professor White, waiting for me to respond.

Just great. I have zero skills. I'm sitting next to the most sexually experienced being on the planet, who, as it so happens, won't give me the time of day physically, and now I have to describe what happens to my hoo-hah when it gets excited.

Karma was making me its bitch, of that much I was certain.

"Vasocongestion will occur." My voice shook as I forced myself to speak loud enough for the professor to hear. "The clitoris becomes engorged." *Oh, God!* "And the inner part of the vagina may expand. The woman's skin becomes flushed." *Yeah, just like mine is becoming flushed now from having to talk about this.* "And she may experience heightened sensitivity in other areas of her body, such as the nipples."

I sensed Quinn's eyes boring into the side of my face as I spoke. Still pissed off from his unwillingness to open up to me, I wasn't about to give him the satisfaction of watching me squirm while I uttered the word "nipple." I was quite sure the sensitivity in my nipples would never be heightened, nor would my clitoris ever become engorged by my faerie non-boyfriend. He couldn't even utter the words "I like you," let alone "I love you," and he wouldn't touch me except to say goodbye, and then only ever laid his hand over my heart. *Damn his iron will!*

Professor White seemed pleased with my answer. "Very good, Miss Pierce, I see you've done your homework. Moving on to the Plateau phase next..."

The muscles in my jaw ached and burned from grinding my teeth, and my entire body flushed hot, not only from the embarrassment of having to speak in front of the class, but from my anger toward Quinn. With each moment that passed, my bitterness grew.

"Moving on to the Orgasm phase... Mr. Donegan?"

Wait. What? Please, no. My heart leaped into my throat and my stomach dropped to the floor. Why? Why did the professor have to call on Quinn?

"Could you please explain what occurs when a woman climaxes?"

"Oh, aye. I surely can." A smug grin crawled across his face and he sat back in his seat, stretching his long legs out before him.

Pompous, egotistical bastard.

The pencil I'd been gripping snapped, eliciting a snort from Quinn before he spoke.

"Well, then. The muscles in the woman's vagina contract, along with the rest of the muscles in her body. Her heart rate and blood pressure peak. And of course, she usually screams my name several times."

Bloody hell!

That last little bit resulted in several hoots and hollers from the male portion of the class.

"Thank you, Mr. Donegan, for your colorful explanation of the female orgasm. Let's try and keep our answers strictly to the physical response from now on, shall we?" Professor White directed a deprecating look toward Quinn before turning to address the class again.

No longer paying any attention to the lecture, I focused all my energy on the smug faerie sitting to my left, my animosity toward him at an all-time high.

I leaned over and whispered just loud enough for him to hear, "You forgot to mention the part where the woman loses her mind and dies!" It was a low blow. I knew it. So thoroughly pissed off, I hadn't bothered to think before I spoke and my words rushed out, unfiltered and cruel.

He met my jab with a cold, icy stare the likes of which I'd never seen. I'd meant to hit a nerve and I did.

The remainder of the lecture was spent in a painful silence, neither Quinn, nor myself willing to make the first move toward reconciliation. When it was time to leave, I shot out of my seat like a crazed woman at a red tag sale. My only thoughts were of how quickly I could get out of the building and away from him.

I was racing toward the quad when he finally spoke. "You can't outrun me." There was no emotion in his voice as he matched my pace with his own.

"I'm angry with you," I said as we made our way toward a semi-secluded grassy knoll in the center of the school.

"Aye, I can see that."

I whirled around to face him. "Why are you hiding things from me about your curse?"

He looked over his shoulder to ensure we were alone, then back to me. "Trust me, *a ghrá*, it's for the best."

"What? What the hell kind of answer is that? It's for the best? I'm not a child, and I don't need you deciding what's best for me. I've dealt with quite a bit in my short life. I think I can handle whatever it is that you won't tell me!"

I wasn't expecting the reaction I got. "Have you ever considered the fact that maybe *I* can't deal?" Quinn completely lost his cool and paced back and forth, angrily scrubbing his hands over his skull. "Fuck!"

"Just tell me. What is going to happen to you when your curse is over? Why aren't you happy?" He should be rejoicing at his imminent freedom and the ability to touch whomever he wished, hopefully me, with no repercussions.

Quinn stared at me, his normally bright, piercing blue eyes now dark and stormy, causing panic to bubble up and boil over.

"Won't we be together?" A huge lump formed in my throat, making my question barely audible. Quinn heard it though, and winced before looking away.

"No," he said.

I stumbled back, a wrecking ball of pain slamming through my chest, knocking the wind out of me and rendering me speechless.

I opened my mouth to speak, but nothing came out. Agonizing pain and utter disbelief flooded every cell in my body. "Why?"

"Because I won't be here!" Unable to contain his emotions, Quinn ripped a nearby bench off the ground and launched it into a nearby tree. A thundering crack echoed through the air as two giant limbs came crashing down along with the now-mangled bench.

I looked around, horrified, making sure no one witnessed Quinn's fit of temper.

He was leaving me. Quinn was leaving me. With all that had happened over the last month, his admission was a crushing blow to my psyche. I couldn't listen to another word.

Shaking my head, I took a few steps back, turned and ran as fast as I could away from him. Probably not the smartest thing to do, but hey, I wasn't firing on all thrusters. It hurt too much to be around him, so I caved and ran.

"Where do you think you are going?" Quinn magically appeared a few feet ahead of me. I stopped too suddenly and lost my balance, ending up a blubbering heap on the grass.

Quinn moved to help me up, but I squashed that notion quickly, scooting back across the damp lawn on my bottom before hauling myself up on my own.

"No! I don't need any help! Leave me alone!"

"Stop your childishness, *mo chrói*. You wanted to know the truth, and now you do. Let's finish this." He towered over me, a mix of anger, pain and determination etched across his godlike face.

"You're leaving me!" Silent tears flooded my cheeks as I stared up at him.

He reached for me, caught himself and clenched a fist before dropping his arm. "I'm so sorry, *a ghrá*."

"Why? Why are you leaving? Where are you going?" I sounded like a desperate child, sniveling away in front of the object of her unrequited love. I didn't care enough to be ashamed. The reality of our situation hurt too much.

Quinn's jaw twitched and he looked away from me, refusing to meet my eyes. "Tell me!"

Quinn's head snapped around, his eyes blazing with emotion. "Dead! I'll be dead! Is that what you wanted to hear? Come the Eve of Samhain, I will cease to exist!"

Time came to a screeching halt. The world I knew faded into nothingness. A gut-wrenching scream pierced through the air. "No!" It took a few moments before I realized the scream came from me.

chapter 13

You're lying!" A mind-splitting ache pounded throughout my skull and I gripped the sides of my head, trying to keep it from exploding.

No. No. No. It can't be. It can't be. I just found him.

"You can't die." I stood before him, trying with all my might to force my will upon him verbally. As if the universe would ever actually bend to my will.

Ha!

The Powers That Be had my ass in a sling, and I knew it.

Quinn's voice was low and full of resignation. "Yes, Ryann, I can."

I rushed forward, invading his personal space until my face was mere centimeters from his own. "I. Refuse. To. Accept. That." I stepped back, grabbed a fistful of hair in each hand and shook my head. "There must be something that can be done. Tell me!" My voice gave out, sounding hoarse and raspy.

The look of pain on Quinn's face nearly broke me, yet he bore his suffering in silence, saying nothing while I ranted like a lunatic. This was the reason for the sadness that always lingered behind his eyes. He knew his fate. Quinn knew he didn't have much time left, and he'd done his best to hide that fact from me. But why?

"No. This conversation is over. Please, Ryann. Let it go."

"I can't." Hot tears engulfed my eyes and I could barely see. "Don't you understand? I love you."

The world fell oddly silent, the air surrounding us stagnant as Quinn stood stock-still, absorbing my admission.

There…I'd finally said it. I'd admitted my feelings to Quinn. This certainly wasn't the way I'd imagined myself professing my love. I'd envisioned something romantic involving candles and a whole lot of kissing, but hey, at least it was out. I'd bared my soul and would have no regrets. My only hope was that he cared for me enough to do the same.

Visibly torn, Quinn raised his arms toward me, looking as though he wanted to pull me into an embrace. He stopped midair, balling his hands into fists. He let out a deafening roar that sent the local fauna running for cover.

Regardless of the fact that I knew I had nothing to fear from Quinn, my body instinctively shied away from his loud battle cry. The look of hurt on his face was clear, but I couldn't make myself stop moving.

My stomach heaved, bile rising up into my mouth. Nothing. I'd bared my soul to him and he'd given me nothing in return. Quinn remained silent, motionless as he watched me inch away from him, crying silent tears with each step. Tears for what I wished we could have been. Tears for what I knew we'd never be. I cried for the love I so desperately wanted him to return, and I cried because in that moment, I desperately wanted a mother that would comfort me and tell me everything would be okay. But I didn't have a mother, and evidently I didn't have Quinn, either.

Regardless of what he did or didn't feel for me, I knew I had to help him. There was no way I was going to sit back and let him die. As long as I had breath in my lungs and a beating heart to keep me going, I'd do all I could to help him.

"Where are you going, *a ghrá*?" Pain fused with confusion in his voice, and though I knew it would kill me to run away from him, I had no choice.

"Away from you!"

"You know I'll follow. I won't rest until I destroy whatever it is that's hunting you. I won't leave you unprotected."

I won't rest either. Not until I help you. Please forgive me.

"I don't want your help," I screamed. "I don't need anything from you. You're just going to leave me regardless. You might as well just leave now." I turned away from him and ran, screaming at the top of my lungs, knowing he'd cloak himself with invisibility to avoid the scene I made.

I ran, balls to the wall, crying, all the way to my apartment, trying unsuccessfully to call Jessica in the process. Occasionally glancing sideways to take in my surroundings, I found my instincts were spot on. I couldn't see him, but the warm ache in my kitty affirmed his proximity. I could find him anywhere by following the tingle.

I picked up my pace as I neared my apartment, reaching into my bag for my keys. I knew if I had any trouble with the new lock I'd be more than able to knock down the door, as upset as I was. My body was pumping with adrenaline, and that shit gives you all kinds of strength.

Finally, for once, fate was on my side, and I made it into my apartment without incident, and, thankfully, alone.

I knew Quinn would never step foot inside, not wanting to risk the possibility of accidental contact. Though at that point, I had to wonder what his motivation was for abstaining. It wasn't like he was saving himself for me. I'd given him the perfect opportunity to man up and share his feelings with me, and he'd failed to do so. Knowing my estimation of his level of affection for me was clearly way off base, I couldn't understand his reasoning for keeping himself from other women. If he didn't want me, why remain abstinent after five hundred years of whoring?

Trying to solve the mystery that was Quinn resulted in a mind-splitting headache. I ceased pondering over his actions and pounded on Jessica's bedroom door, irritated when there was no answer.

"Jess," I hollered. I shuffled toward my room and peered in, hoping to God she was in there. "Are you home? Jess?" My cries were met with silence and I slumped down to the floor, my back resting against the cool wall of the hallway, just outside Martha's door. I'd have to bide my time. I didn't care how long I had to sit and wait. Nothing and no one would keep me from my goal. I was going to find a way to save Quinn. Depleted and mentally worn, I ended up falling asleep while I waited.

A sharp pain in my leg wrenched me from my sleep and I looked up to see Voodoo Martha glaring at me as she kicked me again.

"Hey. Ryann. Wake up. Move." Her embittered voice was cold and sour, as was the look on her face.

I shot up off the floor, knackered and out of it from my emotional confrontation with Quinn. I blocked the doorway where I stood and moved so she could enter her room.

"Sorry. Do you know where Jessica is?"

I got an eyeful of *stay the hell away*. "She's with her mother," she snapped. "I thought you'd know that." Visibly annoyed, Martha grabbed hold of the doorknob, entered her room and swung around, intent on slamming the door in my face.

"Wait." I shoved my foot into the doorjamb and forced my way into the small room, much to the dismay of its owner. "Actually, I'd like to talk to you."

Martha's head snapped back in surprise. "What the hell for?"

"I need your help." I cringed. My life had definitely become a goddamned calamatastrophy if I was seeking out Voodoo Martha. She was the last person I wanted to spend any kind of time with, yet she was the only person I could think of that might be able to help me. That fact made her my new BFF.

"My help?" Martha stood with one foot in front of her, arms crossed, and wearing an expression that boldly shouted, "Do I look like I give a damn?" Her eyebrow rose in question as she waited for my reply.

It wasn't until that moment that I really took a good look at Martha. Sure I'd glanced at her the few times I'd been lucky enough to see her around the apartment, but always ended up looking away because, frankly, she scared me.

Observing her now, I noticed that although her wardrobe and makeup choices were well off the beaten path, Martha was actually pretty. At least, she could be pretty if she'd stop scowling for two seconds, so people could actually see her.

Bathed in black, Martha wore a tight, low-cut black sweater that accentuated her well-endowed chest. She had on a short, ruffled black skirt with large safety pins crawling up the side. Fish net stockings hugged her slender legs and were covered with black and white knee socks, topped off with the most wicked pair of Docs I'd ever seen.

That shit must take forever to lace up.

Martha's head was an issue all unto itself. Her dark, mahogany locks were styled into an emo hairstyle, with longer layers that hung past her shoulders and shorter layers near the crown of her head. Long sweeping bangs fell across her forehead, partially obstructing her hazel eyes, which were surrounded with thick, black eyeliner that distracted from their natural beauty.

A large nose ring jutted out from her left nostril, and another stuck out from her right lower lip, which was painted blood red. And her skin … It was beyond pale and had me wondering just how much powder it actually took to achieve such a look. I wanted to come at her with some bronzer and throw her out into the sun so she could catch a little color. I didn't think she'd be game for a makeover, so I squashed those thoughts quickly.

Martha waved her hands in front of my face, bringing my attention back to the here and now. "Are you done staring at me? What the hell do you want?"

I held up one finger. "Hold on a sec." I walked over to her nightstand and plopped my iPhone onto her docking station, turning the volume up as loud as I could. With Quinn's supernatural hearing, I needed to do what I could to muffle our conversation. I didn't want him to know what I was up to.

"What the hell are you doing? I'm not listening to that crap," Martha snapped.

"Sorry," I said. "I'll explain the music in a minute. I think you might be the only person who can help me, since you know…" I trailed off for a moment, taking the opportunity to look around her room and all the strange paraphernalia it contained. "Since you believe in all of this," I said with a sweeping hand motion.

She met my admission with a scrutinizing glare. Her suspicion was obvious, I'm sure a result of the treatment she regularly received because of her odd lifestyle. If I had any hope of convincing her to help me, I was going to have to dish out something in return. I gave her the only thing I could: the truth. The worst that could happen was she'd think I was bat-shit crazy. In which case, I'd claim substance abuse as the cause of my recent hallucinations. People blamed everything on drugs.

"Look…" I said, taking in a deep breath. "This is going to sound nuts, really out there, but I swear to you I'm not insane. My boy—" I stopped myself from saying the word. Quinn was not my boyfriend. Hell, he hadn't been a boy for several hundred years. Not wanting to stray from the topic at hand, I started again.

"I have this friend, and he's a faerie." I stopped to take in her expression which I was sure would be one of shock and disbelief. To my surprise, Martha stood just as she had the moment before I'd spoken, scowling away at me. I waited for her to ask me if I was joking, but the moment never came.

A small hand sliced through the air in front of me. "Wake up, girl," she said, admonishing me. "This is the twenty-first century. Just because someone is gay doesn't mean they are in need of help. Get a clue!"

What? Gay? Oh!

"No, no. I didn't mean gay faerie. I mean he's actually a faerie. You know, as in mythical creature faerie."

"Oh," she said still wearing a scowl on her face. "You should have just said that in the first place."

She believes me?

My eyes widened. "You believe me?"

She shrugged as if to say our whole conversation was no big thing. "I've seen a lot. Not much shocks me."

"Oh, thank God. You believe me." Relief swept through my veins. "He needs help, because he was cursed and he's dying, and I can't let him die, because I love him." My words ran together I spoke so fast, and I wasn't entirely sure if she caught everything.

With one final glare, Martha turned and walked over to the end of her bed, where her giant trunk lay, closed and padlocked.

"Have a seat," she said as she fiddled with the lock.

Hesitantly, I walked over to her bed and sat, earning a reproachful look from Martha. I slid down to the floor with my back leaning against it. I heard her digging through her case full of mystical goodies and wondered what exactly she kept in the thing. I didn't dare look, worried she might get mad and refuse to help me. I stared idly at my hands, picking at a hangnail on my thumb while she found what she was looking for.

The lid slammed shut and I saw her heavy boots in my peripheral vision as she walked over to sit beside me. She clutched a very thick and very old book to her chest, which she tentatively laid on her lap. The book was bound in dark, worn leather, the edges of its pages appeared slightly yellow and timeworn.

I shuddered to think what the aged manual contained given the contents of the other books she left out in the open. She kept this bad boy under lock and key so it probably held great value. The damn thing was probably dangerous, too.

I swallowed hard, trying to clear the lump in my throat.

"The Book of Light," she smoothed the cover reverently, "has been in my family for over two hundred years."

My eyes grew wide as she spoke. Two hundred years?

"Within its pages are documentations of every encounter my mother, grandmother, great-grandmother, and those that came before them, ever had with otherworldly beings. Demons, warlocks, faeries and the like are all accounted for in this book. I'm quite certain we can find something in here that will aid your dying friend." All trace of hostility vanished from her voice, and I searched her face to find it void of her trademark scowl.

I gaped at her in disbelief. "Why are you helping me?" I'd expected some sort of fight and had readied myself for the possibility of begging. Instead, I sat flabbergasted on the floor next to her as she prepared to assist me in my quest to help Quinn.

"Because. You're the first person that's ever asked."

I stared open-mouthed as she continued.

"People are afraid of me. They think I'm this evil, awful person because of how I look and what I can do. I got tired of trying to prove them wrong. It's just easier to act the way people perceive me, and scare them away."

I blanched. "That's awful."

"Yeah, well … that's just the way it is when you see what I've seen and know what I know."

"What are you?" I'd had my suspicions since my first encounter with her, but wanted to hear it from her lips.

"I'm a witch," she said and smiled brightly.

chapter 14

So do you want to tell me why I'm being forced to suffer through the soundtrack to *Mamma Mia*?" Martha glanced over toward my iPod and back at me, her lips pulled down into a frown.

"I don't want Quinn to hear what I'm up to. He's got exceptional hearing abilities." Images of Quinn popped into my mind as I spoke. Visions of him lifting a park bench over his head, the thick, corded muscles in his biceps straining against his t-shirt, had me drooling and a warm flush crept over my skin. "Among other things," I said, my voice trailing off.

She rolled her eyes. "Let's get on with this then so we can turn that crap off. What kind of faerie is he?"

"He's the Gancanagh."

Martha blanched.

Not exactly the reaction I'd been hoping for. "I take it you've heard of him?"

"Actually … yes. I remember reading about him when I was younger." She opened her antique book and searched through its seasoned pages with determination. "Ah ha," she declared. "Found him!"

It took every ounce of self-control I possessed to not yank the book out of her hands and devour the contents of its pages as quickly as possible. Something told me she might get pissy if I attempted to touch her family heirloom, so I remained still, shaking with impatience. "Well, what does it say? Is there anything in there that can help him?" Frantic and overexcited, I literally bounced in place while I waited for her to respond.

"Calm down," she said, looking at me like I was ridiculous. "It looks like my great-great-grandmother crossed paths with him after he seduced one of her cousins."

"Oh? Well ... what happened?"

Please don't let it be horrible. Please.

Martha ran her finger down the page as she continued reading. "There's not a lot of information here. Mostly, it's my grandmother's account of her unsuccessful attempts to retrieve her cousin's memory. It says here she went calling on her cousin one afternoon and found your boy, scrubbing her memory, the cousin still in an embarrassing state of undress. There was a small skirmish as my great-great-grandmother tried to put a hex on him, but was thwarted. That's when the faerie revealed himself to her as the Gancanagh. According to my grandmother's account, he was exceedingly handsome, horribly arrogant and spoke with a viper's tongue."

Yep. Sounds about right.

I craned my neck trying to read from the book myself. "Are there any other details about him?" There had to be more than just an account of his womanizing. He had to have done something other than blaze a trail of indiscretion through history.

"No." She shook her head. "There's nothing else written. How did you meet him, anyway?"

With an ache in my chest, I filled her in on the finer details of our tempestuous relationship, from our initial meeting at the bar to present day, leaving nothing out. If there was any hope of her helping me, I needed to afford her full disclosure to the intricate details of our connection.

I let my head rest against the side of the bed and closed my eyes, grief-stricken at the thought of not being able to help Quinn.

No doubt sensing my despair, Martha reached out and laid a hand on my arm. "Relax, Ryann. I have an idea."

My head shot back up, and I looked at her with a mix of fear and hope in my eyes as I waited for her explanation.

She closed her book and set it on the floor next to her before turning and sitting cross-legged in front of me. With her elbows on her knees, she leaned forward and spoke. "We're looking for someone who's gotten close enough to Quinn to learn the details of his curse, right?"

I nodded in agreement.

"Well," she said. "It seems to me the person who's come closest to him is you."

I felt my forehead crinkling as I shot her a look that clearly said I thought she was crazy. Then a moment later, I froze in place as her words finally registered. Martha was right on target.

In all his five-hundred-plus years, Quinn had never formed a relationship or gotten close enough to anyone to share the details of his curse with except for me. I alone knew of his all-consuming love of Guinness and fried potatoes. No one else knew of his passion for books and history, or of his fascination with fast cars and small electronic gadgetry. The simple truth of those facts sent goosebumps popping out over my skin.

Excitement spiked and my body shook. "You're right. What can I do?"

"First fill me in on the details of his curse. Who put the whammy on him and why."

"What … is … going … on?" Jessica's voice filled the room, and I looked up to see her staring down at us in complete awe.

So immersed in my conversation with Martha, I hadn't heard her enter the room. I had to admit, it must have been a shock to see the two of us huddled together on the floor over a giant book, with show tunes blaring in the background.

"Ryann? What are you doing in here?" Her sharp tone conveyed her displeasure and I knew she was not only shocked, but a bit peeved as well. Suspicious in the extreme, I knew Jess believed Martha was up to no good.

I looked up at her with a reassuring smile. "Martha's helping me."

Jessica made a "pssh" sound and scowled. "What could she possibly help you with? How to be a freak?"

Whoa. Didn't see that one coming. "Jess."

Martha exhaled forcefully, and I turned to see her glaring up at Jessica with anger filled eyes.

I couldn't have the two of them fighting. I needed Jessica's support, and I desperately needed Martha's help. "Martha is helping me save Quinn. If you want to know what's going on, you'll sit down and listen." I wasn't normally so short and bossy, but I didn't have time to deal with petty prejudices. Quinn's fate was too important.

Returning Martha's icy glare, Jessica tossed her purse onto the floor and plopped down across from the two of us. "What is going on, Ryann? What's wrong with Quinn? Why does he need saving?"

I wrestled for a moment with how to go about telling my best friend I'd left her in the dark for the past month where my new male friend was concerned. I'd never kept anything from Jessica before, and felt guilty on more than one occasion over the past few weeks about my inability to share my experiences with her. The truth of the matter was Quinn's secret was not mine to share, and I'd used that reasoning as an excuse to justify my actions. Now, with Quinn's life hanging in the balance, I had no qualms about spilling his secret to my best friend or our witchy roommate. I needed their help, and I knew they wouldn't blab.

"Jess." I paused for a moment. "What I'm about to tell you may seem beyond all reason, but I assure you it's true. Quinn is a mythical being. More specifically, he's a faerie." I sat back and watched her reaction.

Jessica sat quiet and motionless for several seconds, a thoughtful look on her face before she turned toward Martha, and let loose with a verbal diatribe the likes of which I'd never seen before.

"What did you do to her, you whacked-out freak? Whatever you did, make it stop. Fix her. Now." Jessica leaned forward her face mere inches from Martha's, and shouted with so much force her face turned three shades of purple.

I shot forward across the floor, placing my body between the two of them. "Jess, stop it."

"Back off, Jessica, or you will be sorry!" Martha threatened. All three of us shouted simultaneously, none of us hearing what the others were saying.

Enough of this crap.

"Stop!" My voice drowned them out, and they stopped bickering mid-sentence. Shock and surprise painted their angry faces. Clearly neither thought me capable of making such a loud noise.

"Ryann, I'm sorry, but I'm scared for you." The look of concern on Jessica's face was genuine. "What you are saying is crazy. You can't possibly believe it."

"I know it sounds crazy," I said, "but it's true. I wish there was a way I could prove it to you. I—"

Jessica grabbed my wrist, a look of overwhelming disbelief etched on her pretty face as she shook her head from side to side. I turned to see what she was staring at.

Martha's ancient manual hovered a foot above the ground in front of her while she sat still, concentrating on the book, a smug smile on her pale face. The lamp illuminating the small room suddenly went out, with several candles magically lighting themselves, casting a warm luminescence throughout the room.

Jessica's jaw nearly hit the floor. "I … uh … I …" Words that normally came so easily to her failed, as she looked at me with total shock. "I can't believe it."

"Tell me about it," I agreed. "Now do you believe me?"

"I'm starting to." She turned to face Martha. "Are you … you know, evil?" Jessica's eyes roamed about Martha's medieval-looking room, taking in all of the dark and scary paraphernalia.

Martha rolled her eyes and cast Jess a sardonic stare. "No. I'm not evil. This," she circled her hand through the air, "is just for show. People make assumptions about me," she gave Jess an accusatory glance, "and it's just easier for me to follow along with their assumptions, rather than argue. I act scary to keep people away."

"So, you're not going to put a hex on me?" Jessica still appeared a bit nervous.

"No," she answered, giving Jessica a reproving glare. "I, along with the women of my family, use magic to help people, not hurt them. Unfortunately, when people find out I have abilities, they tend to run the opposite direction before I get the chance. Ryann here is the first person who's ever approached me, seeking out my help." Smiling, Martha concentrated on the book, lowering it to the floor just in front of her.

Happy my roommates were no longer going for each others' jugulars, I was ready to get back to the business at hand. "Can we get back to helping Quinn now?"

"Yeah, yeah. Go on with whatever you were talking about earlier. I'll catch on," Jess said, trying to sound encouraging, but still looking a bit weirded out by everything she'd just seen.

I moved back to where I'd sat previously and tucked my knees into my chest. "Okay. You need to know who cursed Quinn and why, is that right?"

Martha nodded. "Yes."

Something told me she wasn't going to like my answer, but there was no going back. The knowledge I possessed was key in saving Quinn, regardless of how bad it might sound.

I breathed in deeply before answering. "It was Queen Morgana."

A quick intake of breath filled my ears as I watched Martha's eyes grow wide for the briefest of moments. "Why did she curse him?"

Oh, Lord. Here we go.

I winced. "Quinn was a bit of a womanizer, as accounted for by your great-grandmother in your book." Calling him "a bit" of a womanizer had been putting it mildly. The man was to women what Wonder was to bread. "Evidently, he thought himself to be the be-all and end-all of faerie men, and sported an endless string of booty calls, none of whom he cared for. Bragging about his sexual escapades, he got himself into trouble when he told everyone about his plan to seduce the beautiful queen."

"Idiot," Martha scoffed.

"Fool," Jessica growled.

"Hey," I said, feeling defensive. "This is the man I'm in love with here. I realize his actions were foolish and, well, disgusting, but we are talking about things he did five hundred years ago. He's grown immens—"

"Five hundred years!" Jessica shouted over me as I spoke. She waved her hands frantically in front of her as she shook her head. "Wait just a minute. You're telling me Quinn is five hundred years old?" Her head shot back and her eyes threatened to burst out of her skull and jump across the room.

I nodded, unsure of what else to say. Quinn was old, really old. I knew it. Our pseudo-relationship gave new meaning to the phrase "robbing the cradle," but I couldn't find it in me to care. Quinn was hot. Damn hot. Unravaged by time, he was without a doubt the most beautifully made man I'd ever laid eyes on. And not only that, he consistently blew me away with his gentleness and willingness to always place my needs before his own, even when he caught hell from me for doing so. He was the very air I breathed.

"Wow, Ryann. Pretty boy looks darn good for being a fossil."

"Eh, funny," I said with a sneer. I had a feeling I'd be catching a mountain of grief about Quinn's age for quite some time.

Martha cleared her throat. "Ahem … moving right along. So, the faerie queen cursed Quinn." She tapped at the shiny silver ring on her lip and sighed. "That's … well … I'm not going to lie to you. That makes things difficult."

Wobbling on the edge of defeat, I placed my face in my hands and groaned. "Of course, it does. Nothing in my life is ever easy." Why? Why did everything always have to be so damn difficult?

"No," I shouted. Running my fingers through my hair, I sat up straight, determined not spiral down into the black funk of depression I teetered precariously on. I refused to be deterred. Quinn deserved a happy ending, and so did I. I'd no longer be "that girl." The one that had to work so hard for everything, the girl everyone felt sorry for, because she had no family. I was ready to make a change, ready to grab the reins and change the course of my destiny. "You just said difficult. Not impossible. What can we do?"

Martha sat rifling through the pages of her book as I spoke. "Hold on," she said. "I remember reading something about the Faerie Realm ages ago. Here." She pointed to a particularly long entry in the book titled *The Silver Bough*.

Unable to sit still, I moved so that I sat on my knees and leaned forward, peering at the book. "What does it say?" Excitement and relief coursed through me as I chewed away at my bottom lip, waiting to hear what the passage said.

"Read it out loud," Jess said forcefully. "So we all can hear."

"I was going to, Bossy Bessie!" Martha glared at Jess with fire in her eyes. I hoped to God she didn't possess the ability to burn people alive with her peepers or Jess was toast.

"Stop it, you two," I cried. "Please, Martha. What does it say?" I couldn't take the suspense. I needed to know what information lay upon the ancient pages of Martha's book.

"Okay, okay. I'm sorry." She flashed me an apologetic look and began reading. "It looks like this entry was written by my grandmother. The story's not a firsthand account, but merely a chronicle of a myth passed down through the years." She paused for a moment, taking in my intense gaze, before starting up again.

"It's written there's a mystical apple tree that lies deep in the heart of Ireland. A silver bough from that tree is said to open the gateway between our world and the Isle of Apples, the Faerie Realm. Whoever possesses the bough shall gain safe passage between the two worlds until the sun sets, the following day."

My heart plummeted. A mystical tree in Ireland? I couldn't just pick up and run off to another country. That required money. Money I didn't have. The pay from my job was good, but not *that* good. "Crap! Is there no hope? I won't give up," I cried.

I couldn't imagine a life without Quinn. It didn't matter that we'd only known each other a short while. He'd branded himself onto my very soul, marking me for life. It made no difference that he didn't share my intense feelings. I'd help him regardless because he was my light in a world which had recently plagued me with fear and darkness. And sure as shit I'd do all I could to keep Quinn from fading away.

I closed my eyes, took a deep breath and exhaled slowly. "How the hell am I supposed to get a mythical tree branch from Ireland?"

"That's easy," Martha said and smiled. "The internet."

chapter 15

"Well," I sighed, plopping down onto my bed, "that was the last one."

Jessica sat down next to me and placed an arm around my shoulder in an effort to console me. "I can't believe you sold all of your bags, Ryann. There must have been at least twelve Coach purses in that tub alone, not to mention the Dooneys and Juicys." She, more than anyone else, knew how beloved my handbag collection was to me.

When Martha told me I'd need two thousand dollars to cover the cost of the magical bough, I'd nearly pissed myself.

Oh, yeah. Let me just go pull that out of the petty cash I have stashed away under my pillow. Not!

Along with student loans, my job covered my college tuition, as well as rent, gas, food and basic necessities. I had a decent sized savings account, but there certainly wasn't enough to purchase a mystical relic with. The decision to part with my precious handbag collection had been an easy one. Helping Quinn was my single focus, and I'd do whatever it took to save him. Having taken great care to keep my bags in pristine condition, I knew they'd provide me with the money I needed to buy the branch.

I shrugged. "Material things can be replaced. People can't." I knew that fact all too well, having grown up without parents. I'd give away everything I owned and walk around naked and penniless if it meant I could have a family to call my own. My feelings for Quinn were just as strong and I'd hurriedly put together a "shop my closet" sale, posting signs around my apartment complex as well as the student commons on campus. It took just under a week to sell my precious collection.

Jessica gave my shoulder one last squeeze before standing up and peering into the empty tub where my purses once resided. "Well, with the sale of that last bag, you have the money you need to buy the apple thing-a-ma-jig."

"Bough," I said, correcting her.

She rolled her eyes. "Yeah, bough. Sheesh."

I crossed the room and winced as I stood in front of my mirror. I hadn't been able to look at the damn thing without remembering the creepy words scrawled across it just a short time ago. I ran a brush through my hair and met Jessica's eyes through her reflection in the mirror. "I have to head out to work in a few and I'm sure Quinn is waiting for me outside. Can you tell Martha to go ahead and order the bough now that we have all the money? Just tell her we'll pay for it cash on delivery."

I picked up the giant wad of bills sitting on my dresser and turned, handing it to her. "And make sure she gets the fastest shipping possible. Samhain is just around the corner."

"Samhain, shmanhain. Why don't you just call it Halloween?"

I shook the money in front of her. "Don't lose this." I flashed her a severe look as she took the handful of bills from me.

"Oh, come on!" Jess said in protest. "Have a little faith in your best friend."

"I'm sorry," I said and sighed. "I do have faith in you. I'm just on edge. What we're doing is so important. It's Quinn's life." I crossed the room, grabbing the only purse left to my name, a mid-sized, brown Roxy tote. "I gotta go. I'll talk to you in the morning." I gave her a quick hug and hurried out of the room.

I felt a tad anxious leaving my two roommates together. Jessica remained stubbornly aloof where Martha was concerned. Something had to give and I seriously considered locking the two of them in a room together until they decided to get along.

My breath caught at the sight of Quinn as I walked out into the courtyard of my building, into the crisp evening air. I was quite sure there would never come a time when I'd tire of admiring him. How anyone could make a simple white button-down look so amazingly sexy, I'd never know, but he managed it with ease. The top portion of his shirt was unbuttoned, allowing just a hint of his smooth, powerfully chiseled chest to be exposed. The sleeves were rolled and pushed up, and dammit, even his forearms were ripped and sexy.

Get a grip, Ryann.

As I stood eyeballing Quinn, I almost forgot the tension that had plagued us this past week. Almost. After placing my tongue back into my mouth, I managed to meet him halfway, happily accepting his leather jacket which he'd been holding for me. I was surprised he wasn't wearing it himself as the climate had taken an unseasonably large dip.

"Won't you need this?" I asked as I slipped my arms in the sleeves of his coat. I wore the thing so much, I wondered when he'd just give up and let me have it. His delicious scent lingered on the leather fabric still, even though he hadn't worn it, flooding my center with a sinfully warm sensation. I was doomed. Quinn appealed to all my senses in the most primal way. Resistance was futile.

"Please. You insult me," he scoffed, as he swept a stray lock of brown hair out of my eyes, taking care not to touch my skin. "This isn't cold. It's downright pleasant. Ireland in the dead of winter is cold. Fierce cold. That shit will freeze your balls off."

A loud snort escaped my lips as I laughed. It couldn't be helped, and he chuckled in response. Though bright, his smile didn't reach his eyes, and a small piece of my heart chipped away. What I wouldn't give to see him happy through and through. Still, the laughter felt refreshing after a week's worth of uncomfortable, awkward silence between us.

My thoughts traveled back to when I'd gone to Martha for help. After setting my plan of action for aiding Quinn, I'd lost it, given in to my emotions and freaked out. Feeling guilty over the things I'd shouted at Quinn and sick at the thought of possibly pushing him away, I'd rushed out of my apartment in a panicked search for him.

I knew he'd be watching out for me since my demon stalker still lurked about, but wigged out anyway when I didn't immediately see him. Not thinking straight, I ran down the busy street toward the school, searching for him. I took maybe ten steps before Quinn stopped me.

☙

Quinn magically appeared in front of me. "Will you never learn?" He raised his hands in frustration and growled at me. The man actually growled. "Stubborn, irritating, pain in the hole!" Quinn's Irish accent was thick, and though I was still reeling from our earlier confrontation, my knees went soft at the sound of his voice.

"I was looking for you. I wanted to apologize. Stop yelling at me!"

"Stop yelling, yourself!"

I threw my hands up in the air in a fit of temper. "All right, I will." I not only looked like a complete idiot, I sounded like one as well, yelling at the top of my lungs like a child who got caught doing something naughty. Embarrassment and shame crept over me and I hung my head for a moment not wanting to face his penetrating gaze. There was so much I wanted to say to him.

"I'm so sorry, Quinn. The things… the things I said earlier were… awful." I choked on my words, my voice muffled from the giant lump that formed in my throat as I continued to stare at the ground. His eyes blazed a hole into my soul as I continued. "I know you don't feel the same, but I don't care. I don't want you to leave. I… I can't be without you," I sobbed.

I felt like such a loser, basically begging him to stay, knowing he didn't feel the same. Sure, I could have walked away, not looking back, but that would have killed me. Quinn had taken up a space in my heart, a rather large space, actually, and without him present to fill it, I'd be a walking corpse, a shell of my former self, and half a person. Though he didn't share the intensity of my feelings, he did care for me; that much I knew. He'd offered me his friendship and I'd take that over nothing at all.

A large, warm hand gently came to rest over my heart and my head snapped up, my eyes meeting his. Quinn captured my gaze, holding it in his own, his eyes filled with sorrow and something else I couldn't make out.

"*Táim i ngrá leat. Is tú mo sonuachar.*" He spoke gently and with tenderness despite the rich timbre of his voice. The combination of his words and touch moved me immeasurably, despite the fact I had no idea what he'd said.

"So, I'm forgiven, then?" I could only assume he'd taken pity on me and forgiven my earlier outburst.

Quinn gave me a funny look, as if he were confused. A single brow rose, his eyes widened momentarily, before he nodded, the corners of his mouth turning up. "There is nothing to forgive, *a ghrá*." He let his hand drop, a look of pain enveloping his handsome face. "I'm such a fool," he muttered under his breath while shaking his head. "Come on then, lass. Let's get you home."

e

The smell of fine leather yanked me from my recollection as I climbed into Quinn's car. We rode the short distance to Fire and Ice in the Mercedes, my personal favorite out of all his vehicles. The other sports cars were sleek, powerful and fun, but the Mercedes simply oozed style and class.

Quinn parked the car in the small garage up the street, as was his usual routine when taking me to work. Wary of just about anything with two legs and a pulse, Quinn insisted on staying nearby while I worked, constantly reminding me that evil could come calling at any time of the day, even in a public place.

Dedicated to my protection, Quinn had even taken to carrying an ancient Irish Scían on him, which I must admit, was a complete and total turn on. The ancient dagger was not only beautiful, but also deadly, and Quinn proudly flung it about on numerous occasions, trying to impress me with his skill.

From the research I'd done in recent weeks, I'd gathered that faeries tended to shy away from iron and steel, as it served as a kryptonite of sorts to them. When I asked Quinn about my findings, he'd laughed.

"Aye, that's true for most faeries. I'm one of the lucky blokes that are an exception to that rule. When Morgana cursed me, she knew I'd need a way to defend myself against jealous husbands and the like, and cast a spell rendering me impervious to iron. Not only can I grasp a steel blade, I can do a fair bit of damage with it as well."

The club was empty when we arrived, save a few employees. Stan had called me earlier in the day and asked that I come in early to help with inventory again. Thankful for the hours, what with the large purchase I'd just made, I happily accepted the extra work.

Quinn passed by the bar and knocked knuckles with the bartender, Gabriel, as he waltzed toward the back section where I usually waited tables, his iPhone and ear buds in hand. The two never spoke, but, for some strange reason, had formed an unspoken bond. Gabriel, silent and serious, had taken on a brotherly role of sorts, endearing himself to me and gaining the respect of Quinn in the process. Gabriel was the only man I'd ever witnessed Quinn pay any type of respect to, save our professors, whom he was forced to play nice with.

After storing my purse in the break room, I made my way over to the bar, greeting Gabriel, who then headed for the storage room, clipboard in hand.

Grabbing myself a bottle of water from the refrigerator under the bar, I popped the cap and was about to take a swig when a blast of cold air blew over me, and an evil, malevolent laughter filled the large room.

I opened my mouth to scream, but no sound came out. Standing on the other side of the bar was the same dark creature that haunted my dreams just weeks before, the same monstrosity that attacked me during my morning run. A shudder ripped through me as I stared at the hideous embodiment of evil and all things unholy: my demon stalker.

"Ryann." His sinister voice burned my ears and ate away at my insides.

Before I had time to blink, Quinn appeared, seemingly out of nowhere, and stood in front of the hideous demon, pure unadulterated hatred and rage emanating from him.

"Go in the back with Gabriel and Stan, Ryann." Quinn's eyes never left the Zmeu's, who returned his deadly stare with one of his own.

I tried to move, but my leadened feet fused to the floor, rendering me immobile.

"There is no need for her to flee from my presence, faerie. I mean her no harm." The demon broke Quinn's gaze momentarily, turning toward me with a sinister smile. "So beautiful."

Its bone-chilling voice sent my blood running cold while it moved toward me. It lifted its arm, beckoning for me to move forward.

Quinn dove toward the demon, pinning him to the bar, his deadly Scían dagger unsheathed and poised at its jugular, ready to drain its life in one swift plunge. "Ryann, get back!"

A horrible, base laughter filled the room, as the demon lay unmoving on the wooden surface of the bar, seemingly un-phased by Quinn's murderous intentions. "Ahh...so eager you are to slay me, faerie. I wonder, though, if you are just as eager to risk exposing your true identity? You've already unmasked yourself to one worthless mortal. Would you risk exposure to more by slaying me now?"

"I care not for myself," Quinn growled.

Time as I knew it ceased to exist. I'd shifted to another plane of reality where time passed at a much slower rate. Several things happened simultaneously. The muscles in Quinn's arms flexed as he moved to plunge the dagger into the demon's neck, and the door at the front entrance of the club opened, most likely another one of the bartenders coming in to help with inventory.

I screamed before I knew what I was doing. "Quinn. No!"

All it took was that one moment. Upon hearing my scream, Quinn hesitated, and the demon broke away, morphing into a giant black bird that swooped out the front door, forcing the employee trying to enter to dive to the floor to keep from being struck.

"The hell with that. I'll go around to the back," the poor guy shouted and dashed out of the building.

"No!" Quinn roared. "What have you done? I had him within my grasp. I could have ended this!" Rage and fury the likes of which I'd never seen flowed from every inch of him, reverberating off of the walls causing the entire building to rattle.

We stood in silence, staring at each other for what felt like an immeasurable amount of time.

"Earthquake!" Stan raced out from the back with his arms flailing, squealing like a stuck pig.

My boss's howling failed to register with me as I focused on Quinn. "I'm so sorry." Silent tears streamed down my cheeks. "I didn't mean for him to get away. I … I just …"

Suddenly, Stan's face was all up in my business. "Ryann? Are you okay? Did you feel that? Did anything break?" A mix of panic and concern marked his features as he gasped for air, shaking behind the bar.

"I'm fine," I said, barely able to think, let alone form a coherent sentence. The demon had come after me again, risking exposure no less, by attacking me at my place of work. It was either extremely brazen, or desperate. I wasn't sure which was worse.

Of course, I couldn't exactly tell my boss I'd been attacked by a malicious demon that wanted to steal me away to his underworld lair. He'd most likely accuse me of hitting the sauce and fire me on the spot. So I did the only thing I could do. I lied.

"Just a small quake, that's all," I said, waving him off with my hand. "Pretty typical for California. Nothing's broken."

Stan stood eyes wide, scanning the bar for broken glass before letting his eyes come to rest on Quinn, who shook visibly with rage.

"What a geographical nightmare. Good thing nothing was lost in the quake." Stan's attention darted back and forth between Quinn and me.

"Yes. It *is* a good thing nothing was lost," Quinn snapped bitterly, while looking pointedly at me.

His double entendre was not lost on me. I knew I was damn lucky to be standing where I was.

Stan gave me a hearty clap on the back before snatching up a towel to wipe the bar with. "You look a bit shaken up, Ryann. Why don't you go ahead and take the night off. I'll keep you on the clock, so you won't lose any pay."

"Oh," I said, shocked he'd offer such a thing. But given what had just happened, I wasn't about to argue with him. Retrieving my purse from the break room, I walked quietly to Quinn's side, afraid to meet his heated glare. I'd blown the perfect opportunity to put end to the nightmare that plagued me twenty-four-seven by stupidly opening my mouth. Why was I never able to keep my damn trap shut? Ashamed, and aware I'd totally blown it, I followed Quinn out of the club and down the street to the garage that housed his car, a hideous wall of silence separating us the entire way.

Once in the vehicle, I dared a peek in Quinn's direction and found him sitting with his hands on the steering wheel. He stared out into the distance, his eyes resolute, and conviction radiating from every pore.

"I give you my solemn vow." He turned to face me then, drawing his Scían from its sheath, gripping the blade with his hand and holding it to his chest. "On my soul, by my body, by the very blood that flows through my veins, before I leave this earth, I will bleed that devil dry, and set fire to his bones. You shall never have to fear him again."

I stared, awestruck at the blood that flowed freely down Quinn's massive hand onto the soft leather upholstery of the car before launching myself full force at him.

chapter 16

When I was seven, I had a crush on a boy named Nolan. He had bright blue eyes and a crooked smile that sent my little heart all a twitter. He'd give me the Oreos his mother packed him and chase me around the blacktop during lunch. One afternoon during late recess, Nolan and I snuck behind the library and gave each other our very first kiss. It was quick and awkward, and left me wondering what all the fuss was about with regard to kissing. Our fledgling relationship crumbled shortly thereafter, Nolan telling everyone I had cooties. Not to be outdone, I retaliated by telling everyone he had dog breath.

Many years later, I discovered the difference between good kissing ability and bad, and boy, was there a difference. My first real boyfriend, Spencer, was utterly adorable, funny in the extreme, but quite possibly the world's worst kisser. Possessing the sensitivity of a Bull Mastiff, he kissed much the same, shoving his tongue down my throat and covering my mouth and chin with large amounts of drool. Needless to say, our relationship didn't last long as I'd gag anytime he leaned in for a smooch.

Then there was Carson. Handsome and charismatic, he had a way with the ladies, and quickly stole my heart. No stranger to kissing, he'd schooled me in the fine art of making out. It was Carson who taught me a good kiss could be felt all the way down to your toes.

I dated a few other boys, some skilled, some not so much, but none of whom even came close to delivering the mind-blowing lip lock Quinn and I shared.

Quinn's vow to protect me was the most romantic, heart-stopping, passionate pledge I'd ever been witness to in my short twenty-one years of life. Every coherent thought that had been running through my head—the fear, the remorse from my earlier blunder—quickly flew out the window at hearing him utter his promise to guard me from harm.

Acting on impulse, I threw myself at Quinn, grabbing onto his broad shoulders, my mouth crashing into his with a mounting desire. Somewhere in the recesses of my mind, I knew the kiss would be intensely wonderful, mind-altering even, given the nature of his curse. What I wasn't prepared for was just how nearly orgasmic a simple kiss from him would be.

The moment our lips met, a spark ignited, deep within my very soul, exploding outward like an atom bomb, setting my skin on fire and sending my blood boiling. I gasped at the intensity of the sensation, giving Quinn an open invitation to deepen the kiss—an enticement he greedily accepted. He gently traced the contour of my lower lip with his tongue before sucking it between his own.

I unclenched my hand which gripped his shoulder like a vice, and let my fingertips slowly blaze a trail up the contour of his neck until it came to rest at the base of his skull, my other hand following suit. My body's response to the additional skin-to-skin contact was staggering, and my pulse exploded. A low moan emanated from deep within my throat.

Dropping the Scían he still held to the floor of the car, Quinn grabbed me by the waist, pulling me over the center console and onto his lap. Deepening the kiss further, his tongue danced sensually with my own as we explored each others' mouths with a growing fervor. I felt just how excited Quinn was as I sat straddled against his hips, and ground myself against his cock which strained against the seam of his pants.

He snaked one arm behind my lower back, pulling me closer still, and crushed our bodies together while grabbing a fistful of my short brown locks with his other hand. And dear holy Lord, I felt his kiss from the top of my head to the very tip of my toes. I was sure every molecule in my body would spontaneously combust from the sheer pleasure of it.

Lightheaded from lack of breath, my body shook, cluing Quinn in to my rapidly declining state. He broke contact, much to my dismay, and I cried out with displeasure.

"*A ghrá*, you need to breathe."

Frantic, I shook my head. "Breathing is for the birds. I want more kissing," I said breathlessly, moving in for another lip lock. Nothing else mattered. My mind swam with images of his lips moving with my own, his hands searching and exploring every inch of my body. More. I needed more.

The next thing I knew, he heaved me over the center console and back into my cold seat with an agonizing groan.

"Hey!" I complained. "Why'd you do that?"

His expression was one of pure torment. The longing in his eyes was unmistakable, yet he made no move to give in. "Because, *a ghrá*, you were losing control, succumbing to the curse."

"No, I wasn't. It was fine. I was fine. Please?"

I watched him sit back in his seat and shake his head. He looked like I'd slapped him.

Maybe I was losing control. I'd begged frantically like a child who'd had its toy taken away. I was most definitely not acting like myself. "Maybe you're right," I said reluctantly.

"Aye, I know I'm right." A mixture of lust, pain and sadness tore at his rugged face. "I hope you enjoyed that, because it won't happen again."

The bubble I'd been floating on burst, sending me spiraling down to crash and burn against the sad reality of our situation. There would be no more kissing, no more touching. Quinn's curse placed a wall between us he stubbornly refused to knock down. I knew his reasoning, and though I understood and even admired his decision to abstain from contact with me, it didn't make it any less frustrating. I'd be living off the memory of my stolen kiss for the rest of my life.

"Thank you," I said, my voice just above a whisper. "It was beautiful."

He gave me a sober nod and looked away.

"How was it for you?" I felt like an idiot asking such a clichéd question, but my head demanded I ask what my heart desperately wanted to know.

Quinn turned to face me, his eyes full of…love? I couldn't be sure, but whatever emotion, it was intense. "I've never experienced its equal."

The silver bough came two days later via second day airmail. I felt relieved I had tangible evidence of a way to help Quinn within my grasp, yet afraid of what came along with using the mystical branch. Relief and fear made strange bedfellows.

I'd be confronting a queen. A faerie queen, no less, who'd used her magical powers to put a hex on the man of my dreams. Facing her would be extraordinarily daunting. Still, I knew I would go to the ends of the earth, to hell and back, if it meant keeping Quinn alive.

I cranked the speaker on my iPod's docking station and called Martha into my room to finalize our plan for that night. We had the branch delivered in her name in an effort to keep Quinn in the dark, should he take it upon himself to inspect our packages. While rifling through other people's mail was a federal offense, as a faerie, I didn't think Quinn really cared. He'd do what he had to in order to keep me safe, which meant I needed to stay one step ahead of him at all times.

After texting Jessica, reminding her that tonight was the night, I headed outside to meet Quinn so he could take me to work.

Quinn went ape-shit after Monday night's attack, falling into a panic-fueled spiral of rage. Suspicious of anything and everything with a pulse, he'd actually threatened to beat the piss out of an elderly man who he insisted gave me the "evil eye."

It took quite a bit of reasoning on my part to convince him that not everyone on the planet was a demon in disguise, lying in wait to kidnap me. While Quinn had no problem doling out ass-whoopings to an evil monster such as the Zmeu, he wasn't about to punish innocents who had no clue about the supernatural world. He finally admitted I was probably safe with regard to the elderly and infirm. Until Quinn located the Zmeu's lair, we'd bide our time and wait for him to make another appearance, which we were both certain would happen sooner, rather than later.

According to Quinn, cloaking himself with invisibility while he watched over me at the club was the only way to go. His blue eyes darkened, filling with determination as he hovered over me protectively. "We'll take him by surprise," he said, pounding his fist into his palm as we walked up the street toward the club. "The damn shifty bastard won't know what hit him." My guy was ready to fight, and I'd never felt safer.

I cast him a sideways glare as we entered the club. "Behave yourself."

The corner of his lip curled up into a mischievous grin. "Aye. That I will, *a ghrá*, that I will."

☙

Work lingered on for a damn frigging eternity, my heart and mind focused on my secret plan to save Quinn, and not on the job at hand.

Relishing his ability to wander around like the Invisible Man, Quinn took great pleasure in tormenting my lanky boss every chance he got. Ghosting his movements throughout the club, Quinn snatched up Stan's glasses the minute he set them down.

Unable to see without his hideous specs, Stan took out two servers and a scary looking biker dude when he came out of his office and attempted to make "the rounds" as he called it. Later, when he went to sit down at the bar, his barstool shot out from beneath his butt, sending him ass first onto the floor in front of a large group of co-eds, who then mocked him mercilessly.

Unable to scold Quinn, because no one else knew of his presence, I pulled out my phone and sent him a text.

Knock it off! You're freaking him out!

My phone vibrated a few seconds later with Quinn's response.

I can't help myself. The scrawny ape makes it too damn easy.

As bad as I felt for Stan, I couldn't begrudge Quinn the small bit of happiness he'd found in pranking my dorky boss. His ability to goof around and be playful despite his impending fate warmed my heart. Quinn was like no one I'd ever come across before, and I loved him all the more for it. A small giggle escaped my lips as I waited for Gabriel to fill a drink order.

A high pitched, garbled noise coming from Stan's direction startled me, and I looked over to see him frozen in place, his eyes ten times their normal size, threatening to pop out of their sockets. His breath came in short gasps as he stared across the bar.

I craned my head to see what was frightening him so much and saw he was staring at the giant specialty drink menu that hung behind the right side of the bar. Overcome with silent laughter, I looked away for a moment so Stan wouldn't see.

Quinn, doing his level best to scare the tar out of Stan, had somehow gotten hold of the remote that controlled the electronic drink menu and had programmed "Stan, I'm coming for you," placing it on repeat so the phrase continually crawled across the screen in large, bold letters. My boss, unaware there was a devilish faerie lurking around, saw the ominous message and fled the bar in hysterics, leaving shortly thereafter, claiming stress due to overworking.

"You are incorrigible," I scolded Quinn later as he drove me home, earning an impish grin from him as he hit the gas pedal.

"Try to behave yourself," he said as I climbed out of the Mercedes. "Don't leave the apartment for any reason. If you need something, call me."

"Okay, Dad," I grumbled. I shut the door and leaned down to wave goodbye, only to see him pointing at me and then to his own eyes, letting me know he'd be watching.

"Yeah, yeah. I get it. You'll be watching me," I said, and rolled my eyes.

The corners of his mouth turned up and he blew me a kiss before I turned to walk toward my home. In the distance, I heard car tires squealing as he exited the parking lot.

Damn faerie thinks he's Jeff Gordon!

I walked into Martha's room to see her and Jessica sitting on the floor, waiting for me with several candles and the silver bough lying before them. After dumping my belongings onto Martha's bed, I took a seat on the Berber opposite my two friends, completing the circle.

"Well," I said, and exhaled. "This is it, then. Where do we begin?" I looked over to Martha, who smiled and, with a nod, turned the lights off and lit the candles simultaneously using her magic.

"Can we have some music or will that disrupt the spell? I don't think Quinn is coming back, but you never know. I don't want him to hear what we're up to."

I hated keeping such a huge secret from him, but I knew he'd never approve of what I was about to do. Quinn stubbornly believed he didn't need any help and planned on fading out of this world after five hundred long years, having finally made a connection with someone: me. Unable to even think about a world that didn't have Quinn in it, I was forced to keep my plans of crossing over into the Faerie Realm to plead with the Faerie Queen Morgana hidden from him.

Martha scrunched her face as she pondered my question. "I think that will be okay. It'll have to be something soft and mellow though, no hardcore rap or metal. Those would be too distracting." She glanced over our heads toward the docking station that sat on her nightstand and with a look of concentration sent a soft selection of classical music filling the air.

I shook my head and stared at Martha in awe. "Damn . . . can you teach me how to do that?"

"Sorry." Martha shook her head and laughed. "It's a family thing." She held out her hands, palm up. "All right, girls. I need everyone to join hands." Martha gave Jess an annoyed glare when she initially refused her hand.

"Jess." I flashed her a warning look.

Now was not the time for petty prejudices. I needed her on board. I knew she was just being protective of me where Martha was concerned, but she needed to drop the attitude. Quinn's life was on the line.

"Fine," she said with a huff.

"Whatever you do," Martha continued, "Don't break the circle. Our hands must remain joined in order for the spell to work. Now, try to relax and concentrate on the bough."

We both nodded and looked down toward the branch lying on the carpet. The dim light from the candles bounced off the bough, casting ominous shadows about the room.

My thoughts trailed off. What did the Faerie Realm look like? Would Morgana even allow my presence before her?

"Ryann, focus on the bough," Martha said pointedly.

Shamefaced, I refocused. "Sorry." I set my eyes on the large branch that lay before us as I listened to Martha begin the spell, uttering words I couldn't understand. Staring at the bough, I couldn't help but think it didn't look very magical. In fact, it looked like an ordinary branch you might find laying on the ground after a storm, and I had a hard time imagining what was so damn special about this particular piece of wood that made it worth two thousand dollars.

The answer to my unspoken question came with a brilliant flash of light. The force of it threw us back and the circle broke as we all instinctively drew our hands up to shield our eyes.

"Playing around with magic, are we?" I heard someone say with a low chuckle.

The voice was angelic, soft and lilting, pure music to my ears. I let my hands fall away as I turned and saw the most beautiful woman I'd ever laid eyes on, standing in the center of our makeshift circle.

Dressed in a luminescent white gown that accentuated her perfect figure, she was tall with golden hair that fell in long, luxurious waves down her back. Glowing, porcelain skin covered a seraphic face set with a pair of deep emerald eyes. The woman possessed a regal air about her that suggested she was someone of great importance.

"Who are you?" Martha asked, and was cut off.

"Foolish, mortal child. Silence! I am Queen Morgana, ruler of the Fae, Mistress of Avalon."

"Holy—" Jessica started to speak but was silenced when the queen shot out a hand, magically clamping her mouth shut.

Dumbstruck, I looked over to Martha, who appeared to be just as shocked. Though I most certainly was not a witch and had no experience with casting spells, I was pretty certain the queen's appearance in her room was not what she'd expected to go down.

Turning to focus her full attention on me, the queen spoke again. "You may arise, child. I wish to speak with you." As I stood from the floor, she continued. "Everyone else may leave."

Martha opened her mouth to speak. "But—"

"I said silence!" With a wave of her hand, the door to the room flew open, and with another small flick of her wrist, Jessica and Martha shot across the floor and out the door, which slammed shut behind them.

Terrified and intimidated, I stood frozen in place as Morgana floated around me, appraising my appearance with a harsh eye.

"You're much lovelier in person, I'll give you that," she said as she continued to scrutinize me.

"Thank you?" I wasn't sure if I was allowed to speak, but I didn't want to ignore what could possibly be the only compliment I'd ever receive from her.

She smiled at my reluctant answer. "Relax, my dear Ryann. I've been watching you for a while now, and I'm quite pleased with what I see."

Watching me?

Her admission took me by surprise. Why would she be watching me? I was damn sure my existence was of little importance to the Fae. Maybe she'd been keeping tabs on Quinn and was aware of my presence in his life that way?

She gave a slight nod. "Very good, Ryann. You're very smart."

What? Is she reading my mind?

I gazed at her, awestruck.

"Yes, child, I can hear all your thoughts."

A telepath? My mind reeled. How do you act around a mind reader? Did she already know everything in my head? Did she know my feelings for Quinn? Oh, God! Did she see our kiss? My stomach tightened and knots formed while a horrible nervous feeling chewed away at my gut.

She chuckled, a smooth, pleasant sound. "Relax, Ryann. I've seen everything."

I gulped. That couldn't be good.

"I've kept a watchful eye on Quinn ever since I cursed him. You can't imagine the disappointment I've had to endure over the last five hundred years, watching him continue on in his philandering ways." She shook her head. "I take no delight in the punishments I give out." She paced back and forth in front of me as she spoke, and I was once again floored by her beauty. If I were a horny male faerie, I'd probably want to seduce her, too.

The corner of her mouth turned up, and her eyes met mine for a moment as she smiled.

Aw, crap! She heard my thoughts.

Ignoring the ramblings of my inner mind, Morgana addressed me again.

"It wasn't until Quinn met you that I had any hope for him overcoming his curse. You, my child, have shown him what it means to love. Before you, he knew nothing of sacrifice, of what it means to give of yourself unconditionally. He was selfish and full of himself, and thought of women as things to be had."

Overcome his curse? There's a way to lift it?

She stopped pacing, and stood before me, lifting my chin in her hand so I was forced to meet her piercing gaze head on. Her touch was electric and full of power. "You, my precious child, have shown Quinn the meaning of love. You have unleashed a part of him I long feared did not exist, and I am most pleased."

I showed him what?

"He loves you, Ryann."

"No, he doesn't." The words just shot out of my mouth.

She met my hasty comeback with an icy glare. "Do you dare call me a liar?"

I shook my head, pasting an appropriate amount of "Oh my God, I'm sorry" on my face. I needed to watch it or I was liable to become a pile of ash on the floor. "No. Of course not." When she didn't smite me down, I figured it was safe to continue. "It's just that … well, he won't come near me. I think he has feelings for me, feelings of strong friendship, but beyond that I'm not so sure."

"He loves you," she said insistently. "I've watched him tell you so."

Huh?

An irritated frown briefly crossed over Morgana's lovely face.

My stomach lurched. My stupidity was pissing her off.

"Search your memory child, and you will remember."

I stood still in silent concentration as I racked my brain trying to remember when, if ever, Quinn had professed his love for me. Aside from his affectionate pet names for me, I came up short. I couldn't recall any verbal proclamations of love from him.

Unless… Was she was referring to the Gaelic words he'd spoken to me after our last confrontation?

I searched the queen's face, my eyes full of question, and was met with a warm smile and a nod of affirmation. I gasped.

"Really?" Could I dare to believe Quinn shared my feelings for him?

"In the past five hundred years, Quinn has formed no personal ties or bonds with anyone. He's never cared enough about anyone to avoid touching them until you."

My breath caught at her words.

"He craves your company like no other. You are the very air he breathes, and he abstains to keep what is between you pure, safe from the effects of his curse."

Tears streamed down my face as I listened to the queen affirm Quinn's love for me. My heart had never known such joy.

I searched the queen's emerald eyes and plead my case. "But he's going to die! He won't tell me why. I've got to help him. What can I do?" I sobbed. As happy as I was to finally learn of Quinn's true feelings for me, I was beyond terrified at the thought of losing him before we had a chance to start something. Life was cruel, a fact I knew all too well. I'd lost my parents as a child, and now I was going to lose Quinn.

"Don't despair, little one." She moved to stand beside me, wrapping her long slender arm around my shoulder. "You are the key to Quinn's immortality."

"I am?" I asked, a bit taken aback.

"To break the curse, Quinn must join with his soul mate before the sun goes down on the Eve of Samhain."

"Join?" I asked, confused. And then it hit me. "Oh!" A light bulb clicked on and I suddenly understood. Quinn and I would have to make love in order for him to be free of his curse. "Seriously? You mean, we could have made love ages ago and he would have been saved?" The irony of the situation was not lost on me, and the queen gave a low chuckle at my thought.

"The understanding that intimacy is best when shared with someone you truly love was hard lesson for Quinn to learn. Love, my child, is the key to unmaking his curse. Before you, he was naught but a libertine, devoid of such complex feelings. I truly believed him incapable of unconditional love." Her regal face softened, and she reached out to stroke my hair. "I'm so glad he found you, my dear. Though I was just in punishing him, I've suffered great heartache at the prospect of losing such a charismatic man. He's truly one of a kind."

A blanket of hope covered me from head to toe. "Yes," I agreed with a smile. "He is."

Then it hit me like a ton of bricks. I had to tell Quinn the good news. "Oh, God. I have to go to him. I have to tell him." I darted for the door.

"Stop!" Morgana commanded. "Take heed of my word, child. Quinn must never know I've told you there is a key to reversing his curse. No outside forces may sway his actions. In order for it to be lifted, Quinn must make the decision himself to lay with you."

"But—"

My question went unanswered. With a flash of light, Morgana disappeared just as suddenly as she had appeared.

The door to the small room flew open, revealing a shameless pair of eavesdroppers. Martha and Jess fell through the doorway, having been leaning against it heavily, trying to hear my conversation with the queen.

"Oh my God, Ryann." Jessica squealed as she jumped up from the floor and raced toward me. "He loves you." She grabbed hold of my hands and squeezed them before pulling me into a bone-smashing hug.

"Yes," I said, tears of happiness welling in my eyes. "Now, I just need to help him act on it."

chapter 17

With a mere two weeks to convince Quinn his feelings for me were the genuine article and that he needed to act on them as well, I knew I had my work cut out for me. Leaving no stone unturned, I armed myself with knowledge, turning to friends for advice, surfing the net and even shamefully resorting to perusing the latest issues of *Glamour* and *Cosmo* magazines. Sadly, there were no articles on how to seduce your hot faerie boyfriend in ten easy steps, so I was left to my own devices.

The small amount of advice I'd received from friends was all the same. To bag a hot guy, I needed to be myself, but at the same time, show said guy just what he was missing. In other words, I needed to make Quinn jealous, fiercely jealous. Then maybe, just maybe, he'd forget all about the abstaining crap and come at me like a normal boyfriend with delicious kisses, groping hands, the whole nine yards. Heaven!

Two days later, Operation Green-Eyed Monster came to life. Since I was lucky enough to have the weekend off, the girls and I decided we were in desperate need of a night on the town. Aside from our disastrous evening at the Plough when my car was stolen, we'd yet to enjoy any kind of nightlife since the semester began. A night on the town would not only serve in aiding my attempt to woo a very pigheaded Quinn, but would also provide some much-needed fun. Life felt extremely heavy as of late and we were all in desperate need of a break.

Quinn and I spent the better part of the morning together, which had left me slightly worried about the outcome of our devious little plan.

Desperate to make sure I wouldn't look like one of the founding members of Omega Mu (a fatty), I'd insisted on an early morning trip to the gym so I could get in a good workout.

Quinn, of course, accompanied me, and did his best to appear like the rest of us "normal" folk. Not everyone had the ability to pick up a bench press machine, weights and all, and twirl it around like it was a child's plaything. Playing down his supernatural strength and speed, Quinn jogged alongside me as I ran on a treadmill.

My plan was simple. I'd assault each of his senses and wear him down. Donning the tightest sports bra I could find, I flaunted what the good Lord gave me, while praying I wouldn't suffer black eyes in the process, and let my ample cleavage do all the talking. He'd referred to my hips as lovely once before, so I figured I'd flaunt the junk in my trunk as well and squeezed into the tightest pair of booty shorts I owned.

Quinn smiled at me intermittently, but made no mention of my appearance. I'd struck out.

Ugh! He's not even acting remotely interested!

My state of undress did, however, result in more than a few stares from several other males in the building, one of which had the balls to approach me and ask for my number. This, of course, did not go over well with Quinn.

He glowered at the fool, venom coating his voice. "Speak to her again and I will end you. Piss off! Eff'ing cakehole!"

"Quinn." I stared up at him, shock and anger doing a cha-cha across my heart. Seriously…it looked like his head might spin, and I wouldn't have been shocked in the least if he started spewing pea soup. Anger had him by the balls and he was a man possessed. "That was a bit harsh, don't you think?" I had no desire to speak with the bold, yet stupid stranger, but I didn't necessarily think he deserved to die for daring to converse with me.

He glared at me red-faced with a murderous look in his eyes. "No! The gacky fool had no business speaking to you. In fact, the next bloke that so much as looks in your direction is going to lose a limb! Here," he said and yanked off his t-shirt, throwing it at me as I continued my stationary jog. "Put that on."

The sight of Quinn running shirtless on a treadmill was simply too much goodness for one pair of eyes. I lost my footing as I ran and had to grab hold of the handrails to keep from tumbling backward off the machine.

I knew Quinn was muscular, but holy hell. The man was built. Every square inch of Quinn's back, shoulders, arms, chest and stomach was covered in sinewy, well-defined muscle. So beautifully made and so well proportioned was he that I wouldn't have doubted for a moment if someone told me he'd been Da Vinci's inspiration for the Vitruvian man. Quinn was sheer perfection in every possible way.

"I'm sorry to interrupt your eye-fucking session, but you still need to put that shirt on, *a ghrá*," he said with a particularly smug grin.

Ugh ... Irritating male faerie.

"*Póg mo thóin!*" I snapped and stuck my tongue out at him. Verbal throw-downs were a huge part of our relationship. Both of us passionate people by nature, I'd taken it upon myself to learn a bit of Gaelic with which to abuse him, along with a few other special phrases I was saving for just the right moment. I'd just told him to "kiss my arse."

This prompted a deep chuckle from Quinn. "I'd be more than happy to kiss it for you later, if you'd like. But for now, I'd like you to put on my shirt."

I bristled. We both knew he wouldn't be kissing any part of my anatomy. He needed to shut it. "Gah. You are so ..." I couldn't find the right words. "Damn, freaking, sexy, irritating, pushy faerie. Why don't you just dress me in a burqa and move me to Afghanistan?" I mean-mugged him, completely exasperated as I pulled his t-shirt over my head.

"Don't tempt me," he said, treating me to a smirk.

The shirt smelled like him—absolutely divine. He wasn't getting it back any time soon. I jabbed a finger in his direction. "You're not getting this shirt back. So there." That ought to show him.

"Not a problem, love." He hit the stop button and hopped off his treadmill. "I'm quite happy to show all these mollies what a real man should look like." His eyes beamed as he spoke, fully aware he was burrowing under my skin like a chigger and provoking my temper.

I slammed the stop button on my machine with a loud "humph" and hopped off of the treadmill, shooting evil darts in Quinn's direction.

"You think I'm sexy," he whispered playfully as I walked past him.

"Zip it," I grumbled at him under my breath as we made for the door.

The idiot who'd attempted to speak with me earlier must have had a death wish as he approached me yet again with a sappy smile, staring at my chest. I shot him a nasty look. Apparently, some guys never learned.

Quinn quickly got in the idiot's face making his presence known. "I thought I told you to piss off, cake boy."

I sighed. *Not again.*

I reached my arm out instinctively to pull him back until I remembered I was wearing his shirt. As tempting as his muscular chest was, I didn't want to create an even bigger problem by falling victim to his curse while out in public. Visions of me tearing my clothes off and jumping Quinn's bones danced across my conscious thoughts. I used my indoor voice instead. "Quinn."

The idiot took offense to Quinn's derogatory name. "Cake boy?" He stepped forward, ready to fight, puffing out his chest as he pushed forward against Quinn, foolishly unafraid. If he'd known just how powerful Quinn was, he would have run screaming from the building with his tail between his legs.

Not wanting to see Quinn treat the unwitting stranger to a concrete swirly, I stepped between the two, holding my arms out to prevent the fight I knew was coming.

"Quinn." I glared at him and shook my head once. Gratuitous displays of machismo were not going to fly with me. "Let it go."

With one last scowl in Quinn's direction, the idiot retreated, grumbling a low "fucking Irishman" as he left.

It wasn't until we were in his car speeding to his house that I spoke again.

"Why do you do that? We're living in the twentieth century, Quinn. Women are allowed to speak to whomever they choose."

The muscles in his jaw clenched, and I heard him take a deep breath through his nose. He was silent for a bit, focusing on the road as we sped through the back streets of town toward his home. He glanced at me, then back at the road. "I'm sorry, *mo chrói*. I can't help myself. When I see another man near you, I go crazy. I can't stomach the thought of another bloke looking at you." He looked at me again, his eyes tender and full of emotion. "And when they speak to you, I just want to tear them apart."

My heart swelled at his admission.

He's jealous. Maybe the plan for tonight will work.

I sat grinning from ear to ear. I couldn't help myself. I was fiercely jealous over Quinn and hated that every woman who came within a twenty-foot radius of him all but swooned on sight. Women threw themselves at his feet everywhere we went, regardless of my presence. It was heartwarming to know he felt the same about me.

"I completely understand," I said, eyeballing his naked chest. If I thought I could get away with it, I'd carry a drool bib with me whenever we were together. I squashed my lusty thoughts and continued. "I feel the same way when women throw themselves at you. Do you think I like it when some over-processed floozy tries to slip you her number while I'm standing next to you?"

A low rumble emanated from his chest. "No, I can't imagine you do."

"Damn straight, I don't. But you don't see me threatening to shank them either, do you?"

My last comment brought about a laugh, and the tension that filled the air vanished, serving as a prime example as to the nature of our relationship. With both of us being very impassioned, we fought hard, and we loved hard. Or, at least, I hoped we would be loving hard, and soon.

Once we reached his house, I made myself comfortable in his large kitchen. I plucked an orange from a large glass bowl filled with fruit and sat on one of the expensive barstools as I watched him prepare to cook me breakfast. I found it completely sexy that he felt at home in a kitchen and was all the more besotted with him for it. He looked damn hot, he kicked major ass, and he made a mean omelet to boot. The man was heaven-sent.

As I peeled away the thick flesh of my orange, I recalled one of the articles I'd read the previous day about men being voyeuristic, and how they enjoyed watching women eat sensually. Once peeled, I gently pulled apart a piece of the succulent fruit and waited for Quinn to look up from what he was doing.

Once he'd finished chopping whatever it was he was making, he glanced up at me with a smile.

"Mmm ... I love oranges." I took a large bite of the luscious fruit, letting the juices dribble down my chin. I gave him the best sexy stare I could manage, looking at him through my lashes, while simultaneously trying to chew the fruit without looking like a pig. Being sexy and alluring was hard work. And I apparently wasn't very good at it as Quinn burst into hysterics.

"Quit trying to seduce me with food, *a ghrá*."

I chucked the rest of the orange down with a frown, while Quinn resumed his chopping. Whoever wrote those magazine articles was full of crap! I had about as much sex appeal as a wet paper bag.

Sweaty, sticky, horny and incensed, I left the kitchen and headed up the stairs in search of a shower. I felt a bit antsy at first, with the idea of hosing down in his house, but got over my unease quickly. If I planned on getting pelvic with him in the near future, a quick shower in his bathroom was really no big deal. I wandered down the long hallway until I came to what looked like a master suite.

This must be Quinn's room.

His room was much like the rest of the house. It contained massive amounts of electronic gadgetry, from a huge wide screen television mounted on the wall across from where he slept to a giant entertainment center that housed an impressive looking stereo.

His massive bed was unmade. Draped in black silk sheeting that looked beyond luxurious. Delicious heat spread forth from my center out toward my extremities as vivid images of Quinn and myself, naked and writhing between said sheets, bombarded my consciousness. I wanted nothing more than to dive headfirst into the satiny goodness, but held back due to my desperate need for a shower.

Sweaty from my workout and sticky from my debacle with the fruit, I wandered into Quinn's bathroom intent on cleaning up. I couldn't very well seduce him if I stank.

If Quinn's kitchen was impressive, his master bathroom was nothing short of spectacular. It was bigger than my bedroom, and I stood in awe for a moment at its grandeur. What drew me in the most was the giant shower and tub that took up the entire wall opposite where I stood. The shower, entirely encased in glass, contained three showerheads and had a rather large ledge on which to sit.

Or do other things on…Ack! Get your mind out of the gutter, Ryann.

The tub was big enough to fit a small army and was equally as swanky, as it filled from several spouts in the ceiling. I walked over to the shower and turned on the water, all three showerheads blasting toward its center. As the water heated, I took a chance on a nearby closet and was pleasantly surprised when I found it stocked with several plush towels.

After undressing, I stepped into the lavish enclosure and moaned at the wonderful sensation of the scalding hot water pouring over my body. I took my time washing away the remnants of the morning's workout and enjoyed the feeling of three showerheads rinsing me simultaneously.

A girl could get used to this!

As I rinsed the last remnants of shampoo from my hair, a familiar tingling sensation peppered my skin, stealing my breath away with its intensity. And my kitty…yeah, it went up in flames. *Quinn.* Normally, my first instinct would have been to freak out and cover up if I knew someone was watching me in the shower. However, knowing it was Quinn brought on an entirely different response. My breath caught, and a wonderful, erotic chill shot up my spine. A deep aching need sent a rush of moisture pooling between my thighs, hardening my nipples, setting my skin ablaze. My body reacted to his presence before my mind even registered he was there. It was clear my flesh needed him as much as the rest of me.

I turned to see Quinn standing in the doorway. His eyes were dark and hungry as he took in the sight of me naked and wet. His chest moved up and down, each heady breath heavier than the last. His expression was one of extreme hunger and I wanted nothing more than for him to come at me hard and ravish every inch of me with his hands, his mouth.

Flashes of my shower fantasy raced through my mind. I longed for him to cast away his decision to refrain from touching me and climb into the shower, bringing my daydream to life.

I stepped forward, placing one hand on the foggy glass. It was an invitation. *Come to me,* it said. *I need you. I want you.* My body cried out, dying for his touch. My mind screamed the words I couldn't say out loud. *I'm desperate for you. I want you in me. Touch. Take. Fill. I'm yours, eternally.*

Quinn strode forward, his sapphire eyes locked with mine, until he stood just before me. He placed his hand over mine, nothing but a thin pane of glass between us. Silence and longing filled the room. The intensity of it threatened to shatter not only the glass, but also me along with it.

The raw look of desire in his eyes was nearly my undoing. "In all my life," he said, "never, have I seen anything more beautiful. There are no words, *a ghrá.* You take my very breath away." He leaned forward with a pained look on his face, closed his eyes and placed his forehead against the glass. A loud groan came from deep within his throat and he hit his head against the glass several times. "You're killing me," he moaned.

Breathless from the intensity of the moment, I didn't know what to say. "I'm sorry."

He shook his head and chuckled as he reached for a towel. "No," he said, draping the soft terry over the gold handle on the glass door. "No, you're not. Get dressed. Breakfast is ready." He left before I could protest.

He was right, of course. I wasn't sorry. I wanted Quinn like I'd never wanted anyone before. I was more than ready to hand over my virginity to him on a silver platter. If only he wasn't so stubborn! Every man had his breaking point. I'd just have to find his.

I stepped out of the shower and toweled off, surprised to see Quinn had left a clean t-shirt and pair of sweats for me on the tile counter. If I was going to have any hope of seducing him before sundown on the eve of Samhain, I was going to have to pull out all the stops. I smiled as I thought about our upcoming evening out.

He'll never know what hit him.

chapter 18

U gh." I tossed another shirt onto the growing pile of clothes at the foot of my bed. "I have no idea what I should wear." Indecision was my worst enemy at the moment. I struggled with what to wear on a good day. Trying to find an outfit that would woo Quinn into laying hands on me was proving to be a daunting task.

Jessica plucked a shiny silver tank off the floor and tossed it on the bed. "It's not like you don't have a ton of clothes to choose from, Ryann. There's got to be something in that closet of yours that will wow Quinn."

The three of us, Martha included, decided to get ready for our night out together and were digging through my small storage space, trying to find something for me to wear. Loud music from my iPhone blared throughout the room to ensure Quinn wouldn't overhear our plan. I didn't think he planned on lurking about the building, but one could never be sure with him. Precautionary measures needed to be taken.

"I can't take it anymore. Here…"Jessica crossed the small room, pushed me aside and began digging through my clothes. "What about this?" She pulled out a glittery black halter-top. It had an extremely low back and a plunging neckline, and was definitely one of my sexier tops.

"Ooh…I forgot I had this. It's perfect," I said, giving her a high five and a grin.

She smiled in return and pointed toward the black fabric. "That top will have him standing at attention faster than you can say 'didgeridoo.'"

I scrunched up my face in confusion. "Didgeri-what?"

"Never mind," Jessica said, swatting her hand through the air. "You need something hot to wear with that shirt. What about a skirt?" She held up one of my shorter denim minis. "This just screams easy access. Pair it with some hooker heels and you'll have his tongue lolling out his mouth."

I stared at her with a look of mock horror. "Jess! First off, who are you and what have you done with my shy, sweet best friend? Secondly, I want to seduce him, yes. I do not, however, want to look like some ho-baggity freak. I think the top is as daring as I want to go." There was something to be said for the old adage about leaving some things to the imagination. And besides, Quinn had already had an eyeful of my goods.

Jess frowned. "I'm still your sweet BFF. I'm just tired of letting everything scare me. Tired of holding back all the time, trying to do what's proper, you know?" She pointed to the skirt. "I still think you'd look hot in the skirt." She rifled through my closet looking for something else. "Here," she hollered over her shoulder, and tossed a pair of jeans at me. "These are perfect. No complaining."

I groaned. "You're killing me, Jess. I can't wear these. They barely cover my ass." I shook my head in protest. I'd purchased the jeans earlier in the year, but had yet to wear them, as the rise was so low they barely covered my girlie bits. I wasn't keen on strangers looking at my burning bush, no matter how well I kept it groomed.

"That's the whole point, isn't it?" Jessica stood with her hands on her hips, looking at me like I was crazy. "You want to give him a taste of what he's missing. Those jeans scream sexy."

"He's already seen what he's missing," I said and shrugged.

Martha looked up from her magazine with wide eyes but remained silent.

"What did you just say?" Jessica held up one hand and burned me with an intense glare. "What exactly has he seen, Ryann? What are you not telling us?"

A blush crept over my cheeks as I thought back to earlier in the day when Quinn had watched me shower. Aside from the mind-blowing kiss we'd shared, that morning's voyeuristic escapade was the single most erotic thing I'd ever experienced, and Quinn hadn't even touched me. I knew he wanted me. I saw it in his eyes, and in the way he carried himself. I knew he loved me. Queen Morgana had confirmed that herself.

Love and desire were not the problem. Fear was. Afraid of losing the only person he'd ever connected with, Quinn refused to do anything that might jeopardize the only real relationship he'd ever had. Some way, somehow, I needed to help Quinn move past his fear so we could be together. Hopefully, my plan of driving him mad with jealousy would set things in motion. I was running out of ideas.

Jess furrowed her brows after I told her what happened in Quinn's bathroom, took a deep breath and let out a heavy sigh. "He's more pigheaded than I thought." She pointed at the denim in question and then looked at me. "I'd go commando in those jeans if I were you."

"Commando?" My jaw dropped in horror. "Jess."

She gave me a pointed look and shrugged. "I'm just sayin'," she grumbled to herself and sat down onto my bed.

I looked over to Martha, who sat quietly on the floor reading a magazine. She looked up, sensing my gaze and shook her head. "Don't look to me for fashion advice. Do I look like I know how to dress sexy?"

Clad in a short, red plaid mini, a black pleated button down, with a black corseted belt over it, black tights and her trademark Doc's, Martha did look sexy in a completely different way. Though I didn't share her sense of style, I had to admit she looked pretty in her own way.

"I think you look great."

She treated me to shy smile. "Thanks. I can help you with your shoes, though. If you'd like me to, that is."

"My shoes?" I shot her a look of confusion. Did girlfriend think she was Geppetto?

She walked over to my closet and pulled out a pair of black flats. "Just watch." She waved her hands over the shoes and, with a bright flash of light, my simple flats transformed into a wicked looking pair of Docs.

"I don't really know designer stuff, so if you want something specific, you'll need to show me a picture of what you want."

"Oh, snap!" I said in total awe. "Wicked cool."

Jessica raced over to my laptop, which sat on my desk. Wasting no time, she brought it to the edge of my bed while she logged on. "I know the perfect pair of shoes for that outfit. Look here." She beckoned me over to where she sat while Martha looked on.

I looked over her shoulder and saw a stunning pair of Manolo Blahniks. Made of black leather, the cut-out sandals were adorned with three silver rings and had four- inch heels. The shoes screamed "vampy" and were the perfect addition to my sultry ensemble.

"Ooh … they're sling-backs too. Perfect," I said and looked over to Martha. "Can you conjure these?"

She nodded with a smile. "You bet."

"You are my freaking hero." I motioned toward my black flats she'd already worked her mojo on, beckoning for her to do it again.

"Shoot. You think you can glamour me a bigger set of boobs?" Jessica asked. She was doing her best to mend fences with Martha, and I cast her a look of approval.

Martha eyed Jess for a moment, probably shocked at her continued attempts to make amends, before answering. "Yeah, actually, I can."

Jessica's eyes grew wide. "No. Way," she squealed, and shot off the edge of the bed like a rocket, sticking her chest out.

For a minute I was tempted to have her zap me a size two ass, but changed my mind. Quinn would notice, and that wasn't something I wanted to explain.

An hour later we were all dressed and ready for a rockin' night on the town. Jess decided to sport a denim mini, insisting that one of us needed to show some leg. She paired it with a dark blue, backless top that accented her pale skin and a pair of black boots.

"Who needs *Dr. 90210*? We've got Martha," she said while admiring her newly glamorized breasts. Normally a small B cup, Jessica sported some very full C's thanks to our witchy friend.

"Okay," I said and took a deep breath. "This is it. Operation Green-Eyed Monster is a go. Let's do this." Nervous, I looked over to Jessica. There was no need for me to speak, she knew me well enough to know just how anxious I was about our evening out.

"Relax, Ryann. You look great. When Quinn sees how hot you look and how other guys respond to that hotness, he's going to break. I just know it."

I took a deep breath and sighed. "I hope so."

Because I have no idea what else to do.

"Bloody hell!" Quinn grimaced as we walked toward the entrance of Fire and Ice. The loud bass thumping of the club's music floated through the air. Legions of scantily dressed women flooded the establishment, gawking at Quinn as they passed by, drooling over him as though he were standing alone, and not with three women.

Quinn shot me a pleading look.

"It'll be okay," I said, smiling. "Trust me."

I didn't go commando for nothing.

"Come on, Quinn," Jessica said. "Loosen up a bit."

Quinn zeroed in on Jessica, his eyes narrowed and a frown on his face. "Something's different. You changed something, yes?"

"I … uh … I … nothing's different." She stammered nervously, while flashing me a look of panic.

I didn't think she wanted to explain her temporarily enlarged breasts were the difference in her appearance, so I threw her a lifeline. "Tonight is all about letting go and having fun, which is something we all are in desperate need of. Too much work, not enough play. C'mon, let's go." I tried to be as encouraging as I could, hoping to ease the tension I plainly saw Quinn trying to hide.

He was on edge about not locating the Zmeu's lair. Believing we only had just over two weeks left together, Quinn would rather have spent the evening elsewhere, just the two of us. To be honest, I would have preferred the same. But given his stubborn refusal to get physical with me, I had no choice but to pull out all the stops and trigger the jealous side of his nature. It was underhanded and low. But hey … a girl had to do what a girl had to do.

Of course, he wasn't privy to my plan, or the fact that my roomies were in on it, as well. In fact, Quinn had no idea my friends knew his true identity. I hated keeping him in the dark, but if I had any hope of saving him from his stubborn self, secrecy was not only necessary, it was essential. I looked up at him, giving him the most encouraging smile I could muster.

Quinn didn't appear encouraged. In fact, he looked like a man walking toward certain doom. I knew he dreaded the unwanted attention that was sure to come as soon as he entered the building. Women went after him like strung out crack-whores looking for a fix. By accompanying us to the club he was practically throwing himself into a lion's den. But instead of facing savage predatory cats, he'd be facing a hoard of oversexed gutter sluts, none of whom he had any interest in. I didn't know which was worse.

He heaved a sigh. "Very well, then."

I leaned in and whispered in his ear. "Don't worry, I'll protect you."

"And I you, *a ghrá*. And I you," he said as we entered the club.

It felt odd entering Fire and Ice as a patron and not an employee. I brushed off the urge to grab a tray and start taking drink orders.

Packed to capacity, the club was very dark, and very crowded. I felt slightly claustrophobic as we wove through the crowd, having spotted a table at the far end of the room. I'd never seen the place so busy.

Quinn navigated in and out of the sea of single women who made up ninety percent of the crowd, keeping me close the entire way. His hand rested on the small of my back, and although our flesh never came into contact, I still felt an incredible electric pull between us. We were like two live wires, each of us charged, full of desire, but somehow incomplete. Once those wires came together, sparks flew, electricity flowed and magic happened.

Figures he'd find an area that was covered to touch.

I'd purposely worn the halter top because it bared quite a bit of skin and was more than a little disappointed when he found a "safe place" to touch me. Quinn was a tough nut to crack, and I had my work cut out for me.

Once we reached the table, Jessica dropped her purse and started jumping in place. "Oh! I love this song. Let's dance." She grabbed hold of me by the arm and pulled me toward the dance floor.

I wrangled my wrist out of her grasp and shook my head. "Sorry, girlie. I'm sitting this one out."

With a shrug and a "pssh," she disappeared into the massive crowd of dancing bodies, leaving Martha, Quinn and me alone at the table.

Quinn leaned in close, his delicious, masculine smell sending my thighs up in flames. "I don't like this. It's too crowded. There is an overwhelming sense of evil in here, and it's coming at me from all directions."

I stiffened. "You think the Zmeu is here?" A Mack truck filled with panic ran me down at the thought of my demon stalker hiding somewhere in the crowd.

"Possibly. Along with a few other buggers as well." He placed his finger to his lips and looked over to Martha, who sat staring out into the crowd. He didn't want her to hear our whispered conversation.

A few others?

My mouth felt dry. "Others?"

"Aye, love," he said and pointed toward the bar. "You see those two shites dressed in the black leather jackets?"

I nodded.

"Vampires," he huffed, and scowled with disgust.

"Vampires?" I shouted over the loud din. "Really?"

From the corner of my eye, I saw Martha's head snap toward me after my outburst, her brows furrowed. Was she afraid of vampires? Why I hadn't given any thought to the mythical, bloodsucking beasts before, I wasn't sure. I was sure, however, that I didn't want anything to do with them. One evil stalker was enough for me. I didn't need any more, thank you.

"Goddammit, *a ghrá*," he said, casting me a fierce shut-the-fuck-up glare. "Could you maybe shout a bit louder so the rest of the patrons can hear?"

My hand shot up to my mouth. "Sorry," I said through my fingers.

I looked over my shoulder to where Martha sat, and though she still appeared to be looking out into the crowd, acting bored, I knew different. I saw her chewing on the inside of her lip, something I recently learned she did when she was nervous. Upon closer inspection, I saw her eyes darting through the crowd in the direction of the bar.

What is up with that?

Deciding we'd sat long enough, I hopped out of my seat and stood in front of Quinn.

"Let's dance."

Quinn snorted. "Do I look like the type that dances?"

"Well … I …" I didn't want to agree with him out loud. He *didn't* look like the type that danced. He looked, well, he looked intimidating. With muscle on top of muscle, Quinn looked like someone capable of reducing you to a bloody stain on the floor. He was deadly and sexy all rolled into one, and I suddenly felt flushed as I stood there gawking at him.

"Only cake boys and mollies participate in this type of dancing. Real men dance between the sheets."

"So teach me to dance between the sheets." I leaned forward, treating Quinn to a perfect view of my cleavage. I'd forgone a bra, something I never do. My bodacious tatas were enjoying a bit of freedom.

Quinn stared at my chest like a starving man at an all-you-can-eat-buffet, before closing his eyes and taking a deep breath. He sat silent for a moment and then opened his eyes to look into mine. "You know I cannot. Why do you torture me so?" His normally smooth voice sounded strained and I felt a pang of guilt for flaunting myself in front of him, though I knew I had no other choice. I needed him to take the bait.

"Yes, you can. You love me. Trust in that love, Quinn. Believe in me, in us," I whispered.

I watched as he warred with his desire to connect with me on a physical level. He believed if he gave in he would not only lose me to madness, but also die with me no longer remembering him.

I knew the moment he found his resolve, as his jaw clenched and his face became hard and serious.

"No, I won't take that chance. I can't lose you."

I whirled around with a groan. *Stubborn faerie.*

"C'mon, Martha, let's dance," I shouted over the loud music. I grabbed her by the hand, pulling her into the crowded abyss. Quinn's fiery gaze burned a hole through me as we wove in and out the massive sea of bodies, looking for a place to dance.

"So what's up with you and vampires?" I didn't see any point in wasting time. Martha had looked visibly disturbed when Quinn and I discussed the vamps at the bar, and I wanted to know why.

Martha met my eyes with an icy stare. "A vampire killed my mother."

Way to stick your foot in it, Ryann.

"Oh, God, Martha. I'm so sorry. I shouldn't have asked." I felt like an idiot. Not only was I completely incapable of seducing the love of my life, but I was also a horrible friend to boot. I groveled some more. "I'm so sorry."

"It's okay, Ryann. Really, relax," she said, trying to reassure me. "It happened when I was a little girl. I don't remember much really, just his face, and the face of the vamp that was with him. I've been on the hunt ever since, searching for the monster that took my mother from me so I can kill him." Her voice was cold and determined, and I knew she was deadly serious. Martha would have her revenge.

I drew Martha into a hug in the center of the dance floor. I knew what it felt like to go through life without parents. It sucked ass, and I felt bad that she'd suffered such a terrible loss. "I'm so sorry, Martha. I'm here for you. Any time you want to talk, okay?"

I felt her nod as she returned my embrace, and in that moment I knew we'd be friends for life.

"Oh, hell yeah. Girl-on-girl. Kiss! Kiss!"

We broke apart to see a large group of idiots staring at us, beer in hand and eyes wide.

I heard a familiar voice shout, "Shut up, Tyler."

The idiot from the gym emerged from the center of the band of creeps and strode over to me, a sheepish look on his plastered face. "Sorry about my friends. They're a bunch of tools. Wanna dance?" He held out his hand, and smiled at me with glassy eyes. Idiot Boy was no Quinn, but he had two legs and a pulse and would do the job when it came to making my stubborn faerie jealous.

I looked over to Martha, who was already hightailing it toward the bar. "I'm gonna go check it out," she hollered over her shoulder and disappeared into the crowd.

"Well, since my friend just left me, I guess I'm free. Sure, I'll dance with you." I took his sweaty hand, and followed him deeper onto the dance floor.

I felt Quinn's eyes on me, even as we moved, and I knew he'd left the sanctuary of our table to keep a watchful eye on me.

I'll give him an eyeful. Stubborn, irritating faerie.

Along with zero interpersonal skills, Idiot Boy also lacked rhythm, which was sort of necessary when dancing. While I swayed my hips to the beat of the music, he flailed around like a dead fish, thrusting his pelvis forward like a maniac. His frenzied air pumping continued until he pulled me forcefully against him so that my back pressed up against his chest. For a minute, I worried he might try and rub his junk against my backside, but I relaxed a bit when he settled down and grabbed hold of my hips, and swayed us side to side along with the music. Maybe I still had a chance to make Quinn jealous after all.

Closing my eyes, I raised my arms so they circled Idiot Boy's neck, letting my head rest against his shoulder as we moved. It was wrong of me to take advantage of him, dancing so sensually, but I didn't know what else to do.

As the music drove on, I continued grinding my hips against Idiot Boy, giving myself over to the music. I stiffened when his hands traveled from my hips, blazing a trail up my sides, his fingertips brushing against the sides of my breasts. That was most definitely not what I was looking for.

"Get your fucking hands off of her, boy." My eyes shot open to see Quinn standing in front of the Idiot and me, his eyes wild, his fists clenched, anger rolling off him in spades.

My arms dropped to my sides instantly and I stepped forward, placing space between Idiot Boy and me. I wanted to make Quinn jealous, yes, but I didn't want the poor boy to die in the process.

"Quinn," I said, doing my best to try and calm him with my eyes. "We were just dancing."

"Yeah, relax, bro. It's all good." The Idiot was blissfully unaware he was about to become a broken bag of bones.

"Touch her again," Quinn said as he pointed to the Idiot, "and I will tear you the fuck apart and make sure no one finds the pieces."

I stepped forward and got in his face. "Quinn. You can't just … Hey!" He grabbed me by the waist, threw me over his shoulder and stormed off the dance floor, depositing me in my seat at our table.

"What the hell did you do that for?"

"I know what you're doing, *a ghrá*, and it won't work. We're leaving." He picked up a bottle of beer that sat on the table and downed it.

"But I don't want to leave."

"Too bad. I've endured this cesspool long enough. I refuse to sit and watch you be groped by worthless idiots. I refuse to share you."

"Share me?" I shouted as I shot out of my seat. "You won't even touch me. At least Idiot Boy over there thinks I'm sexy. Unlike you, he's not afraid of getting physical. Maybe I should go back and find him."

The bottle of beer that Quinn gripped shattered in his hand. "Enough!"

"Hey," Jessica shouted as she hurried over to where we stood. "What's going on? Why are you two fighting?"

"We're leaving," Quinn snapped. "Now."

Wide eyed, Jessica nodded and grabbed her purse from the table. "Yeah, okay. I just need to hit the little girl's room before we go. Ryann?"

I grabbed my purse and attempted to follow when Quinn stepped in front of me, halting my movement. "Where do you think you're going?"

"I have to pee, Quinn. It's a bodily function that I have no control over. I'm not holding it, sorry." I sidestepped him, treating him to a nasty glare. I followed Jess toward the restroom, Quinn's eyes burning a hole into my bared back the entire way.

The restrooms were located in the very back of the club, at the end of a long hallway. Staying close together, we hurried into the crowded bathroom to take care of business.

"What happened?" Jessica asked as we washed our hands.

"Not now," I said, fighting back tears. "If I talk about it now, I'll just lose it." My grandiose plan to seduce Quinn failed miserably and I was dangerously close to falling into the shiteous realm of hysteria.

She nodded and we exited the restroom in silence.

I'd taken all of two steps into the hallway when I saw Stan round the corner, his eyes cast downward to the floor.

"Hi, Stan," I called out, anxious to catch his attention.

Stan looked up from the floor with a dangerous smile on his face, and I gasped. Two soulless black eyes stared at me, chilling me to the bone.

"Ryann," Jessica screamed, but was quickly silenced.

With a crushing backhand blow, Stan sent Jessica flying backward. She crashed into the nearby wall and fell to a lifeless heap on the floor.

Stan stood inches from me in the empty hallway. I froze, a mixture of shock and horror gluing my feet to the floor. My demon stalker, the vicious creature who haunted not only my dreams, but my every waking thought, was none other than my lanky, bumbling boss, Stan.

"No—" I opened my mouth to scream Quinn's name but everything went black.

chapter 19

Over the years, I'd heard endless accounts of what it was like to face death. Some said significant events that happened in your life came barreling into the forefront of your mind, while others merely saw flashes of their loved ones. Some felt an overwhelming sense of peace, as if some higher power controlled the outcome of their situation, guiding them to safety, yet others said they'd never felt more alone.

Me? I felt angry. Crazier than a shit-house-rat. Actually, anger didn't even cut it. I was a ticking time-bomb filled with enough rage to make an atom bomb look like nothing more than a firecracker. I wasn't going down without a fight. To hell with that, there was too much at stake. I was not about to lose Quinn when there was still time to save him. I needed to get away from Stan, or the Zmeu, or whatever the hell the thing was, at all costs.

I woke up a few seconds after blacking out to find myself being dragged out the back entrance of Fire and Ice by the demon who still wore a Stan suit.

"What do you want from me? Let me go." I screamed as loud as I could, kicking and punching, doing everything I could to try and escape the demon's iron grasp.

The evil dirtbag looked down at me with its soulless black eyes and let out a ghastly chuckle. "It is you I want, Ryann. Such a pretty little gem, I find I cannot be without you. I must have you as my own. You are mine," it hissed with a baleful voice. "Cease your screaming, for it will not save you."

"I don't belong to anyone, you demon freak." With a deep breath, I screamed as loud as I possibly could. "Quinn!"

An icy, cold hand clamped over my mouth, its clammy, leathery skin squelching my cries for help. "I said, silence!"

Once outside, the Zmeu scooped me into its bony arms and took flight, launching itself from the darkness of the alley behind the club, into the cool night air.

Petrified with fear, I clenched my eyes shut and curled into myself with my arms covering my face. I didn't want to see the Zmeu, and I sure as hell didn't want to look down. I had problems flying in commercial airliners due to my fear of heights and lack of control, so I wasn't about to take in the sights while being stolen away by some underworld freak.

The cold night air ripped across my body as we flew through the air, freezing me to the bone. My body shook and spasmed, fighting to keep warm.

"Cease your incessant wiggling!"

"I…c…can't help it, I'm f…freezing." My teeth slammed together painfully as I spoke, and I was certain I would die of hypothermia if I didn't get out of the cold.

We flew for what seemed like an eternity. The wind that tore through me slowed to a breeze and moments later we were on the ground. I opened my eyes to find we were standing in an industrial area near an old abandoned warehouse.

"Where have you taken me, you ugly-ass bastard?" My teeth continued to clank together as I struggled to free myself from its hideous clutches.

"Somewhere where your faerie lover will never find you."

The Zmeu set me on my feet, and I struggled, somehow managing to twist my body so I faced it. I grabbed hold of its shoulders and brought my knee up hard into its groin, causing it to double over with a shriek of pain.

I wasn't gonna waste time; I turned and got the hell outta Dodge, running as fast as my legs would carry me, across the pavement toward the front of the abandoned building. I made it all of fifty feet before the demon appeared in front of me, having swooped down from above.

Enraged by my escape attempt, the Zmeu raced forward and clutched me by the neck. Lifting me several feet off the ground, the demon threw me sideways, sending me flying into an old Dumpster.

A loud cracking sound rang through the night as pain the likes of which I'd never felt before shot up and down my left arm. I lay in a heap on the cold pavement. I tried to lift myself up and fell back, crying out from the pain. A terrible wave of dizziness came over me as I looked down at my broken arm. A cold sweat broke out over my skin and my stomach churned, threatening to unload its contents. Twisted like a jigsaw puzzle piece, the lower half of my arm stuck out in odd angles, my hand hanging lifeless from the wrist down.

I rolled over and threw up, the force of my heaving causing more pain to shoot up and down my arm.

The Zmeu hissed. "Tut, tut, little one. Look what you made me do. Do not force my hand again, or I will have no choice but to damage you further." Kneeling down, the creature took hold of my broken appendage, inspecting it carefully before snapping the broken bones into place. The force of the snap sent a shockwave of pain throughout my entire body. A bloodcurdling scream ripped through my lungs, and I once again fell into unconsciousness.

Unsure of how long I was out, I woke and found myself lying on a broken down couch in the center of what was, no doubt, the abandoned warehouse I'd been taken to. The building was huge and largely empty save a few metal barrels that were strewn throughout. A rusted out staircase rose from the floor on the far side of the abandoned repository, leading to what once must have been an office of sorts. The cold night air billowed in through several broken windows that sat high above me and served as an entrance for a family of crows I heard fluttering and squawking.

I looked down to see my broken arm, cradled against my chest, a makeshift splint holding it in place. Taking care to not place any pressure on it, I lifted myself into a sitting position. Careful or not, my arm still hurt like hell, and I cried out in agony.

"Silence. Enough of your sniveling."

My head shot around to see the demon glaring at me from across the room. Standing on some type of workbench, it paced back and forth as if it were nervous.

You should be nervous, freak. When Quinn gets his hands on you, you're dead.

"You broke my arm," I shouted, my voice filled with hatred for the despicable creature. "It hurts!"

"Pain is merely weakness leaving your body. Embrace it, for it will only make you stronger." He leaped from the workbench, sailing through the air, and landed in front of me with an evil grin smeared across its face.

I flinched, turning my face away as it moved to touch me. This only served to make it angrier.

"Do not turn away from me." It grabbed hold of my chin, forcing my head around so I had no choice but to look into its evil face. Except it was Stan that looked at me. The face of my goofy looking boss stared down at me with a mix of malice and dominance, his Coke-bottle glasses gone, his eyes a lifeless obsidian.

I whimpered. "I can't look at you. You make me sick."

"As you wish." He cast an evil sneer at me. There was a brilliant flash of light so intense my eyes felt like they were being singed. Covering my face with my good arm, I cowered on the dilapidated couch as the demon shifted forms just inches away from me. The horrible, crunching sound of bones snapping and changing filled the air.

"There now," a familiar voice called out to me coolly.

No!

"No," I screamed. "Not her. You can't be her. No!" Standing before me with a sinister smile, was the exact likeness of my best friend, Jessica. Once again, her eyes were replaced by two empty, black holes.

"Are you not comforted by the likeness of your best friend?" It hissed as it paced back and forth in front of me. She…it…whatever the hell it was, glanced over its shoulder every so often before turning its attention back to me.

Yes, be afraid. Quinn will come after me and when he does, you'll be sorry.

Filled with disgust, I turned my face away from the demon once again, knowing my refusal to look at it would piss it off but good.

"No," I said, my voice filling with contempt. "I am not comforted. I'm disgusted."

Jessica's voice echoed off the walls of the empty building as the demon shrieked, and once again shifted its form with a blinding flash of light.

"Perhaps I've been going about this wrong. Maybe you prefer the face of your faerie lover?"

Quinn's voice filled the room and my traitorous body felt drawn to it, letting out an involuntary gasp, though my mind knew it was an illusion. That was, most certainly, not the voice of my soul mate. I shook my head like a madwoman, smashing my face against the moldy fabric of the beaten down couch, and stubbornly refusing to look upon the demon's face.

The sofa shifted and I felt its cold presence leaning toward me as I sat hunched over and cowering. Its cool, rancid breath tickled the back of my neck.

"Look at me," he whispered coolly.

"No," I screamed and pressed my face further into the rank fabric.

"Look at me." The voice that screeched into my ear was terrifying. Though on the surface it sounded like Quinn, it held an undertone of pure evil Quinn's voice could never possess, and it chilled me to the bone.

"Never," I cried out, tears spilling freely down my face. It would take nothing short of an act of God to get me to look at the Zmeu while it wore the face of the man I loved. The idea of seeing two gaping black holes where Quinn's vibrant blue eyes should have been made me sick to my stomach.

Bile shot up into my mouth, choking me. Gasping, I struggled to pull precious air into my lungs as I sobbed. A pair of cold hands wrenched me from the refuge of the musty sofa, forcing my head and body around, leaving me no place to hide.

"You will look at me, my pet, and you will love me, one way or another." The demon clamped down onto my broken arm, sending waves of searing pain throughout my body.

I cried out in agony and my eyes shot open to see an evil replica of my true love sneering at me with a nefarious grin. Not once had my Quinn looked at me with such malevolence. The sight of the demon's poisonous grin sent me reeling, but it was his eyes that shoved me off the deep end.

Gone were the deep sapphire blue eyes that brightened Quinn's godlike face. Gone were the eyes that so thoroughly bewitched me, that captured my heart and filled my soul. Dark, lifeless orbs devoid of any semblance of goodness stared at me now, and it was more than I could bear.

"No," I screamed. "You are not him. I will never love you. You are nothing to me. Nothing!" Filled with uncontrollable anger, I spat at the demon and swung my good arm back to hit it.

The Zmeu deflected my blow with ease and sent me flying over the back of the sofa with a powerful backhand blow to the head.

I held the side of my face that throbbed with my good hand, as I lay dizzy on the cold cement floor. Another flash of light exploded throughout the room, and then a low, sinister chuckle made its way around the couch toward me.

"Foolish child. I gave you the chance to look upon a familiar face to ease your transition into your new life, and you spat upon me. I will coddle you no more. You will look upon my true self, and you will love me for all eternity."

My right eye swelled shut from the beating I received at the demon's bitter hand. I struggled to see the dark figure that stalked forward, its labored breaths bouncing off the walls of the warehouse. As the evil freak came closer, I gasped, wracked with revulsion. The same devilish being from my dream the month before looked down at me.

Bathed in black, the Zmeu towered over me. Black, spidery veins covered his waxen skin and crept across his face and neck, somewhat obscured by his long, greasy, ebony locks. A mouthful of razor sharp, jagged teeth smiled down at me as he spoke.

"Look upon the face of your new lover, my pet, for you are to be mine, both in body and soul. You will be my bride and will reside with me for all of eternity."

The Zmeu moved to lower himself over me, and I screamed with every ounce of air and strength I had left in me.

"Quinn!"

The demon's mouth hovered just inches from my own when the double doors that led into the warehouse exploded into the large room with a deafening bang. The walls of the structure shook violently, and the few glass windows that remained imploded into the room, sending a shower of glass raining down into the room.

"Faerie!" The Zmeu let out a grizzly howl as it tore itself away from me to face its opponent.

Quinn!

I rolled over, pulling myself forward along the cement floor with my good arm until I was able to see past the edge of the sofa into the center of the storehouse.

Like a powerful tempest, Quinn's anger and wrath filled the large warehouse. Channeling his anger along with his supernatural strength and speed, Quinn flew across the open space like a rocket, delivering a powerful strike to the Zmeu, sending him flying up and back into the empty office space that sat high above. Blind with rage, Quinn continued his attack, leaping to the top of the metal staircase, and again into the office space where he'd thrown the Zmeu.

I cursed my wretched mortal eyesight and swollen eye. I couldn't see a damn thing that was happening above me. Several loud crashes, followed by a high-pitched keening, rang out into the night.

As I pulled myself up onto my knees, I was finally able to see Quinn as he wrenched the Zmeu from the office floor and threw him down onto the concrete slab below. With a running jump, he followed behind, landing just in front of the demon that writhed on the floor. Pulling his Scían from its sheath, Quinn stood over the demon ready to strike, when it suddenly whipped around, kicking Quinn's legs out from under him, bringing him to the floor. The Scían slid across the floor out of his reach.

Wasting no time, the Zmeu launched itself onto Quinn and pummeled him with a barrage of vicious blows.

There was no way I was going to sit on my ass while the demon attacked Quinn. I shot up from the floor, adrenaline pumping through my veins, and raced over to the edge of the building where the glass from the shattered windows fell. Grabbing a large shard of glass, I whirled around and raced toward the ensuing fight with the sole purpose of killing the underworld bastard or, at the very least, maiming it.

As I approached the fight, I saw that the Zmeu had Quinn in a chokehold, doing its level best to strangle the life from him.

Blood boiled beneath the surface of my skin and I gripped my weapon tighter in my hand. The jagged glass sliced through my palm, sending sharp, stinging pain pulsating up my arm. I didn't care. The pain energized me, cleared my thoughts and fueled my rage. Pure undiluted fury flowed through me, and I flew at the demon, burying the shard of glass deep into its neck.

Howling in pain, the Zmeu released its hold on Quinn and, with a flash of light, transformed into a large dragon-like creature.

"Get out of the way," Quinn shouted and shoved me to the side as he leaped up from the floor to face the deadly beast.

I fell to the floor, inches away from Quinn's dagger. Without hesitation, I grabbed hold of the knife and screamed. "Quinn! Your dagger!"

Shooting up from the floor, I threw the dagger as hard as I could toward Quinn, who cloaked himself with invisibility and caught the deadly blade midair. As if by magic, using his supernatural speed, he appeared in front of the large beast and sank the blade into its middle, gutting it from navel to neck in one powerful slice. The beast made a horrible gurgling noise, shifting its form several times, before dropping like a stone to the floor, in its true form, that of the dark stalker from my dream.

It was over. I'd never have to fear my demon stalker again. There would be no more nightmares, no need to look over my shoulder every time I left my dorm room to venture outside. Quinn had defeated the Zmeu.

I was safe. My other half, my love—Quinn—came for me, saved me. The adrenaline that pulsed through me earlier ebbed, and the reality of all that had happened hit me like a powerful blow to the face. I broke.

"Quinn." I reached for him, my voice ragged and strained as I cried. My knees gave out as I desperately gasped for air in between the uncontrollable sobs that took over my body.

Quinn stood before me in an instant. He dropped to his knees and held me by my arms to keep me from falling.

"You're bleeding." He grimaced as he held the hand I'd used to grasp the shard of glass.

Bleeding? I glanced down at my hand to see a deep diagonal gash running the length of my palm. I vaguely remembered cutting myself when I went after the demon, but I couldn't bring myself to care. Quinn had rescued me and my nightmare was over.

In that moment, I felt no pain. It didn't matter that our skin made contact where he held me. The effects of his curse took a distant back seat to the effusion of love that flowed between us.

"You came for me." My voice was barely audible, as I looked up into the face of my hero, my love.

"I will always come for you, *a ghrá*. You are my life, the very air I breathe, and I cannot be without you. *Táim I ngrá leat. Is tú mo shonuachar.* I love you. You're my soul mate."

chapter 20

No, no. I don't want to get up, too tired." A faint beeping sound tore me from my hazy sleep. I moved my hand to shut the annoying alarm clock going off.

"Oh, God. She's waking up."

Jess?

My mouth felt dry, like someone had shoved an entire bag of cotton in it. When I went to swallow, my throat burned and ached all the way down into my chest. I moaned, trying to reach for it, but my left arm felt weighted down and I could barely move it.

"No, honey. Leave it be." I felt a warm hand on my forehead, and the soothing sound of Jessica's mother, Karen, filled my ears.

A thick fog clouded my head and the right side of my face felt like someone had taken a sledgehammer to it and it was ten times its normal size. It took a few tries, but I finally managed to open my eyes. The bright fluorescent lights of the room stung them and caused me to blink rapidly. "Where am I?" The last thing I remembered was Quinn kneeling before me in the center of the abandoned warehouse, finally confessing his love.

His love? He'd finally admitted his feelings for me. Oh, God.

"Quinn." I sat bolt upright, immediately feeling dizzy.

"Whoa! Whoa! Whoa! Take it easy, Ryann." Karen's voice rang out in alarm. She gently guided my back and shoulders down to the pillows I'd been laying against.

"Quinn," I shouted, feeling out of breath. "I need to see Quinn. I have to go to him."

"Honey, you can't go anywhere. You're in the hospital. Who's Quinn?" Karen asked with a puzzled look on her face.

"He's a friend, Mom," Jessica said, stepping in front of her mother. "Can we have a few minutes alone?"

Karen nodded and kissed my forehead before leaving.

"Quinn's been here every day. He comes and sits with you at night when everyone else leaves," she whispered. "He has to cloak himself or the nurses go crazy and forget all about their patients." She brushed a piece of hair from my face and sighed. From the way she spoke, I figured Quinn was now aware that she and Martha both knew of his mythical identity.

Her expression became serious all of a sudden. "I was so scared for you, Ryann. I…I…" Tears filled her eyes as she spoke. "I woke up on the floor near the bathrooms just after you'd been taken. Quinn was…oh, God, Ryann. He went crazy. You should have seen him. He heard you scream right before the demon whisked you away. He came running, but you were already gone. I…I've never seen anything like it, Ryann. He ripped the door off the back exit to the club and smashed it into the side of the building. There's a giant hole there now." Her eyes grew wide as she recounted the aftermath of my abduction.

She took a deep breath and exhaled heavily. "Thank goodness for Martha. She came racing out and worked her voodoo magic, so Quinn could find you."

I shook my head. I wasn't following.

"Martha told Quinn he needed to find a map so she could scry for your location. You know, work her mojo to find you magically. Quinn ran around, ripping doors off cars until he found one. Martha yanked out this weird crystal thingy she wore around her neck and held it over the map. It took a few minutes, and then all of a sudden, the map lit up, and we knew where you were. Before I knew what happened, Quinn was gone."

"Wow," I said, in complete awe of my roommate and new friend, Martha.

"So…do you want to talk about what happened?" Jessica's voice held a cautious tone, and I knew she didn't want to push me if I didn't want to talk.

"That thing," I said hoarsely. "It was awful. It kept changing shape so that it looked like you and—" I winced at the memory. "I couldn't look at it; I wouldn't look at it," I said, desperately trying to keep the awful image from resurfacing.

"Quinn, he.. ... oh, God, Jessica. You should have seen him." Tears streamed down my face as I recounted the deadly fight between Quinn and the Zmeu.

"The way he attacked the demon was so ... so ..." I couldn't find the words. Quinn had been heroic and fearless, savage and unrelenting, and entirely lethal. How could I describe all that with just one word? I shook my head. "He practically gutted the thing in one swipe. It was amazing and scary and horrible and—" I broke off. Silent sobs shook through my body as Jessica cradled me in her arms as best she could. "He told me he loves me, Jess."

Quinn's declaration of love inundated my thoughts. The memory of him kneeling in front of me, confessing his love, played on a continuous loop, over and over again in my mind. If he admitted his feelings to me verbally, then maybe he'd forgo his stubborn refusal to be intimate with me as well. I could only hope. Our future together depended on it.

"Wait a minute," I said, panic filling my voice. "How long have I been in the hospital?"

Jessica looked away and then down at the floor.

"Jess, how long?" I pressed.

Her eyes darted about the room and she fiddled with the edge of the hospital blanket. "Ten days."

"What?" I shouted. "No! There's not enough time. I need more time. What day is it?"

"Relax, Ryann. You still have time. It's Tuesday. The doctors said they'd release you on Friday, barring any unforeseen complications."

"Friday? But that's the day before Halloween. The Eve of Samhain. That doesn't give me enough time, not nearly enough. I need to leave now."

I tried to sit up, only to fall back against the pillows moments later, woozy and out of it. "Why am I so groggy? I feel like I've been drugged."

Jessica snorted with laughter. "That's because you have been, silly. You were pretty messed up when Quinn brought you in."

I looked down at my arm, which I knew had been broken. It was wrapped in a cast from the tip of my fingers to just under my shoulder, a sling carefully cradling it against my body. "Well, I knew my arm was broken," I said bitterly.

"Not just broken, Ryann. Shattered, and in several places. You've had a couple surgeries over the past week to place a metal plate and some pins in your arm."

I grimaced.

A plate? Pins?

"I know what you're thinking, Ryann. I can see it on your face. Don't worry about what you will or won't be able to do with your arm right now. Just be happy you're alive. That demon could have killed you."

She was right. With everything else going on in my life, worrying about what I may or may not be able to do with my arm seemed pointless.

"So I've been holed up in the hospital for ten days for a broken arm?" It seemed a bit excessive.

"And your head," she said grimly.

"My head? What's wrong with my head? Did they shave my hair off?" My pulse thrummed in my ears and my stomach rolled as visions of Mr. Clean and his shiny chrome dome clouded my vision. Whimpering, I lifted my gauze wrapped hand and sighed in relief when my fingers gripped a handful of hair.

"Well, I don't really understand all the doctor lingo and jargon, but I think they said something about multiple contusions and possible swelling. You were coming in and out of consciousness for a few days. Then, with the surgeries for your arm, they've kept you pretty drugged up and out of it. This has been your longest wakeful period since you've been here."

I cried like a baby again. Yeah, I was relieved, hell, overjoyed that my days of being tormented by the Zmeu were over. But lying strapped to a hospital bed, unconscious and helpless, I'd lost precious time with Quinn. Time I'd never get back. Time I desperately needed to save him. I was despondent.

The door to my room breezed open and a short, stout nurse bustled over to the opposite side of my bed.

"You're awake." She smiled brightly as she checked my vitals and fiddled with my IV bag. "Are you in pain? Is there anything I can get for you?"

I shook my head, wincing from the movement. I was in pain, but I didn't care. Unless she could produce a time machine that allowed me to procure more time with Quinn, there was nothing she could get for me.

"A stubborn one, I see," she said and stuck something into my IV. "Time for you to rest, dear. Your friend can come back later." She ushered Jessica toward the door.

"Wait. I—"

"You'll see her later. Trust me. In about ten seconds, you are going to get real sleepy and you won't be up for conversation." With that, the portly nurse laughed and exited the room.

I was out before I had a chance to protest.

⌁

I woke to the same incessant beeping that plagued me before. It was nighttime and the room was dark, the only light, aside from the machinery, coming from the small window at the far side of the room. Using my bandaged hand, I searched for the remote that controlled the bed and TV, chucking it at the source of my irritation. I missed, and the beeping continued as the remote clattered onto the floor, skidding across the room.

"Ugh," I groaned and yanked a pillow over my head.

"You're cranky when you wake up." A deep, velvety smooth voice chuckled as it moved toward my bed.

"Quinn," I said breathlessly. My throat still felt raw from being intubated. My voice strained as I spoke, but I couldn't bring myself to care. "You're here." I reached for him. The air filled with an electric charge and my body came alive. My breath caught and my heartbeat kicked up a notch, causing the machines that monitored me to beep even louder.

"Aye, love. I'm here," he said, taking my hand in his own. The effect was instantaneous. Warmth radiated throughout me the moment our skin touched, and an all-encompassing sense of comfort and security came over me. I felt the effect of his curse as well, but it took a distant back seat to the intense outpouring of love that flowed freely between us. My body eased, and all traces of tension and worry vanished. His touch was truly magical.

Quinn leaned over me, and cradled my head with his free hand. Resting his forehead against my own, he breathed me in, relishing our nearness. He pulled back slightly and placed a gentle kiss on my forehead before sweeping a stray lock of hair out of my face.

"You gave me quite a scare, *a ghrá*." It was dark in the room, but I made out the features of his perfectly sculpted face. His eyes were tired and his jaw slack. He'd been worrying over me.

"I'm so sorry, Quinn." I couldn't bear to see him upset and wished there was a way I could magically take his pain from him and give us more time together. As far as he knew, he'd be dying on Friday, and the majority of our few remaining days, I'd spent laying unconscious in a hospital bed.

"We have so little time left, and here I am strapped to a frigging hospital bed," I whispered hoarsely. "This is all my fault. We never should have gone out. I never should have gone off without you."

"Sshhh." He placed his finger against my lips, silencing me. "Quit trying to take responsibility for things you had no control over. The fault is mine." He pulled back, his lips drawing thin. "Fuck! I should have been able to pick up on the demon's presence, to sense that Stan was no good, but I got nothing. Damn fucker must have been really old to be able to mask its identity the way it did."

"I'm so sorry," I said, reaching out to comfort him.

"Shhh … It's over now. You're safe." His hand flinched as it traced my cheek where the Zmeu struck me.

"Is it bad?" I asked, turning my head to the side to avoid his gaze. "I must look awful." I closed my eyes, unable to bear a look of pity from him.

Refusing to let me look away, Quinn held my face gently as he spoke. "Look at me, *a ghrá*. Don't hide your eyes from me."

I felt his gaze and knew he would persist until I gave in to his wishes. I met his stare and was blown away by the tenderness it held.

"In the entirety of my pitiful existence, you, Ryann, are the most beautiful creature I've ever had the privilege to look upon. The mere fact that you grace me with your presence makes me the luckiest bastard that ever walked this planet."

I opened my mouth to speak, but he pressed his fingers to my lips once more.

"The reality that you could love a deplorable creature such as me is beyond anything I can comprehend." He paused for a moment, shaking his head. "Though I can't understand it, and I know I don't deserve it," he sighed and looked at me intently, an enormous smile creeping across his face. "I'm just so fucking happy that you do."

His hand moved from my mouth to cradle the side of my face, his thumb gently tracing across my cheekbone. "Thank you, Ryann."

I should have rejoiced at his words, but I couldn't. A sick feeling of dread wormed its way into my heart and stomach. The way he spoke felt too much like a goodbye. It wasn't his words, but the tone of his voice and his eyes. Sadness lay beneath the careful façade he was hiding behind.

I fiddled with the edge of the thin hospital blanket. "You can thank me in person on Friday, when I get out of this place."

Quinn looked up at the ceiling with a sigh before meeting my gaze once again. He said nothing, leaving my nervous reply unanswered. The atmosphere between us shifted, and an awkward, uncomfortable silence permeated the air.

"Quinn?" My voice broke and the monitors started beeping wildly as my pulse jumped out of control.

He moved to stand in front of the window, looking out into the night. He ran his hands over his head repeatedly and paced back and forth, giving the impression he was torn over how to answer me.

"I'll see you Friday when I get out, right?" My body shook as my anxiety escalated. The longer he remained silent, the more concerned I became. "Right?" Warm tears trickled down my face as I waited for him to say the words, to tell me he was leaving.

Quinn moved to my side. He knelt alongside the bed, and cradled my good hand in his own, wiping the tears from my cheeks.

"Sshhh, *mo chrói*, don't cry. I'll see you on Friday. I give you my word." His voice was tender and soothing. "There's something I need to take care of so I won't be able to stay with you the next two nights like I have been. I hate to leave while you're still recovering, but the matter is pressing and won't wait."

"That's okay. I understand," I whispered, still anxious about his odd behavior and unwillingness to answer me. His body language conveyed the exact opposite of what he told me. Something was up, and I didn't like it.

Quinn lay holding me in his arms on the hospital bed for most of the night, taking care not to touch my skin and only leaving my side temporarily when the nurses came in to check my vitals. Though I felt safe and comforted in his embrace, I couldn't shake the nagging feeling that no matter what I did to try and stop his horrible fate, I would fail. The thought that Quinn wouldn't be with me in two days' time frightened me more than the Zmeu ever had.

The days that followed dragged on for what seemed like an eternity. A wretched mess, I did nothing but lay silent in my bed, unwilling to speak, eat or cooperate in any way with the nurses. What did I care if they wanted me to eat? I wasn't hungry. What did I care if they needed a urine sample? My life was ending, and as far as I was concerned, they could take their urine sample and shove it where the sun didn't shine. My head felt better and my arm would heal eventually, but my heart ... well, that was another matter altogether. I shuddered to think of what I'd become if my worst nightmare came true, and I somehow failed to save Quinn from his curse.

Too anxiety-ridden to carry on any kind of conversation, I sat in silence while Martha and Jess did their best to try and pull me from my funk. I was surrounded with flowers, chocolate and the latest celebrity gossip magazines, none of which held my interest in the least. I wanted to be left alone. I wanted to sulk. I wanted Quinn.

"I'm sorry, guys. I just want to be alone. Do you mind?" I felt bad sending them away, but I felt even worse pretending to be interested when I wasn't. Not to mention, I'd never been the type of person who could pretend to be happy when I wasn't. I was a terrible liar and an even shittier actress.

"No, that's okay," Martha said, and bit her lip. "I need to head back soon anyway. I've got a test I need to study for. Oh, and hey…I managed to get notes from the lectures you missed and the homework assignments for each of your classes, that way you can catch up once you're out of here." She flashed me an encouraging smile.

"Thanks, Martha." I cast her a halfhearted smile. School was the last thing on my mind at the moment, but I couldn't tell her that. Not after she'd gone to so much trouble. "I really appreciate it."

"No problem. I'll catch you tomorrow then," she said before leaving Jessica and me alone in the room.

"I don't like seeing you like this, Ryann." Jessica grabbed her purse and stood up from her chair. "It's not like you to just roll over and give up."

"Give up? How am I giving up?"

"I can see it in your eyes. You're already preparing yourself for failure. You've already accepted defeat before you've even tried to help Quinn."

"I'm scared, Jess. I know this is going to sound a tad melodramatic, but I don't think I can live without him." Saying I was scared was an understatement. I was absolutely terrified. If I couldn't break Quinn's resolve and get him to be intimate with me, my future looked pretty bleak.

"A tad?" she said with a laugh and moved to stand in the doorway.

"This isn't funny, Jess. There's too much at stake, too much to lose. I…I just don't think I can deal if something happens to him." My voice cracked as I spoke.

"I know it's not funny. I'm sorry. Listen, you and Quinn share something very few people ever find. Hold on to that, Ryann. Fight for it. More than anyone else I know, you deserve to be happy. I know you won't give up." She closed the door behind her, leaving me to my stupor.

I lay anxious in my bed, replaying my conversation with Jessica over and over in my mind. I knew she was right. I was rolling over, giving up, and the realization made me sick to my stomach.

I never gave up when things got tough. I always persevered, digging my heels in with a stubborn tenacity that sometimes bordered on irritating. When I wanted something, I usually got it. Why was I giving in so easily now? Why was I accepting defeat? Quinn was the best thing that had ever happened to me. He was my light, my joy, my heart and my soul. Was I just going to give him up without a fight?

"Hell, no," I growled loudly and startled the nurse who'd just walked in to check my vitals.

"Sorry, honey. Got no choice, it's my job." She cast me a sideways glance, frowning as she went about her business.

By the time she left my room, I'd made up my mind. I wasn't going down without a fight. I wasn't going to lose Quinn.

chapter 21

"There." I tossed the blue Bic on top of the giant stack of release papers I'd just signed. "I feel like I signed my life away."

The stout nurse gathered up my paperwork. She had warm honey-colored eyes and wore a bright pink scrub top with crazy geometric designs on it that made my eyes feel like crossing. "Yep. I get that every day. Now just sit tight while I go get your wheelchair."

"Wheelchair? I can walk just fine, thank you. I broke my arm, not my leg." What the hell was she thinking? I might have been a bit broken, but I was no invalid.

She pointed a pudgy finger in my direction and shook her head. "Honey, even if you were treated for an ingrown toenail, hospital policy states you must leave in a wheelchair. Now, like I said before, sit tight." She waddled out of the room before I could protest further.

"Damn." I looked over to Martha, who appeared equally taken aback.

"Someone's not getting any," she muttered under her breath.

Jessica strode into the room, twirling a set of car keys on her pointer finger. "Why do you look so pissy? What'd I miss?"

I didn't feel like rehashing the wheelchair issue so I focused on the bigger issue at hand: rescuing Quinn.

She took a seat on the edge of my hospital bed and patted my leg with a smile. "My mom's car is parked out front and ready to go."

A deep ache wormed its way through my gut at the mention of the word "car." My own vehicle, my precious Mint Mobile, had been found just outside the city limits the day before, mangled and crushed like a tin can. I might have been sporting a head injury, but the lightbulb was still on upstairs, and I understood the demon's motivation. The Zmeu wanted me on foot, making it easier to attack me. But dammit, why couldn't he have just disconnected the battery? Why'd he have to destroy my only means of transportation? I hated bumming rides off my friends. Stupid underworld rat bastard!

I turned to Martha, who stood and moved toward me. "I'll help you with your clothes and hair."

Due to my cast, my wardrobe choice was limited. I wore an oversized t-shirt and pair of sweats. My outfit was not exactly what one might refer to as sexy and definitely not conducive to seducing the man of my dreams. I cast her an appreciative smile. "Thank you."

After Wheelchair Betty rolled me outside and saw that I was securely belted into the backseat of Jessica's car, we took off toward Quinn's place without delay. I'd been away from him long enough, and with his impending death hanging over our heads, there wasn't a second to spare.

Martha turned in her seat as we sped away from the hospital. "First things first. Let's do something about those ratty sweats you're wearing."

I heaved a giant sigh of relief. "Please. I'm all for comfort, but if I have to wear these damn things another minute, I think I'll lose my mind."

Jessica squealed from the front seat. "Wait! I have an idea." She rifled through a magazine as she drove. Not the smartest thing to do, but hey, desperate times called for desperate measures. I was in the middle of a fashion emergency. "How about this?"

Martha leaned forward to look at her suggestion. "Hmm...I don't know." She turned her head and cast me a worried glance.

"Oh, come on," Jessica cried. "It's perfect. She needs to look sexy and this, right here, screams sex."

Warning bells rang in my ears and my stomach rolled with unease. What the hell did she want to dress me in?

"Fine," Martha said and focused on me intently.

The next thing I knew, my aging sweatpants and t-shirt were gone, replaced by a satiny red push up bra, and matching skirt, that sported ruffle upon ruffle of flowing red taffeta.

"What the hell!" I exclaimed. "What magazine were you looking at?"

Jessica held up a copy of Victoria's Secret and shrugged as she focused on the road ahead of her.

"I. Don't. Think. So! Zap me out of this please. Now."

"Oh, for crying out loud. That outfit would have Quinn on his knees and begging," Jessica grumbled from the front seat. "Whatever! Hand me the *Cosmo*."

Martha tossed over a copy of the magazine, which Jessica ripped through while stopped at a light. "Here," she said, chucking the magazine into the backseat. "Put her in this."

I grabbed the dog-eared fashion magazine, making sure her selection was safe and appropriate before passing it over to Martha. The last thing I needed was to end up in some sort of black leather lingerie nightmare.

A few moments later, I sat dressed in a slinky blue top, which sported an open back, a pair of Seven jeans and some fancy black ballet flats.

By the time Jessica dropped me off in front of Quinn's estate, I was coiffed, fluffed and ready to put an end to his stubborn foolishness. There was no way in hell I'd let him go gently into the night. I'd fight for Quinn's life until there wasn't a breath left in my body.

There were only a few hours of sunlight left, so I rushed to the front doors, slamming my bandaged hand against the wood and ringing the doorbell.

"Quinn!" I shouted and continued to pound away at the giant doors. My efforts were met with a deafening silence. Where was Martha when I needed her? At least she could zap the doors open so I wouldn't have to wait outside.

I zeroed in on the doorknob and thought "what the hell?" I grasped the knob and was surprised when it opened. I stepped into the foyer and called out again. "Quinn. Are you here?"

I heard a faint "Aye, I'm here" coming from the back of his large home, in the direction of the kitchen.

I raced toward the voice and came to a screeching halt as I entered the kitchen. Seated at one of the barstools along the large island with his head in his hands and a small folder in front of him was Quinn. He looked absolutely awful. Actually, awful didn't come close to describing how bad he looked. In truth, Quinn looked positively wretched. He lifted his head as I entered the kitchen and cast me a warm smile that didn't reach his eyes.

My stomach lurched.

"A ghrá." He stood from his chair and walked forward to meet me. Quinn's deep and powerful voice was tainted with sorrow and pain. Several days outgrowth covered his normally smooth face and head. Dark circles lined the undersides of his tired eyes, making it painfully obvious he hadn't been sleeping. He wrapped his arms around me gently, avoiding my bulky cast.

I gasped at the myriad of sensations flooding my body and filling my senses. Raw heat and desire coursed through me at his touch, yet it was overshadowed by the all-encompassing aura of love flowing between us. This man was as essential to my well-being as breathing. We belonged together, I was certain of it.

"I missed you." I lay my head against the large expanse of his chest, breathing in his heavenly, masculine scent and basking in the warmth of his embrace. It wasn't until I was in his arms that I realized how incomplete I felt without Quinn. He was my other half, my home, and I knew that even if I had nothing else in this life, if I had him, I'd be complete.

"And I you, love." He held me close and took a deep breath as he rested his cheek on the top of my head. His hands rubbed circles up and down my back, soothing me with the thing I'd craved for so long—his touch. Much to my dismay, he pulled back and walked over to the counter to retrieve a thin folder. "Here," he said, handing it to me with a sigh. "Everything is in order."

"What's in order?" I looked down at the folder in confusion. "What is this?"

"The deed to this house … among other things."

The house? Other things?

I reached my arm out, pointing to the thin, cream-colored folder he clutched in his hand, not wanting to touch the damn thing. "Is this what you've been working on the past two days?"

"Aye. I had to make sure you'd be taken care of when I'm no longer here."

I was beyond confused, and to be honest, a little bit hurt he'd spent the last few days we had left together away from me. "You didn't have to do that. I can take care of myself just fine."

He blanched, as if I'd slapped him. "You didn't think I'd leave ye with nothing, did you? I may be a womanizing bastard, but I'm not cruel. In the short time we've known each other, I've done nothing but bring you down, bring danger to your life. This…" he shook the folder through the air, "this is the one good thing I can do for you. The only thing I can do for you. Please, Ryann, don't refuse it."

He wore an agonized look of defeat on his handsome face. It was evident he believed himself to be the lowest of the low, a contemptible creature of no value. How wrong he was. Quinn was without a doubt the most selfless, thoughtful, caring person I'd ever known. Stubborn to a fault and fiercely passionate, he was my match in every way. We just fit.

I slapped the folder out of his hands. Paper scattered across the white tile flooring. "I don't want your house. I want you." My words were harsh and came barreling out before I could stop them. I knew his actions stemmed from concern for my well-being, but I couldn't help the way I felt. I wanted to spend what little time I had on this earth with the people that I loved, Quinn topping that short list.

He stepped forward with his hand outstretched, trying to reason with me. "I've seen to it that you will be well taken care of for the rest of your days. You'll never want for anything."

"Yes, I will," I cried out. "I'll want for you." How could he not see that? Why couldn't he see that nothing else in this world mattered to me, but him?

He stiffened at my words before losing all control, punching a large hole in the nearby wall. A loud groan emanated from deep within his chest, and he stormed over to the nearby island. "Why? Why now? For five hundred years, I've walked this earth a lonely, miserable bastard, caring about nothing, caring about no one. Then, just as my worthless existence is finally about to end, you come waltzing into my life like a breath of fresh air, pulling me out from the dark cloud I've been endlessly trapped under."

I stepped forward and raised my arm toward him. "Fate." There was no other way to explain it. Quinn entered my life when I least expected it, showing me I was capable of laughing, hoping and most importantly, loving. Quinn was quite literally my angel, and I was not about to let him go.

His face twisted with rage. "Fuck fate!" He slammed his fists onto the marble counter, sending a large chunk crumbling to the floor. With anger pouring off him in waves and his muscles still flexing from the destruction he'd wrought upon the counter, Quinn looked deadly.

I should have been afraid, but I wasn't. I'd never desired him more.

He came at me quickly, pinning me against the wall as he slammed his fists above my head. "The Fates hate me," he said, his voice filled with agony. "Why else would they give you to me, only to take you away so soon? It would have been better if we'd never met." He hung his head in defeat, resting it on my shoulder.

His pained words cut through me like a knife. "I should be screaming that, not you. I'm the one who'll be left behind." He wouldn't have to live out his life knowing what once was. Knowing he'd found his soul mate, his one true love, the only person who could truly make him whole, yet couldn't be with. If fate hated anyone, it hated me. It was taking away my beloved Quinn. I hated fate.

His eyes met mine, full of sadness and longing, and he cupped the side of my face, rubbing his thumb across my cheekbone. "I'm sorry, love." He leaned forward, placing his forehead against mine as he spoke. "I don't want to leave you. For the first time in my pathetic life, I have something to live for. You've touched a part of me, Ryann, that no one else has. I never imagined I'd care for another being as I care for you." His voice was low and gravelly, full of pain. "You've brought meaning to my life and a happy end to my miserable existence."

A painful ache took up residence in my chest and I fought to breathe. It felt like someone was tearing me in half. I gasped. "Quinn."

He placed his hand on my mouth, silencing me. In a swift movement, he pulled a small object from his pocket and brought it to my hand, the light reflecting off the top of the silver metal.

It was a ring, an Irish claddagh. Placing the ring on my right hand, the heart facing inward, he spoke. "My heart belongs to you, *a ghrá*. Wear this always and remember me. *Tá mo chrói istigh ionat.* My heart is yours, eternally."

He lifted my hand to his mouth, kissing the ring and my fingers tenderly before releasing my hand and pulling away. Quinn looked exactly the way I felt: as if someone ripped his still beating heart directly from his chest.

The pain in my heart was unbearable. I knew what Quinn was doing as he stepped back. He was saying goodbye, and I'd be damned if I was going to sit back and let him walk out of my life without a fight.

"Don't you dare walk away from me!" Anger swept through me as I watched him turn his back to me. How could he just walk away? How could he turn away from me? I felt the same pain he did, yet I remained. "Coward!" I screamed.

He whirled around to face me, misery and resignation marring his face. "What would you have me do? Lie down and let you watch me die? I'm not a coward because I want to shield you from what's to become of me. I love you too much to let you suffer such a thing."

"If you loved me, you'd stay."

"I do love you!" He stepped forward like a man on fire, eyes dark and full of a mixture of anger and desire.

My heart threatened to jump out of my chest, and my breaths came in quick, shallow pants.

"Then prove it, you stubborn bastard. Love me!"

He came at me like a lion attacking its prey, fierce and powerful, full of hunger and need. His mouth claimed my own, kissing me with a fevered passion that stole my breath away. In that moment, nothing else existed. There was only Quinn and me.

He growled as our tongues danced, exploring each others' mouths with a ferocity that bordered on desperation. Having denied ourselves for so long, our need to claim each other was monumental.

My back still to the wall, and he lifted me off my feet with ease. One skilled hand squeezed my backside, while he ground himself into my center; his other hand fisted my hair as he deepened our kiss even further.

God, but he felt good! I felt like screaming from the rooftops. Finally! I moaned in delight at the feel of his mouth and hands on me.

"Is this what you want?" he growled in my ear. His lips blazed a trail of feather-light kisses down my neck, while he continued to thrust his rock hard cock against me, our traitorous clothes the only barrier between us and Quinn's salvation.

"Yes," I whispered breathless as I held his head to me with my good arm. "God, yes."

"Good." He lifted his head so our eyes met. "Because I can resist you no longer."

Still holding me against him, he carried me to the large island and set me down atop the cool marble counter. Cupping my face in his hands, he kissed me tenderly, brushing his lips over my bruised cheekbone, as if trying to kiss the hurt away. Pulling away momentarily with a devilish grin, he took hold of the thin fabric of my top and ripped it from me, taking care not to jostle my injured arm.

I sat topless before him on the counter as he stared at me, his eyes dark and full of desire.

"Beautiful," he breathed out softly. "In all my life, I've never known an equal to your beauty."

My breath caught at his words, sending a shiver down my spine.

"Here," he said, taking my hand and placing it on his chest. "Feel what you do to me." His heart hammered a wild rhythm against my palm, and his breathing was choppy and ragged like mine.

"Never once, in the entirety of my existence, have I ever wanted to make love to someone more." His voice was low and seductive, his sapphire eyes dark and smoldering. Pushing me down so that my back was flush with the cool marble, I watched as Quinn removed my jeans, emitting a low growl when he discovered I'd gone commando.

Taking his time, Quinn explored every inch of my body with his hands and mouth, memorizing every curve, every dip, and every detail. He worshiped me with a reverence that nearly shattered me. As he devoured my flesh with his mouth, I couldn't help but think how happy I was I'd saved myself for the one person I truly loved. There was no other person I could imagine sharing such an intimate part of myself with.

Any and all thoughts of the outside world vanished when I felt his warm mouth on me, exploring, teasing and deliciously torturing a part of me no man had ever touched before. He held me still as I writhed on the countertop, back arched, crying out in pleasure. With one powerful hand beneath me, the other explored the contours of my chest and abs, setting fire to my skin as his mouth prepared me for what was to come. Before I knew what happened, my body stiffened, every muscle contracting as wave after wave of sweet, agonizing bliss washed over me.

Moving up to devour my mouth once more with his own, Quinn pulled me up so I was once again sitting, then hastily removed his jeans. He broke away for just a moment, ripping his shirt over his head and tossing it to the side.

Still trembling from the pleasure he gave me, I sat in awe as I eyed Quinn in all of his naked glory.

Beautifully sculpted, he was a heaping mass of raw power and sinewy perfection.

And I wanted him, desperately.

He pulled me forward, placing himself just at my opening and paused. "You'll hurt for a moment, *a ghrá*, because it's your first time. But after that, I promise, you will feel no pain."

Crushing his lips against my own, he thrust into me hard, claiming my innocence. I cried out from the pain as he held me in his arms, patient and still. The burning subsided quickly and my body relaxed against his as I reveled in his magical embrace.

Ravishing me with his mouth, paying tribute to every inch of my upper body, Quinn slowly moved within me, schooling me in the art of love, teaching me what two people were capable of when they came together as one.

My breaths came in short pants as I teetered on the brink of the same earth-shattering feeling I'd experienced before at his mouth.

"Quinn," I cried out.

He slid his hands up my body and cupped my face in his hands, staring deeply into my eyes. "I love you, Ryann, always. Now come for me."

That was all it took. I fell over the edge screaming his name, pure, undiluted ecstasy enveloping me.

Quinn followed me into oblivion moments later, shouting as he experienced his own release.

We sat, molded to one another, for what seemed like an immeasurable amount of time, caressing each others' backs and sharing kisses, oblivious to everything but each other.

"Thank you," I whispered, completely spent. "That was amazing."

He brushed his lips across my cheekbone, trailing them down until he nuzzled my neck. "No, *a ghrá*. You are amazing. *Tá grá agam duit.* I love you."

A brilliant flash of light filled the room.

I clung to Quinn, clamping my eyes shut to shield them from the light. When I opened them again, I found we were no longer in the kitchen, but in Quinn's bedroom, lying atop his bed. My arm no longer wore a cast, healed as if by magic.

"What the—" Quinn shot up, taking a defensive stance, ready to attack anyone or anything that might harm me.

With another brilliant flash of light, Morgana appeared before us, standing at the foot of the bed. "It is finished." Her majestic voice filled the air, cutting Quinn off mid-sentence.

"My queen," he said, completely taken aback.

I grabbed for the sheeting to cover myself, but found both Quinn and I wore black silk robes.

Just as before, Morgana stood dressed in a flowing white gown, her long hair cascading in perfect waves past her shoulders and down her back. Her expression was soft, and with her, she carried an air of benevolence that eased me at once. "Yes. It is I."

On hearing the majestic voice of his queen, Quinn jumped off the bed and knelt on the floor with his head bowed.

Morgana stepped forward and addressed him. "Quinn. At long last, you have discovered the true nature of love. You have learned that love is selfless and unconditional, patient and kind. Love requires sacrifice and the ability to put another's needs before your own."

My hand shot up to my mouth as the queen's musical voice filled the room. Could I dare hope to we had overcome his curse?

Morgana held out her hands as she continued. "As you gave of yourself freely to Ryann in this manner, and she to you, I hereby release you from the bonds of your affliction. You are cursed no more."

I gave a loud sob at hearing her words. Quinn would live. Overwhelming joy and relief washed over me, and I wept like a child.

A giant tremor wracked his body and his voice cracked as he spoke. "Thank you, my queen."

"Furthermore, I should like to bestow upon your mate a gift."

I stared at the queen in confusion. "A gift?" What else could she possibly give me? I was already eternally indebted to her for rescinding Quinn's curse. As far as I was concerned, I had everything I'd ever need.

"Precious child." She smiled at me as she spoke. "You truly possess a pure heart, and it pleases me all the more to bestow upon you my gift. As a faerie, Quinn ages differently than a mortal. His life will go on for a great while, while your mortal body will age quickly and eventually perish. I find it cruel that one of you should die while the other lives on, so I bestow upon you the gift of life. From this moment on, you shall age as Quinn does, so that you may remain with one another always, and leave this world in the same manner—together."

I sat dumbstruck atop the bed.

What would that make me? I wasn't a faerie, but would I still be human?

A low chuckle filled the air as the queen read my confused thoughts.

"Be of ease, child. Though you will age as the Fae do, you will not possess our magical abilities. Your humanity shall remain intact, and you are free to live out your life as you so choose. May your children be blessed as well and enjoy my gift of long life."

Warm tears of happiness flowed down my cheeks and I choked on my words. "Thank you."

"Yes, my queen, thank you," Quinn said, echoing my response.

Morgana stepped forward, and placed a hand on top of Quinn's head. "You are most welcome, Quinn Donegan. I long feared you would fail to overcome my punishment. It brings me great joy to see you embrace the true nature of love, and with such a worthy mate. Cherish each other always, never forgetting the journey that brought you together."

With a smile and a flash of light, Morgana disappeared, leaving Quinn and me alone in stunned silence.

One moment Quinn knelt on the floor, the next he was cradling me in his powerful arms, holding him to me as if he'd never let me go.

"We did it," I sobbed, kissing every inch of his skin my mouth could find. "You're safe. You're alive." I was certain there wasn't a person on the planet who'd ever felt as happy as I did at that moment. We'd overcome his curse. Quinn would live. And I—I was on top of the world.

The electric spark flowing between us whenever we were near flared, but gone was the magical pull his curse once brought about with his touch. The euphoria I felt, as his hands cupped my face and his mouth claimed mine, was all Quinn's doing.

We held each other for what seemed like an eternity, touching, caressing and enjoying our newfound ability to explore each others' bodies without repercussion.

Perfectly content to remain in his arms for the rest of my existence, I frowned when Quinn pulled away. "Where are you going?"

Quinn glanced toward his enormous bathroom and the glass shower that took up the majority of its back wall and turned back to face me, a rakish grin on his face. "You're not wearing a cast any more."

A blast of heat scorched my skin, and I sent a silent prayer of thanks to the queen for magically healing my arm. I knew what he was thinking and I was all for it. I shifted in place. Eager. "No. No, I'm not."

He groaned, a low rumble that sent my pulse skyrocketing and my nether regions aching with need. "I haven't been able to get the picture of you standing naked in that shower out of my mind for some time now."

My heart leaped in anticipation of what was to come, and I cast him a wicked grin. "You know what they say: Practice makes perfect."

I squealed as he scooped me up into his strong arms and carried me into the bathroom to fulfill my shower fantasy in real life.

He nipped playfully at my neck and flashed me a hungry smile as he turned on the water. "It's time for a wee bit of fun, little girl," he said and stepped into the shower.

ACKNOWLEDGEMENTS

First, I'd like to thank God, without whom I'd be nothing.

I'd like to give special thanks to the two best critique partners a girl could ever have. Kaiti, Kristin, you girls rock my world. Kaiti, without you, this book simply would not be. I'm forever grateful.

I'd like to give a hearty WOOT to my girls in The SC: Deanna, Karen and Edie. Thank you for reading those early drafts over and over and over again. More importantly, thank you for your friendship. It means the world.

To my mother, my sisters, Diana and Jan, and my best friend Sarah, who is more family than friend. Thank you for your encouragement. I love you dearly.

Most importantly, I'd like to thank my husband, Ryan, and my three daughters Kendall, Taryn and Irelynn. You inspire me daily. Thanks for putting up with a messy house and a mom who can't tear herself away from her laptop. I promise, no more chicken nuggets for dinner! I love you all more than words can say.

ABOUT THE AUTHOR

Lisa's lifelong love of writing, coupled with her ability to weave together an intricate and compelling story has led to the release of her first published novel, *Eve of Samhain*.

In her role as a busy stay-at-home and self-proclaimed "cheer mom," on any given day Lisa wears a number of different hats. From taxi driver to chef, nurse to seamstress, laundry-woman to enforcer, and, of course, writer, Lisa manages to keep everything together all while caring for her husband and three children. The few spare moments left in her day are usually spent reading or writing, and if she's really lucky, possibly even catching up on some much needed sleep.

Lisa and her family currently reside in Tracy, California.